PINK LADY BLUES

Maurice from Jim

Pink Lady Blues

James Willis

Arkst Publishing

First published in Great Britain 2003 by
ARKST PUBLISHING
LONDON

© James Willis

The right of James Willis to be identified as the author of this work has been asserted by him in accordance with the Copyright, Designs and Patents Act 1988

This book is copyright. No part of it may be reproduced in any form without permission in writing from the publishers except by a reviewer who wishes to quote brief passages in connection with a review written for inclusion in a newspaper, magazine, radio or television broadcast. All rights reserved.

British Library Cataloguing in Publication Data
A catalogue record for this book is available from the British Library

ISBN: 0 9525243 3 3

Printed and Bound in Great Britain by
ProPrint, Riverside Cottages, Old Great North Road, Stibbington. PE8 6LR

For Nuala and Fiona

CHAPTER ONE

It was an important day, well it had to be for God's sake, everyone in the media had said so, and that was it, so what more do you want? *The Times* had declared it as being ... *an auspicious occasion in the calendar of the established Church, a day dedicated to the celebration of a New Era of Greater Religious Understanding in a time of change and strife*...and you can't say fairer than that.

A distinguished congregation had been solemnly assembled in Westminster Abbey in attendance at The Service of Dedication of the United Nations Congress of Ecumenical Understanding and Global Moral Fellowship or something like that - the name doesn't matter, since it was the thought that counted. Consequently the congregation was packed with representatives of numerous worthy causes, including many relevant workers engaged in the pursuit of the enhancement of interracial understanding, the promotion of good fellowship and mutual respect between Christianity and Islam, and also those good forward-looking folk who were opposed to foxhunting, the eating of flesh meat, smoking, excessive self – abuse, homophobia - you get the picture. No sweat, this important and meaningful winging was an influential get together of carefully chosen punters who weren't going to accept any old shit that was thrown at them. No way buster.

There was also an extensive selection of less privileged but equally well-meaning assholes, hanging in and around the plenary but less *hochgeboren* meeting which was being held down the road at the Central Hall amidst all the Styrofoam coffee cups and crumbly biscuits, where the fire exit doors banged and clattered all the while, as opposed to the serenity of the Abbey where all was silent, except for the occasional rustle of the odd chasuble. Those poor souls who were marooned down at The Central Hall were mainly a bunch of dumb *schmucks* who were denied access to the big roadside attraction because they were a shade unwholesome, having questionable armpits, halitosis and so on, but no one could say as much, since that would have been un-Christian, not to say well out of order Squire.

And now, in the Abbey, the Archbishop commenced the delivery of his important homily. It was you might say, the ecclesiastical equivalent of being the keynote speaker at a conference on the future of the advertising industry, or new trends in Management Consultancy, but it was possessed of considerably more *gravitas* than either of those topics. The Archbishop took this particular duty extremely seriously – the whole interdenominational relationship whoop-de-do was, in his book, pretty heavy shit, in case you might not have guessed as much. Later someone was to remark that on this occasion the good man looked almost seraphic, 'globally at peace,' as someone else said in a moment of total idiocy, eyes shining with divine love and stuff: quite a change from his customary slightly harassed, feeling the pain of a troubled society that has lost its way variety, which he had retained since he had been unexpectedly, and rather uncomfortably buggered by the Principal at Theological College all those years ago.

Truly, as he had often reflected, there is indeed no gain without pain in this sinful world of all worlds. Everyone cleared their throats so as not cough and need to gob out and disturb the speaker. They looked attentively at the august figure of the worthy cleric who was about to address them.

'Good Friends and all Folk of a concerned and caring nature – Greetings,' he began, 'there is something that I need to share with you, a concern and a source of deep hurt which has been occupying my mind for some time now, touching as it does on matters of great personal relevance at this point in time and having, as you will understand, certain possible wider social implications, and here I should say that we need to consider carefully the meaning of time in a truly spiritual and meaningful sense, as related to ecumenical values of an ongoing sort in a troubled world.' He was definitely going to sock it to them, as he continued, 'I refer to a state of persistent discomfort and itchiness in the region of my genitals and areas adjacent thereto ...' and then totally unexpectedly, he began to scratch the affected part vigorously. The congregation was considerably taken aback at this amazing lapse, and even more so when the good man unexpectedly dived into the recesses of his vestments and, producing a banjo from beneath his underpinnings, began to strum tunelessly and sing with great gusto,

'My old man's a dustman,
He wears a dustman's hat,
He wears gorblimey trousers
And he lives in a council flat...'
A murmur of surprise ran throughout the congregation.
He continued:
He looks a proper nana
In his bloody great dustman's boots
He has to bend and pull them up
And he calls them daisy roots
He was just about to start on a song that seemed to refer to a bloody great wheel, or as some people later claimed, to a kidney wiper, when a kindly deacon bore the poor man away to a place of greater safety. What a world, everyone exclaimed with one voice, as The St Johns Ambulance took over. They were well able to deal with the shocked and stressed out attendees, treating everyone with hot sweet tea. What a bummer it all was.

In the Stock Exchange, the CEO astonished a visiting delegation from Germany when he climbed on to a desk top, dropped his trousers and urinated splashily on the nearest VDU whilst singing:

'I don't want to join the Air Force
I don't want to go to war
I'd rather hang around
 Piccadilly Underground
Living on the earnings of a high born lady
I don't want a bayonet up my arsehole
I don't want my bollocks shot away...'

Something was seriously amiss. His colleagues put it down to stress and concern regarding a possible takeover from the bloody krauts in Frankfurt. Fortunately, the Footsie remained unchanged.

In the House of Commons, during Prime Minister's Question time, The Prime Minister took a total change of direction whilst answering a question about illegal immigration when, out of the blue, so to speak, he dropped his trousers as he mooned at Her Majesty's Opposition and broke wind.

What in heavens name, everyone said, is going on around here? The papers were full of it, and on Television there were fist fights on 'Any Questions' as angry Moslems demanded to know why they had not been consulted about things in greater depth, and more frequently if it came to that, not to mention the obscene display of the partially uncovered form of an infidel. Talk about loss of face.

CHAPTER TWO

Most people would have told you that Croke Parker was generally reckoned to be the card carrying shit of the month. On a good day, if you had said that he was an egocentric narcissistic tosser, that would have about wrapped it up. He was about as ill-mannered and amoral as too many smart ass townies frequently are; particularly if they have a hangover or their burger hasn't got enough ketchup. Yesterday, he had felt irritable and ratty, when he checked out his answer phone after another day spent hanging around waiting for nothing to happen. And on this day there had been a message that irritated and perplexed him: of all things, an invitation to lunch at a flash place, and not only that, at a most unlikely meeting place for the likes of Croke Parker.

In his infrequent visits to restaurants he avoided such places. This one was what you might call a downmarket Caprice, where people go to be seen rather than to eat; where they can chatter and scream. His natural arrogance was affronted that anyone should think that he would want to visit to such an eatery at all. The very idea, if you bloody please. Some nerve. What would his friends think; not that he had all that many? What a snobbish bastard I am he thought, for he knew that he was and was proud of it. The whole idea offended the puritan streak inside his well stuffed shirt. Podgy git. His carefully folded copy of *The Guardian* became ruffled at the very idea.

And another thing, he didn't like celeb gaffs, even bogus ones. It was said that this was one of the reasons that he was called Dag by those who despised him, Dag being the New Zealand slang term for the lumps of sheepshit matted around a sheep's ass in case you didn't know. More in the meat and potatoes line was Croke, so long as he wasn't paying,he preferred honest bitter to bourgeois champagne any day of the week. Give me a good working-class drink, he'd say. He'd know about the working class wouldn't he, with his minor public school and an unheard of Oxford College? Not that he was against self- indulgence. He just didn't reckon the poncey - eatery where the you- kiss- my- ass- and- I'll- kiss- yours- axis hung out, and that was bloody that. In any case he was amazed to have heard from Bill Poynton after so many years. Bill, that was all anyone had ever called him in the old days. Many affected not to know what was his real name. 'You know who I mean – Bill' they would say and smile 'you know - with Jock and that awful bloody man from Central...' There would be a pause, and someone would say 'Bloody Hell. Bill. Is he still around? I thought he went at the time of the last...' and trail off into silence while everyone looked embarrassed until someone like George Jorgensen might say, 'Well enough of that. What about one of you buggers buying me another drink for once in your bloody life? I don't know.' George had always had it in for 'that sodding Bill' as he called him. Then it would be time for the uneasy laughter, relief all round, and the subject would be dropped. Well what could you expect?

That was well before Bill had left so suddenly. Absolutely no warning. The people at Head Office were reputed to have foamed at the mouth and gibbered with anger, 'Absolutely apeshit Old Boy, they were, believe me.' said Nick, 'old Bill let the bloody side down in spades if you follow what I'm saying.' Croke had never really understood what this meant. Perhaps it was that he understood, but preferred not to let on, even to himself. About Bill that is.

He'd always rather liked Bill, in a way though, despite the unkind comments. When he had first started in the job it was Bill who had spotted that he was ill at ease in an unfriendly place, and he was friendly from the off, and invited him to lunch in a nearby pub where they had sausage and mash and Guinness. Croke had sensed that Bill would probably have been happier with a good claret, but he appreciated the sympathetic consideration shown to a newly joined member of the team. Not that your man was patronising. Not at all. Just friendly and keen to see a new boy settle in. They met infrequently but regularly after that. Bill was impressed by Croke Parker's cast iron schedules, pithy minuting and attention to detail. Many thought that Croke Parker's promotions had been engineered by Bill but dared not say so. He had too much clout for that. As they said 'Bill knows how to drown the kittens, in case you didn't know.' And some added 'and he knows where the bodies are buried: I'm only joking you understand.' and then they'd tail off.

Yes, it had been amazing when Bill had left - just like that. And now here it was years later, or so it seemed, and here was Croke in the bar waiting for Bill. Time had always been a problem for Croke. Why was that, he wondered? The barman said rather patronizingly, 'Mr Bill said that you'd be here before him, and he ordered a drink for you. He said you liked a Martini on the rocks. Is that right?' He smiled. Everyone called him Bill, even barmen it seemed.

How odd that Bill would have remembered my only excursion into high living, he thought piously, and nodded his acceptance of the drink. A difficult chap to make out: no one ever quite knew what he might be up to next, and then he heard a remembered foot step and turned to meet Bill.

After all those years he seemed unchanged in appearance, as ever he was tidily dressed, nothing overstated - a well cut suit, a shirt from Turnbull and Asser - affluent looking, but not showy: that was him sure enough.

Bill Poynton smiled and shook his hand quite firmly. He looked at him and half smiled. 'All those years' he said 'Yes Dag you look pretty bloody good. The Wunderkind has come to maturity. No, please don't look so embarrassed, I heard about how well you've been doing. Stick at it at is my advice. I suppose the others are all still there?'

'More or less,' he replied. Jesus he thought he's not going to want a full run down on everything that's happened since the day he left. His thoughts were interrupted by Bill. 'Why don't we go into lunch. I was going to suggest the Garrick but I imagine you're fed up with nursery grub.'

He winced. He'd never felt easy when the man had tried to get funny. Never quite worked really. In any case he knew very well that he was never into clubs. On the other hand, he'd heard that this place was good at Cumberland sausages, and said that it was OK this place would be just fine thank you Bill. At lunch they talked a good deal about the old days, but as the meeting progressed Croke felt progressively more puzzled as to the purpose of the meeting. Bill gave no clue as to what he'd been doing since last they met, and seemed preoccupied, he even looked mildly bored when Croke filled him in on what had happened to the buildings, details of his own promotions and snippets of gossip about those who had left and those who had stayed.

'I've often thought of going back to the old place and seeing everyone again,' said Bill, redirecting his attention with an effort, '*recherche du temps perdu* you know.'

'Jesus' he thought, that bloody does it. I'd forgotten that he was also an arsehole, and made a non-committal reply. Surely Bill must know that he wouldn't even be let past the bloody door, let alone see anyone. Clearance went forever if you left at your own request – and that was it. Rule number bloody One. No coming back; surely he remembered that. And as for seeing everyone, stuff that for a game of soldiers; that was totally out of the question. He could imagine what the likes of George Jorgensen would say if they heard that. He looked at Bill more closely. His appearance had coarsened a bit, and the more he looked at him the more he realised that he was not as smart as all that. Maybe the shirt and tie weren't Turnbull and Asser after all. Odd thing, his hands looked a shade coarsened too. Perhaps he'd been ill. There had been rumours, but Dag had ignored them.

By now he was beginning to weary slightly. Perhaps it had been a mistake to have this meeting. It had turned out to be a right bloody let down.Sort of going nowhere really - that was it. What was the point of it all? He felt unease creeping in.

He aroused himself to find Bill looking at him.

'Croke' he said 'you know I've really enjoyed this. I wish I'd kept in touch more but you know how it is.'

He wanted to say that he really didn't know how it was at all, but forbore. Bill said 'Sorry to grind to a halt so suddenly, but I have to dash. We'll meet again soon.' He paused, 'I used to enjoy those evenings at The Pink Lady, didn't you? It was all such a long time...' And then he was gone.

He'd left. Just like he'd left when he left the Office. Croke felt strangely angered, puzzled and dismayed by the meeting. He finished his drink and the last of the coffee, and made his way out. As he passed through the lobby the barman passed him an envelope.

From Bill of course - always one for the last minute memo, the last word, and out the door, thank you very much. He stuffed it into his pocket angrily. Bill had always shown promise of being a card carrying shit, yes that had been the general verdict. Perhaps the others had been right after all. Yet, why did he have feelings of uneasy regret?

And The Pink Lady, for Christ's sake, why did he have to bring that place up after all those years? What was such a big deal about The Pink bloody Lady? A bloody boring club that Bill always wanted you to go to, and no one ever knew why, or did they? And then he remembered. It must have been because you might just get to meet Elizabeth Odalisque. Wasn't that her name? Couldn't have been her real name surely. Funny that, remembering her name after all that time. Well you would. Hadn't Bill developed some sort of special relationship with her or something, wasn't that it? Though he'd heard otherwise about Bill's likings for the unusual. Hard to say after all those years, and in any case according to the likes of George Jorgensen, old Bill's tastes lay in a different quarter, as if it bloody mattered. What a load of old gossiping old women that shower had been. He didn't get around to opening the envelope until later that evening, what with one thing and another.

The note inside said only, 'Croke - for God's sake please help me I'm in deep shit. You can call me at the old number. Please come round and see me tonight if possible. I'm appealing to you. Bill'

And he thought that perhaps he should take a look at what was going down with Bill; just for old times sake. He wondered why it was that Bill could be appealing to him about anything for God's sake. Didn't make sense at all.

CHAPTER THREE

Croke stood outside Bill Poynton's door. He felt aggrieved about this and felt the need to think things out for a while. Anger and uncertainty were rising within him as he wondered why the hell he had bothered to come. What concern were Bill Poynton's problems to him? He hadn't seen him for years. What was it to him if good old Bill was up to his eyebrows in it? And why did he have to pick on him to ask for help? As he climbed the stairs he'd been thinking about how long it had been since his last visit to the place, and he began to feel refreshed, even uplifted in some odd way by its strangely tacky atmosphere; he'd forgotten about that. The apartment was situated on the top floor of a block of prosperous looking mansion flats on the south side of Battersea Park, with a good view of the gloomy recesses and ambiguous sculptures in the least appealing of the London Parks

The place was by now a bit run down, probably a safe haven for lunch time shaggers - the sort of place that you might have seen in nineteen sixties movies where a sadistic gangster loves his dear old mum one minute, and next thing he's beating the shit out of his minder, just before he fucks his ass. Right up Bill's street, he thought and then wondered why did I think that? And then he discovered that the lift was out of action. Now that surprised him: the maintenance in these places was usually pretty good.

As he climbed the stairs from the first floor he could hear Heavy Metal, and on the second floor, a string quartet. On the top floor there was silence and the smell of incense. The place was clean and well kept; also solid and quiet, except for the unexpected music below. Apart from the incense there were no smells. He remembered that Bill was renowned for the rarity of his invitations, he'd visited there only once to pick him up and take him to a meeting in Whitehall at the MoD. He pressed the bell and receiving no answer, he was surprised to find the door open, so he pushed it and went right in. He now felt some slight stirrings of unease, and for no particular reason became concerned about the smell of incense. Bill Poynton burning incense for Christ's sake, why would he burn incense? Not one of your incense burners is Bill, he thought. And then he felt sorry about the dishevelled Bill and that perhaps he should have tried to visit him earlier, maybe there was something wrong here after all.

And if there had been something, why should he suddenly make contact with him after all these years? So he pressed on through the poorly lit entrance hall, passing one or two unremarkable prints, he was never much of one for your art, he remembered. 'Bloody Philistine, if you ask me old boy.' Nick used to say; then he remembered, bloody Nick, as if he should talk - all he did was shag the girls in Central Registry. He called them girls. He would. From one of the rooms he now overheard low amplitude, unidentifiable music; this heightened his feelings of unease.

He called out, 'Poynton, is that you. It's me, Croke Parker - you remember you asked me to come over...' There was no reply. Then he heard another sound, at first he couldn't make it out, it was low and fuzzily reiterative. It was the answer phone, repeating the same message over and over like it was in Los Angeles airport telling you where to park. Funny the way you think of daft things when you're a bit, well not exactly apprehensive, but it was a bit strange, you'd have to agree with that. Also there was something wrong with the tape and he couldn't hear what was being said. In any case he couldn't make out where the phone was situated. Oh yes, there it was. He now started to feel unaccountably alarmed. One would. He passed the kitchen, glimpsing a dripping tap and a conglomerate of unwashed dishes

And then, in the living room, he was immediately made aware of the reason for Bill's failure to reply. He'd had most of his head removed, probably by several expanding bullets.

What a bloody mess. A right old mess, he thought. Sod this, I'm out of here: don't touch anything. No prints, nothing. He was pleased by his own callousness, and relieved by his cool. Not wishing to get involved in any way with anything that had happened here that was the best thing. He needed time to think, he told himself. Why would that be? And what was he meant to think about at this stage in the game? Someone had taken Bill out. It was nothing to do with him. Bill's brains all over the floor.

He remembered George Jorgensen, 'One day, believe me, that guy will find himself in a situation where he can't talk his way out of things this one time, and that will be bloody it, as far as Bill is concerned. You wait...' How would he know that? So? For the moment it seemed important to leg it as quickly as possible, or perhaps call the Law? No bloody way, not the Law. He preferred not to do that, but if you'd asked him why he'd have been reluctantly unable to give you a satisfactory answer. If someone felt the need to top Bill, the Law was the last lot you needed, I mean after all that trouble with the Iraqis at the funeral when the brother had freaked out and said that Bill had arranged for the girl to be topped. Bloody nerve. He had enough street sense to get in and out of the room without leaving any sign of entry, he hoped, having read books on the subject, quite apart from his own training.

And then the phone rang, that was a right bummer. Just like in a bloody book he thought. Well no way was he going to pick it up and all that shit. Pull the other one, it's got bells on it. We all know who's calling, some bugger opposite who can see me through his scope and put a large one up my ass.

And then he remembered that there was only the Park opposite. That did it. Time to go. There was no sign that there was anyone in the building; that was a bit odd, he thought absently and then it's time for the off and he was down the stairs and out that bloody door like shit off a hot shovel, no question. By now he was even thinking in whispers. He was confident that he had been unobserved, but you can never be sure he thought, as his bowel contents leaked gently into his underpants. Talk about a crisis of confidence; only the washing machine would know its extent.

But nevertheless he had this strong feeling that he should return to try and find out what had happened. It was wise, he thought, to have gotten out immediately but, as he recalled certain features of Bill's past, he realised that he must have a second look. There might even be something lying around in the place that might give more of a clue about that inscrutable, unhappy dead man. The chances were strongly in favour of his having continued to lead a solitary life, for too many reasons, as everyone knew. From his brief eyeballing of the place, he had seen virtually no evidence of recent visitors beyond the dead man. The flat was comfortably furnished, bookish and that was it. Some classy furniture mind you, good quality antiques, now there was a surprise. No signs of fun and games though; now that was a surprise.

Yes he would definitely visit later that night. He was glad that he had extinguished the incense burner and switched off the answer phone with his pen, or should he have left it on? He would come back in his car, sus things out. And then he wondered why it was that he was so curious, why was it that he felt the need to find out what was going on here. Maybe he owed him. And he knew that there was no maybe about it: he did owe him.

When he came back later that evening, he felt more confident, as he had now had the time to think things out and prepare a plan of action. What action? That was what he kept asking himself. He had brought along a flight bag full of assorted things, a video cam, a Polaroid, plastic bags and plastic gloves to collect anything that he might find. Also a Makarov which he'd acquired in Liverpool. At this stage he had no clear idea what he was going to do; it all seemed to become more ridiculous the nearer he approached the bloody place. What did he expect to find? A note saying, 'I did it because I hated his guts. My address is Number One Ramilles Gardens NW1. Knock twice and ask for the man who murdered Bill Poynton.' There was no obvious sign that anyone else had entered, until he got into the living room when it became obvious that someone had entered the place and had a bit of a look around. Poynton's body had gone. It was as if nothing had happened.

First things first. Getting back in had been no problem: he'd picked up a spare key which he'd found conveniently hanging on a hook in the kitchen: in any case doors were never exactly a problem. However, as soon as he entered he knew that something was going down, you could smell that it was different; he was glad that he'd brought the shooter. What was it Danny Glover kept saying in the Lethal Weapon movies? '... I'm too old for all this shit...'

Once inside the door he was relieved to see that apart from there being no body, the room was unchanged. That is, except for one other thing - a white envelope on the floor where the body had lain. It was addressed to N Parker Esq. He took it up, opened it, thinking OK, we got a comedian in the house, well who'd have thought of that? Inside was a plain white postcard. It contained a simple message. 'Stay out of this Judas.' You can't argue with that, thought Croke and then he felt an unexpected surge of anger and fear. OK so Bill had his not so good points, but he didn't deserve to end his days like that with his brains all over the Isfahan, for God's sake.

It would be nice to say that at this point Croke made a noble resolve to avenge the death of Bill, but life is rarely quite that simple. He reasoned that whoever they were, and he had a fair idea who, the people responsible for all this, the killing, the message, they would be unlikely to turn up at this moment. Putting the frighteners on would be enough for the moment. Killing him could wait. This might be the opportunity to have more of a look around. Unless they were watching the place. On balance, he thought that this was for the moment unlikely- sod it here goes. His next thought was to ask himself what it was that he was looking for. Or rather where best to look.

Bill's library seemed like a good start. One wall was lined with books, so he decided to eyeball the lot and see what came up. Not much. He had no idea of where Bill's literary tastes might have lain. For that matter he had no idea of where any of Bill's tastes had lain. The books provided little to go on. A commendable selection of reference works of the Oxford - Companion -to variety. Put them on the shelves. Look at the covers now and again and never open them, secure in the knowledge that you can enjoy the safe feeling given by a store of answers for a quiz that you'll never enter. A safe feeling given by the certainty that you can look up Stewart Milner-Barry's Chess opening if you feel like it. Or the Treaty of Brest Litovsk. A selection of contemporary fiction of staggering dullness. No Erotica, no verse. The only surprise was a shelf full of Comparative Religion.

Enough of that, thinks Croke, now is the time to open Bill's computer and have a look around. It would be totally encrypted, but that would present no problem. Besides, he had brought along his lap top and could download whatever took his fancy. The first password was dead easy. It had to be pink lady. And it was. Funny how easy it is, he thought. Best now to get into his online banking stuff as soon as possible. He'd always wondered about Bill's fiscal arrangements. He had never seemed short of the stuff, except that you could never work out what exactly he spent it on.

And here came surprise number one. His banking on -line ins and outs contained an odd series of entries. For instance there were regular payments received from the Religious Affairs Cultural Studies Group aka (RACSG), whoever they might be. Now there's a thing. An odd income source for the likes of Bill surely. So what next he's thinking and realizing that he may need to get a butchers at Bill's confidential files at the Office. No one's going to like that he realizes, no way are they and he thought Christ imagine what George Jorgensen and the others would say if they knew I was planning all this, I mean looking at personnel files, unheard of and thought, in any case personnel is for assholes; isn't that what Clint Eastwood had said? Bloody right too. He thought things over and decided to leg it. He would have done a lot better to mind his own business, the stupid shit.

And then he wondered if perhaps he should contact that spook who was meant to be one of the head Honchos in The Box at Vauxhall Cross. What was his name, Mr Sarno? FX Bloody Sarno. He was bound to know something. It was definitely worth a shot, no matter what people said. He would take a chance on it and see if anything came up. After all, it's all for the good of the Service as they say; that was what he thought.

As soon as he arrived in FX Sarno's office the next morning he realized that he had made a big mistake. The chill of hostile indifference and outright dislike would have stripped the paint off a battleship. No way was he going to get much out of this man, nor out of his sidekick, a Mr Ted Blunger. A right bloody waste of time. They both looked at him as if he was a pool of sick outside the local tandoori on a Saturday night after closing time.

'And how may we be of help?' says FX Sarno, sounding not as nice as bloody pie. Croke started off as breezy as he could manage, having just lost a dead body that he'd not bothered to tell anyone about. Hardly a good beginning to a delicate interview with this pair of oddballs: from what he'd heard about them they sounded a right couple. So he bangs in with, 'Right well I'll get straight to the point Mr Sarno. It's about old Bill Poynton you remember Bill?' Seemingly Mr Sarno didn't, or if he did he was keeping his cards well into his chest at this stage in the game. 'You'll have known him.

I'm sure that he was in your division at one time I believe, at least I'd heard he that was, or had been.' He began to get flustered The guy Sarno was now looking at him with even greater distaste. 'Poynton,' says FX. 'I don't know anyone of that name. I think that you must have come to the wrong department. What did you say your name was? Ah yes Parkness. An unusual name isn't it, but I digress. Yes the wrong Department, no doubt of that. He's not one of ours is he Ted, I can't believe that he would be?'

Ted shook his head and smiled.

Croke said loudly, anger overtaking him, 'Of course he's not one of yours you pompous prat, he's not in anyone's bloody department, as of bloody now because he's bloody dead. Shot in the head, and his brains all over the place.' said Croke. Oh Christ he thinks, I've lost my cool in the first minute. 'It's important Mr Parkside that we must all remain calm at all times. Don't we all agree?' Ted smiled and said, 'No doubt about that Guv.'

'Don't fuck with me Mr Clever arse Sarno.' says Croke, very angry already. FXS ignored this and asked quietly. 'Have the police been notified may one enquire?' Croke says, 'I was coming to that. No they bloody haven't. And the body has gone. Sounds like one of yours from what I've heard.'

FX just looked and said only, 'I cannot possibly imagine what you might mean by that, can you Mr Blunger?' He paused He looked at Croke as cool and nasty as possible with it. And said very quietly, 'I must now inform you that this conversation is now over Mr Parka if that is your real name. Let me say one thing: you appear to be in a state of inappropriate excitement; a shade below par, if not somewhat overexcited, no doubt the death of a close personal associate whoever he may or may not have been, whoever he may have been, but apparently no longer is, if what you say is true. Clearly this experience whether real or imaginary, has to some degree upset you. But there is no need to burst in here and behave like a silly schoolgirl who has received the wrong A level results and failed to secure admission to the University of Hairdressing. Come back and see us when you are feeling a shade calmer. For the moment let me ask my colleague Mr Blunger to help you. He is a caring person, despite your obvious misgivings regarding his homely appearance. As to that, let me say this, "never judge a book by its cover." You will do well to remember that in the difficult times that may lie ahead. He will escort you and find you transportation to your point of origin.'

And that was the end of the interview. Two minutes on, and Croke was on the street. He'd heard about Sarno. They were double right. The man was a right bastard and obnoxious with it. Bloody clever arse university git no doubt. And Ted was doing his nut, I mean totally his head in with helpless laughter as he said, 'Good job whoever it was got shot of the stiff immediately.'

Agreeing, FX said to Ted, 'Always keep things tidy is my belief' he sighed and said icily, 'We may need to say tinkety - tonk to that fellow. Nasty little piece of goods if you ask me. A right specimen of the double glazing profession; and no doubt from Carshalton. I'm sure Fizzer would love to take care of him for us, he likes doing over what he regards as the upper classes.'

Ted said 'Where did they dig that little cocksucker up from I wonder?' 'What does it matter,' said FX, 'It's amazing the sort of people they let into universities these days. And in any case it's none of our business.' He looked out of the window. 'Better ask Mr Fizzer to speak to him and square it all away. He could be an awful pain I fancy. Probably it should be done as soon as possible before the silly prick starts blathering to the wrong people.'

'I thought you'd want to do that, so I called Fizzer and they're picking him up when he leaves here. Ted replied 'the word is that the Poynton job is one of Karbnis' numbers. It certainly has his fist written all over. The stupid bloody postcard, who did they think that would fool? K likes to think he's funny when he takes anyone out. Also the man is a nutter called Steve. I don't know where they get them from.' FX replied, 'The trouble is Ted they none of them have had the benefits of a good public school education. And another thing about the late Poynton are his fiscal affairs and all these monies that he shifted to and from the Religious Group.'

'Blackmail is my guess. They had something on him and no doubt, he on them.'

'Good enough. What a way to supplement an income. But it leaves unanswered the question as to who killed the man. My money is on one of the loose cannons in The Department of the Love that Dares not Speak its Name. They have a few weirdoes over there: far too many in my opinion. It's a disgrace and an unfair burden on the taxpayer. See to it Ted; I mean and straighten things out.'

'Thanks a Bunch Guv. Just what I need I mean barging into their bloody place and asking who killed Poynton? Which of you ponces did him in?'

'Well I don't think that you'll need to put it quite like that.'

'I suppose,' said FX, 'One might wonder what might have been done with the body might one not? My guess is that the well known idiot Karbnis is in somewhere amongst all this. He always was something of a hothead. He may need to take a short holiday. Perhaps that can be arranged via, say Mr Edwards. I wonder who Maestro Karbnis employed. We should find him too. Quite a bit of clearing up to do. And it's all so bloody stupid. It's all about nothing.'

'Tell me about it,' said Ted.

At that moment Croke was leaving the building. He was probably not all that surprised when a car pulled alongside him, and a voice said, 'May we give you a lift somewhere Mr Parker? My name's Edwards, by the way and don't get any fucking stupid ideas about buggering off sunshine.' And he was about to leg it until he saw the man behind the voice, and got in helplessly, thinking what next I wonder? He'd heard of this guy Edwards and started to shake. Fizzer smiled and said, 'We need to talk Mr Parker. I hear that you've been upsetting Mr Sarno and his people. And, as I work with them some of the time on what you might call the PR side, they asked me to explain to you about that, and why it's not considered to be a good idea to upset them: sort of straighten things out, know what I mean squire?' And he laughed as they drove off. Croke Parker didn't laugh however.

CHAPTER FOUR

Ted Blunger knew it was going to be bad trouble the moment he had swiped his card when he entered the Vauxhall Cross spookhouse, and as things turned out, it was also the day when Ted seriously began to wonder if FXS was losing his grip on sanity. Bad vibes in the Anti Terrorist world. This worsened the minute he walked through the door when FXS, without looking up, says all icy and cheery like at once, 'There's a brave new world out there you know Ted if you get my drift.' Even mild sarcasm was never a good sign on such a day.

'You can do better than that Guv. Had a rough night at the Athenaeum did we, is that it? They should never have let the women bishops in. It's not meant. I always said it would never work out.'

FXS continued, 'Nonsense. There is far too much surveillance going on in our world.'

'You amaze me. What you doing Chief? Talking us out of our jobs. That it?'

'Now it's your turn to be original,' replied FX. 'OK so I'm not bothered with the morality of whether we breach the civil rights of a bunch of wankers in NW3. It's the bloody inefficiency I don't like. Satellite coverage, signal sweeps. Doesn't amount to a hill of beans -did I get the quote right?'

'Yes. What we do is a good living for some of us.'

'Don't be so bloody crass Ted. We are drowning in garbage - email, satellite signals, phonetaps, you name it. One email with the wrong word and it's red flagged for ever. And where does it get us? We can't even catch a few psychopaths in caves, or sus out a plot to take out the Trade Towers. And you want to know why?'

'I imagine that we would all like to.'

'Too much information and no imagination. That's bloody why. And no need to be sanctimonious Ted.' We are in a right pet aren't we? Give me the strength to get through this day Dear Lord, thinks Ted.

FXS paused, 'Try this for size then. One slight change of direction and we could learn a lot from the likes of la delice Gilli, whom you may remember. Dolphins for starters and she worked in The Rugforth healing place. Mildly wacky, I'll grant you, but a first class brain inside a perfectly formed head.'

'Nicely put Guv. Of course I do. I was hoping to catch up on her one of these days if you want to know, not that it's any of your business.'

'You might want to do that, catch up on her. We may have need of her view of the world I suspect.'

Ted later confided to Sandra, tactfully omitting the references to Gilli, 'And then FX comes on with a right load of old crap – without so much as a what do you reckon to this.' FX said, "What about this then Ted? The Archbishop's banjo and all the other stuff: could we be looking at a conspiracy thing here Ted?"

He's really flipped his lid this time. I suppose it had to happen what with all the pressures we're under – it's the stress – it gets to us all in the end they say. He's bloody unhinged. Someone's going to have to tell his family, not that anyone knows who they are. Awkward sod. And he'd replied, 'Leave it out Guv, we don't need to go down that road, you talking the little green men story I mean? What's so wrong with it's just a bunch of jerkoffs having a laugh? The most we've had so far is an Archbishop making an asshole of himself in public – nothing new in that I believe – the CEO of the Stock Exchange drops his pants and recites Eskimo Nell or whatever.' And added, 'He pissed all over a VDU, wasn't that it?'

'Probably,' said FX, 'the details hardly matter' adding, 'Oh yes, and the Prime Minister dropping his kecks. That keeps *The Mail on Sunday* in business.'

Ted continued, 'OK Guv, lets go further down that road. Someone wants to take the country over by driving us all bonkers is that it? Didn't they try that in Los Angeles, plus the CIA tried it all over the US in the Sixties, in case you'd forgotten?'

FXS merely said, 'Who can say what they did? I understood it happens most weekends in that place' He always called LA 'That Place, I wont even fly over it you know.' But FXS is thinking that whenever Ted starts calling him Guv it means he's worried, and so he says quite deliberately. 'All I know is that we have nothing to go on and we're asked to get it sorted, imagine a Minister saying get it sorted ASAP. So far what have we got? Nothing.'

Unrelenting he continued, 'In any case, lets get back to the outside agencies. What concerns me about these bits of exaggerated jokery, is the absence of hallmarks. We've trawled everything and found nothing. No connections of the sort we can pull in an hour flat. Not even a loony in Bedford for instance.'

'Funny that, it's always Bedford, or Luton.'

'And another thing, I don't buy all this Bilderberg stuff, and I don't believe in six foot lizards conspiring to take over the world, whatever the Southend nutter says. I just have a feeling about this one. It's more than a few funnies pissing in the window. Only someone who is deadly serious would try a thing like this.'

Ted thinks, sod it he's serious I don't believe it, and said, 'Let's have it then Guv, give us the whole bit.' And said 'OK if it's aliens why aren't they here running the world? Jesus, I don't believe I'm saying this. What's happening here? And another thing Guv, aliens don't exist: it's official. *The Fortean Times* said so, it has to be true. No abductions, no gynaecological exams of trailer park trash and the UFO Society is wound up. What more do you want?'

FX came back with, 'Is nothing sacred? The Internet says they're running it anyway. But that's not what I'm talking about Ted. I'm not talking about anoraks with Roswell on the brain. All I'm saying is that after exhausting all the known possibles, shouldn't we be looking for something new to our perceptions of that which we assume to be reality.'

'I don't know what you're talking about Guv, but you're beginning to worry me: why don't you just leave it out and cut out the funny bits? They're not your thing. 'Why can't he get some tablets? Everyone else here takes the bloody things.

'You disappoint me, I thought you'd know about all this crap Ted. Aliens exist, they can travel, but aren't interested in us. Isn't that what they say? Now supposing that were the case, why shouldn't they be interested in us? Science isn't the ultimate in human understanding. Make what you like of that, as my mother used to say. OK forget it, but I suggest you look at a few websites. A bunch of determined conspiracy theorists might just try something like this, to see what happens. That's all I am saying. A boy's best friend is his mother Ted.'

'Jesus Chief you had me worried there.' Thank Christ that's over, he thinks. What the hell does he get up to at the weekends? Perhaps he needs a hobby. Like DIY? I think not. Shit a brick. It really could do your head in, working in a place like this: it must do sooner or later. This is where they invented the déjà vu, I know it.

Today was the major-heavy- shit –meeting-of-the- week day. Anyone might have thought like this if they'd been present in the spookhouse on that afternoon, or was it morning? The September rains had stopped and the sun was ready to bugger off. You can always tell when summer is over when the sun stays red in the evening but it's not hot any more. A long train of barges drifted slowly downstream taking tons of crap to the landfill sites of Dagenham or Tilbury. It certainly wasn't the Royal Borough of Kensington, you could be sure of that. The traffic drifted slowly up and down the embankment: the odd police siren called out. And things would undoubtedly get worse. Ted knew that.

And it had all seemed to be going along smoothly enough until, for no reason, FXS had to start out with this load of crap about conspiracies. 'I don't often give lectures,' he had said quite solemnly, 'but in this case I make an exception as we live in absurd times.'

'Nice one,' says Ted 'Oh yes chief, and what would they be then?' And FX said, a shade harshly, 'For Christ' sake Ted please don't get funny with me. Here's the full SP.'

Why is he getting so shirty I wonder? I bet he's nervous and all. It's an age thing I suppose. Happens to us all. It's all this having to get up for a piss in the middle of the night. Has to be, I mean we're all at it.

But FXS went on, 'A practical joker is making fools of revered figures of the establishment; at least that's how it looks. Take the bloody Archbishop a silly enough little piece God knows, quite a laugh I'm told, but it froze the VIP's in their scented tracks. The word from our friends in the Special Problems affecting the UK Department, for that is what they are called, is that we should be on our toes. *They expect us to clarify the ongoing scenario in the event national security is being compromised* -I swear it, that's what one of them said this very morning, that is if they don't come blundering over here in white plastic suits.'

'I heard about it,' said Ted 'but I still can't see that it's anything more than someone fooling around.'

FXS said, and ratty with it, 'Well of course you can imagine who's most bothered about this thing.' He paused and hummed a few fragments of *Grabstein für Stephan und Stele.*

'The upmarket end of the boys in blue I suppose,' said Ted.

'Right. The belief is that a bunch of punters are spreading alarm and despondency amongst us to upset the fabric of our society, I swear that's what one of them said: not that they could be just taking the piss. No one knows why, and we have to find out. All I'm saying is it could be a wealthy group who are collectively paranoid. Someone up there thinks it's serious.'

Ted said, 'I don't believe all this. The Merry Pranksters on the road again? Christ that dates me.'

'It does.' FX said, 'Here's the rest. It all started a few days ago with certain highly placed persons getting email messages that said "We want to blow your minds and improve your health you assholes: you got it?" So far no one has a clue where that's coming from. The strategic view is that it's not International Terrorism, since there are, as yet no, associated demands nor references to the Great Shaytan: more likely a bunch of eccentrics with a tiresome idea of a joke, is the most popular theory amongst those where imagination is preceded by major brain surgery. I have different ideas however.'

He looked at Ted. 'Thus far we are adrift, and I think that we must forget about revolutions, anarchy and the starving masses and so on, and by the way we are ordered that whatever we do not to offend the Moslems.' Ted said, 'Well that's normal, OK, I'll buy that if it's going to save us endless meetings with them, but I still don't see what it has to do with the Archbishop and...' FXS only continued as if unstoppable, 'A hundred years ago, the bicycle was superior to the horse and if you talked abut space travel you were straight down the loony bin. That's all I'm saying, I mean about conspiracies you see.' He paused. 'We must all keep an open mind.' Ted replied, 'Come on Guv, you can't be serious. Are you telling me you believe that little green men are behind a bunch of practical jokers?' He thought, this is ridiculous, why am I even bothering?

'Listen to what I'm bloody saying Ted, and stop behaving like a stupid tosser,' FX losing his cool? Unthinkable. 'All I want you to consider is that certain things we now consider cast iron may one day turn out be a load of cobblers. It doesn't seem much to ask. It isn't as if I was asking you to visit Roswell High.' He paused and said, 'Sorry Ted, but I was impolite.' And then, 'And while we're on the topic of things that neither of us understand, consider the possibility of Parallel Universes which are only a millimetre away. The eleventh dimension. I find that idea rather appealing.' He laughed, 'I wish I'd paid more attention to Physics at school. OK back to our problem.'

'That's OK,' said Ted, relieved that they were back on safer ground, 'We all have our bad days Guv,but we've come a bit down the road from the Archbishop and his banjo if you ask me. I mean, you have to concede that it's a bit weird to dive straight into a load of speculative crap right from the off.'

'Fine,' said FXS, 'That's OK ,but don't overlook my liking for the unexpected. That's why I'm so good at my job. It's the open mind thing you see.' Ted thinks, he's losing it, he really is, and replied, 'Is that right?' And desperately almost, he blurted out, 'Why don't we ask Fizzer Edwards what he thinks about it? This sort of thing is right up his street?' Anything to get away from the little geezers in funny hats. What is the man on about?

FX said, 'Fizzer? Am I hearing you right Ted?'

'Yes,' replied Ted, 'OK, so Fizzer is a difficult sod, but he knows what's going down, plus he's got more clout than any Inspector on the Force. They say he's so cool, when he goes to bed, the sheep count him. A born cop. He'll come up with a few suspects. He's got a nose for villains, though sometimes I'd wondered if he's as hard as he likes to make out.'

FX said, 'Less of the psychology Ted, it doesn't suit you dear.' And said. 'Let's call him if that's what you want. Sheep indeed; I know what movie that comes from.'

'You amaze me Guv. I called him already,' said Ted. 'You didn't think this was news to me, did you Chief? I'm not that clapped out you know.' For he had called Fizzer and the hard man was in his unhelpful *I'm only a simple copper rooting out toe rags while all you cleverarse sods get the bloody OBE mode. And his message was,*' And you can tell Mr Bleeding Sarno not to come the sodding acid with me. If he wants me that's down to him, he can ask me straight up like any one else can't he? I've got problems to deal with this end including, if you must know, a new man who they bloody dumped on my manor. Some smartarse ponce fresh out of Bramshill who's after my job. No doubt his bloody lordship hadn't copped that one. My name's Hunt in case you didn't know it.'

FX had laughed when he heard that, 'I can hear him saying it. So reassuring, isn't it, to find that Mr Fizzer always runs true to form. If he came in all sweet and wholesome, I'd be no end put out, you may be sure of that. I wonder who the new man is, God help him.'

'There's no doubt that Fizzer makes the most of his reputation. Ted. You and I perceive him exactly as he wants us to. He confirms our expectations, but in reality, OK so he's not meek and mild, but his reputation for violence and so on is based on one event, the killing of Zeinab the Iraqi terrorist in Damascus. He cultivates that hard nose image to excellent effect. I agree he's an aggressive bugger, but it's all studied. At least that's how I see him. Let's not forget, he started out as the best hostage negotiator in the business, and that all began more or less by accident. There was no one else to do the job, and the Merseyside Force gave it to him. They created him.'

'And then gave him to us as a present,' said Ted. 'For God's sake Guv, the man's a loose cannon, can't you see that?'

'Not so Ted: it's entirely a reputation that he has created for his own reasons, is my view,' says FX, 'Until Damascus happened all he'd done physically, was broken a few heads and polished up his action man image. Don't forget that he had that awful fellow Manson for a Chief, an envy ridden impotent little piece who damn nearly lost him at Damascus airport. Inspector Edwards is a good policeman. He's never let us down, even if he has been somewhat abrasive. Also he keeps well away from the media. Imagine Fizzer on Crimewatch. He'd have the presenter's knickers off in five flat.'

'Chief, sometimes you amaze me. Let's hope he'll deliver this time.'

'If he doesn't, God help us.'

'How about this prick The Met have sent down to keep an eye on him?'

'Amateur night. Fizzer will have his balls in a bucket, be sure of that.'

He laughed, 'Oh yes Maestro Fizzer is always assured of a warm welcome here. Come now Ted, don't be so cheesy, the Fizzers of this world are the at the cutting edge of the maintenance of law and order and you know it.' Ted replied, 'I think you mean the Iridium tip.'

'Get a load of you everybody' says FX. He wasn't smiling now. 'What's Fizzer really doing these days as if I didn't know?'

'Rooting out corruption in the force and doing any dirty work they can find for him I hear. If there's some bad bastard around who no one dares touch, Fizzer will always nail him to the ceiling. They reckon he pulled in the Dagenham crunchers in one day.' FXS said, 'I think you're right and the sooner we speak to him the better. He can find baddies by how they smell, as far as I can make out, and who knows, this one may turn out to be nastier than, at first appears. It usually does.' He added, 'I find many aspects of this whole affair more puzzling than I like.'

Now it was time for an FX sudden change of direction as he asked, 'And what do you make of that bloody idiot Poynton being topped?' Ted replied, probably too hastily, 'And about time, some say. It's nothing to do with us Guv, never mind what they're saying. For a start, he was never really one of our lot, particularly with his hanging around that nutters club, the one full of total misfits and I don't know what, as far as I could make out.' What was all that about? FX replied,' Never mind, I have often found that places like The Pink Lady turn out to be good clearing houses. You'd be amazed at the amount of good stuff we've picked up over the years in places that are far worse, believe me Ted.' And continued, 'God knows the man Poynton went around the planet telling everyone that he was some sort of an unrecognised genius. I don't remember much more that that about him, do you?'

'There never was any real connection with us worth a damn,' said Ted, 'He was hired to do some research when an idiot MP came up with the idea that the Dalai Lama was a KGB agent, and we were forced to look into it to keep the peace with the Foreign Office.' FX said, 'I know, and he wasn't.I hope we did something about the MP.' He knows bloody well what happened, thinks Ted. 'Oh yes,' says FX going on, as bold as bloody brass, 'Didn't he pass away in a brothel or something?' Adding piously, 'and serve him right.'

'No need to be so vindictive' says Ted, '… and as to Mr Poynton, I'm sure that Fizzer would love to take that one on. One of Poynton's old colleagues found the body, as you no doubt remember – a right nosey sod, Croke Parker who they should have pensioned off years ago to the Costa del Sol to write his memoirs. He had his hand in the cookie jar for years.'

'Well I knew that' says FX, 'What I can't make out is what the connection was. Poynton was booted out years ago after that "little problem" of his, and I had assumed that the whole thing had been buried. And the man Parker was not one of our better hirings.' Ted then said, 'And another thing Guv, I should mention is that the news is that there's a contract out on Fizzer. I heard that one only this morning from the man himself.' FX said, 'Not best pleased I imagine. I cannot imagine what Fizzer will do to the perp when he finds him, as he undoubtedly will. Screw his balls into a light socket and switch on I imagine, that is before he starts reading him his rights.' Ted said, 'For God's sake Guv, death threats to Fizzer aren't exactly front page news: I thought he got them weekly.'

'He's taking this one extremely seriously, is that it?'

'Well he would wouldn't he? He reckons it's the Arabs.' FX said, 'We must remember to ask him about it when we see him. Shows compassion. He'd know about the Arabs though, what with him killing that ghastly woman on the aircraft in Damascus, and a few more after by all accounts that never showed in the records. Which Arabs if it comes to that? Home grown yobbos from Oldham?'

Ted replied, 'He says he's not sure, but he means to find out and nail their balls to the ceiling whoever they are: that's what the man said, and he reckons it's a big shot.'

'Don't tell me Ted, I can guess who he has in mind. And as to the ceiling; he would.' said FX, 'One might have hoped that he would have calmed down a shade since his wife has now taken silk.' Mrs Sylvie Edwards had at last been rewarded for her years of hope and struggle, as she called them.

'A token thing wasn't it?' said FX.

'That's not right Guv,' said Ted, 'She's a shit hot lawyer so they say.' Ignoring that FX asked, 'Are things calmer within the Fizzer household these days?'

'The last I heard was that it's armed neutrality and Fizzer having blood tests every month.' FX said, 'While we're on the subject of our Arab pals, there is one person who we shouldn't forget. I refer to His Excellency.' Ted replied, 'I thought we'd given up on him. He's just another harmless Arab big shot who needs two Lebanese to hold his dick in case he pisses himself.'

'I never just give up on suspects Ted. You know that. And I know that this man is bad news. My guess is that he is Fizzer's prime suspect for the contract.'

'Mine too.' Said Ted. 'Let's wait and see: I think it's time His Ex went home and had his ass kicked a little.'

At that moment His Excellency would have fainted dead away if he knew what was being said about him. He was in his Club writing a letter to an influential weekly found in all the best clubs: a favourite read amongst the Tories of the public school foxhunting -is –great- fun -and –very- liberating- but at heart -we –really- love- Keats and Trollope sort. He liked their weekly because it was covertly anti semitic but employed a mad Jewish pro-Israeli columnist, in much the same way that certain gays marry silly women. The Excellent Official whom God preserve so to speak, took deep offence at the anti-Arab remarks that the fiery Semite penned in his weekly rants.

His Excellency was a man of literary pretensions. He posed as a former admirer of the West, drank fine wine and wrote bad verse: disappointed fan sort of chap, who had taken it upon himself to correct the ways of the decadent West in the columns of the national Press, using leaden humour and feeble attempts at irony.

A soft target, but a dangerous son of a bitch, was what FX thought of him when he arranged for him and his bastard bloody chummies to have a higher level of surveillance than was strictly permitted under whatever protocol covers such matters, as if anyone gave a toss, as he delicately put it. 'I want his bloody raghead ass in a sling Ted,' he said in a rare moment of indiscretion.

Ted thought that this might be going over the top and said as much 'This lot have been friendly on the whole and they do have the oil Guv' as he, a shade cynically for him, put it. 'In which case there's all the more reason to watch the buggers,' said FX, 'In my book after September Eleven all the dirty thob brigade are suspect. If he makes intemperate remarks of the sort that he's been dishing out lately, he must expect us to keep an eye on him. After all his bloody lot aren't exactly bleeding hearts liberals. Three separate Secret Police forces, underground prisons where you never see daylight, torture, you name it. Fuck them that's what I say.' And added, 'that is if they're not stoning you. I want us to know every bit of SigInt that goes in and out of his bloody place and more.' Ted said, 'Listen Chief, I have to ask this. I'm getting an impression here that there might be something personal in all this. Would I be right?' FX replied wearily, for it was getting on, 'Anything is possible Ted, in this Vale of Tears.'

And then he said, 'I don't like zealots Ted. As far as I'm concerned most of the useful work we do is attempting to get back at people who want to kill us all, and anyone handy because we don't share their goofy beliefs. It is as simple as that Ted. I've never revealed too much of my self, as you know. And I'm not likely to, beyond conceding that possibly I was influenced by too many zealots in childhood. And another thing, one of the features about friend Fizzer is that he may be a major crosspatch, but he is not a bigot. That's all.'

Ted replied, 'I understand Guv.' And he noticed that FX looked quite sad at that moment. A rare sight. And FX said, 'And that is why I want His Excellency's ass. That man is an evil bugger. He peddles cheap anti-Americanism and makes pious statements about Islamic Fundamentalism, and so on. I think he may turn out to be one of the worst of the lot.' Ted thought, that's it, he's losing it and then again you never know.

And he added 'We might need to set something up for him.' FX nodded 'It's time we met Mr Parker again.' Said FX, changing the subject. 'We can meet Fizzer later.'

Ted continued, 'On the contrary my guess is that the contract on Fizzer is nothing to do with the Arabs. My money is on someone like Hacker Tuke's brother. I bet you didn't know he had one did you? And we can't meet Parker- he's out of town, remember?'

'Didn't know nor do I care, one way or the other about petty criminals: it's probably both of them. Fizzer makes enemies.' said FX, a trifle huffily. 'Yes,' said Ted. He's just another villain: nothing special, but he was well choked when Hacker went down and in consequence he wants Fizzer done away with. Though I gather the brother is not exactly the brains of the family, but they are connected.'

'I suspect he might regret that. As a matter of fact Fizzer asked if he could utilize the facilities in the Fulham Road, if it was felt that it might be necessary to ask Hacker a question or two. He sent a coded memo. Very correct I have to say.'

They both felt slightly uneasy but said nothing.

'That will be OK, if that is what he wants. Or here. And as to the aliens that gave you so much grief. It's OK, I'm not losing it. I wasn't being one hundred percent serious as you will have realised, but while we're on the subject, it wouldn't hurt one of us to have look at a cast iron madman, a certain Doctor Horatio Bargs: all he does is give lectures about abductions, and what's more, he's well in with these people that Gilli contacted us about in that letter to you, that you don't know that I have seen. Another of life's meaningless coincidences I suppose, but it's worth more than a glance. He may turn out to be another waste of time. Who knows?' He paused and said, possibly too casually, 'Yes and regarding the Pink Lady. As we know it was one of Poynton's haunts. Bill had some odd habits which he found easy to indulge in that unsavoury environment. I think that was the case.'

'Well you ought to know.' said Ted. FX passed that over. 'Any way consider it done Guv. Even if you do read my mail,' said Ted, 'I mean with this guy Horatio, a right idiot by all accounts I can have a look at him.' And thinking where do we go now I wonder? And FX said, 'In any case you should remember that Poynton had to leave us, sooner rather than later, I mean it wasn't just the pretty young chaps that bothered people, but his having sold some of our best stuff. And we never found out who he was selling it to. I think that it's time that we did; don't you, that is as long as that the idiot

Parker hasn't screwed everything up and put the evidence in the shredder just to tidy things up.'

'Had it ever occurred to you Guv, that certain people might say that sometimes we tend to be a bit casual here and there?'

'It had.'

'And another thing. This outbreak of graffiti all over Town,' said Ted, 'it has to be our people.'

'Who else?' says FXS. 'What I like about it is that it shows us they are getting cocky, which in my book is always a good sign. I mean for God's sake how about "Watch this space for more news from the Jokemaster."? That's bloody infantile. I expected something better from this lot.' Ted replied, 'We checked their hits again, and sure enough Batman came up twenty times in the past twenty four hours.' FX paused; he'd been about to reply and he said, 'The buggers are taking the piss, that's it, isn't it Ted?'

'I'm not so sure Guv, this lot don't seem to follow any rules. I mean take when we interviewed them. They never even got mildly angry, more in the way of slightly miffed and low key outraged dignity, as far as I could make out, and that was it and they were up and away. They weren't taking any bloody notice of us. Didn't give a toss one way or the other.' Then added, 'in any case I'm not so sure that it's them.'

'Also,' said FX, 'the references to Jokemaster in the email announcement intrigues me in that it suggests an undue degree of interest in the most sinister of the Batman characters, I refer to The Joker, who has always seemed to me to be the worst of the bunch, Mr Nicholson wasn't it?'

'If you say so Guv,' said Ted. And he thought sometimes I wonder I really do. And then, as he usually did whenever he came up with something else, FX said abnormally quietly, whispering now almost, 'Of course, you realise Ted, that all this is, I suspect about to turn very nasty. They, whoever exactly they may turn out to be, aren't going to all this trouble just for a few laughs. I suspect these people are after mega bucks, you see. OK, so this far it seems little more than a set of rather silly pranks, they aren't going to stop at this. Take it from me Ted, there's a lot more to come, and probably ghastly with it, and we may need to brace ourselves for something really awful, that is my guess.'

'I know.' said Ted. 'That's what's worrying me.' And added, 'You know sometimes Chief I wish you could be a bit more optimistic.'

FX thought, bugger me old Ted's worried. Not like him What did I say I wonder?

And Ted thought, and another thing what's all this crap about bloody Parker, we know where he is. We arranged a meeting with Fizzer. Has he forgotten already?

CHAPTER FIVE

Lucy Creedmore had been brought up in Tunbridge Wells and educated at a flash Private School dedicated to the education of the better off and to the maintenance of good standards of personal and social behaviour. Personal hygiene and being a jolly good sport also counted for a great deal. At games of lacrosse or cricket, the young women were expected to cheer modestly, clap lightly and call out 'Hurrah', but never 'Hooray'. The latter would be likened unto blasphemy. It was like being in a time warp, and what's wrong with that in smallish doses?

'It sure beats the crap out of Grange Hill', as the Head Teacher sometimes remarked over a large G and T. Once you had copped these critical features of Lucy's background you were no longer surprised, for they explained many things about her. They accounted for her air of having been well brought up, for her easy good manners and her tendency towards wanting always to be doing the right thing. In Tunbridge Wells this is considered to be pretty heavy shit, in case anyone doesn't know. That and her unshakable adherence to the use of received English of the sort spoken so long ago, that some people might have found its clipped syllables and odd vowel sounds as incomprehensible as Sanskrit. Her family members were similarly affected on the linguistic side.

Brother Hugh was a successful consultant surgeon in Bath or somewhere, and mostly talked balls. He patronised his sister and made helpful comments about his sister such as, 'poor Lucy, she's such an underachiever.' And Lucy would think 'Who needs it?' say nothing and smile. The other brother, Cedric, was a parson in Lincolnshire and played cricket most of the time. And they all hated each other's asses to bits, but met once a year en famille at Christmas where they exchanged hostile glances and got pissed out of their minds. It usually cost Lucy a bloody fortune in cocaine did Christmas, plus she couldn't bear the parson's unspeakable wife Alicia, all teeth, incessant comments on her heavy periods and good works, even worse were their children, Jonty and Cissie, two right little bastards who were just plain hateful, or so she thought. They openly mocked Lucy's good manners and imitated her mode of speech as Lucy dreamt hopelessly of better times that would probably never come

the sun is shining, the grass is green,
the orange and palm trees sway,
there's never been such a day in Beverley Hills L.A ...

Poor Lucy, some bloody hope of a White Christmas with that shower for family Her parents lived in Tunbridge Wells: her father had been the Headmaster of a minor Public School in Sussex, famed for its open air productions of Greek classical plays and the promotion of homosexual behaviour amongst the boys, as a way of fostering in them an enduring love of the drama. After leaving school she had entered one of those Drama Schools that prepared young women for unemployment, after which she had worked briefly in rep and had made two or three negligible TV appearances in aga land serials.

Then it all came to a halt. Sadly, the problem was that she wasn't really much good, and her luck ran out, which can too often be the case with those who fancy acting as a soft option. She hadn't got it, as they say in the business. All would have been well if she had left it at that and accepted the way in which things had turned out, kicked her ass into shape, and got a job - instead she hung around waiting for a boat that never came in, and although she had one or two good ideas of what she might do with her life, somehow they never amounted to much.

Each good idea was thwarted by her tendency to drift into bed with some asshole with his eye on a quick shag, and inevitably she ended up dumped on, with an occasional dose of clap or non specific urethritis. Thank God she never gets pregnant, her friends all said. She was blonde-haired, but she had reached that critical stage in life when blondness had lost its appeal - it no longer counted for anything: playing the real-life role of the blonde ingénue with theatrical pretensions was something that she'd hung on to for too long. She was a good natured, attractive person, of whom older men said, when looking for a piece of her ass, 'Isn't it amazing that no one ever asked her to marry them,' as they tried to feel her up. 'What's wrong with the men nowadays?' asked women.

She often looked puzzled and unhappy, but soon cheered up and could talk about wine. 'This is a good one,' she would say knowingly and smile: never a good sign. She drifted through a variety of jobs but her heart remained in the acting even when she finally settled as a self-employed teacher cum dragoman organizing upmarket cultural visits to antique lands and sites. But lately, sometimes she woke in the night sweating and uncertain. Would anything interesting ever happen to her? This is a dangerous state for anyone to be in, particularly a vulnerable, not so young woman.

But now it seemed that her luck might be changing for the better, for she had received the offer of an interesting well-paid job which had good prospects for Lucy, fed up with a succession of moderately lucrative blind alleys. This one looked pretty good. She had found the job, more or less by accident, at party given by one of her Sloaney friends. Someone, was it Poppy or was it Susannah, had yelled, 'I heah yah looking for a job Darling. There's this fantastic clinicky sort of thingy sort of place, you know, meditation and yoga and colonic cleansing. You know, and Giles said they were looking for a Social Director so I said "well why not call bloody Lucy?" I mean, your name is Lucy isn't it? How stupid of me.'

At first glance the idea of the job didn't appeal, because of the 'clinicky' bit, but you never knew, it might just turn out to be a laugh. It was situated in an agreeable place in the countryside, forty miles north of central London. Now there was a problem: Lucy didn't like anything that was North of London apart from Primrose Hill or grouse moors in the Land of the Jocks. But she steeled herself, choosing to ignore the warnings of friends who shrieked despairingly, 'But you wont be able to get polenta or meet any of us at Harvey Nicks,' and off she went up the M11 in her green BMW 315 rear spoilers, alloy wheels and all. She was feeling pretty good at the time, and she looked good too: Prada jeans, Hackett sports jacket and a pink shirt - the healthy intelligent look aspired to by those happy members of the upper classes who never have to work for a living and go to Art schools.

The letter from the Shufi Center for Holistic Enrichment and Inspirational Bodywork had been short on facts but long on reassuring generalisations, *'...health wellness, integrity, sanity prosperity happens naturally when we are living in a state of balance...'* was the opener... *'Our aim: to achieve those goals and ensure their maintenance and harmonic resonances in your life space and self-realisation in an increasingly emotionally and spiritually impoverished world...'* After this, it listed the activities available to those fortunate enough to be admitted to the care of the establishment. Who would quarrel with that, she thought as she read through the feast of treats that the place offered you?

The general objectives included... an opportunity to discover the essential truth of who you really are, a fully experiential experience in which you could listen to your inner world of bodily feeling and intuition, access your own true self, activate your body with Sacred Sound... you could even have a bash at a Tibetan Singing bowl, no less. All in one week, or three days if you were in a real hurry. And all for a grand. It was a snip. There was also a pool, a sauna and a fitness Center. Lucy's problem was that she felt unqualified for the post. She knew from nothing about Yoga, Reiki and didn't know a shaman from a hole in the ground, but the Executive Director, Purdue Gould, a brisk American voice, cheerfully dismissed all that over the phone. As he put it, 'Listen Honey, we are looking for a dynamic person with attitude - a pragmatic attitude. My guess is that you meet our needs, judging from your CV.' After he had settled an agreement regarding her dietary needs, he said, 'Hey Lucy why don't you come down and see us? We can talk about money and stuff then.' And he put down the phone thinking she sounds like a nice piece of ass. Lucy had been nonplussed by this breezy attitude from someone whom she had down in her book as a flat- earther who probably lived in a Tipi and ate seaweed or worse. Nevertheless, she went along for the hell of it, thinking that it might be a change from evading the gropings of alcoholic hoteliers. It might even be fun.

The Shufi Centre was one of those places that you might often see, well set back from the M4, M5 or M6. Usually they are about three quarters of a mile away, on a gently sloping hillside, situated in parkland through which you can see the approach roads, with tidy white post and rail fences, and you think, I wonder what that place is? It looks quite nice. As you hurtle onwards you wonder more about it. Is it a private facility for the detoxification of bimbos and prats, a rather dodgy private school, or a conference centre? And then you drive on and forget about it, until the next time you pass by. And there it is, but this time it has horse jumps. In truth, it's probably been all of the places you had wondered about. Anyway, it was now The Shufi Centre for Holistic Enrichment and Inspirational Bodywork, full stop. The main building was grandiose Edwardian, and there were extensions and annexes that had been added on each time that the place changed its function. This gave it a certain wacky attractiveness: it was as if you never knew quite what to expect next.

When she arrived at Reception Lucy noticed the music; you could hardly fail to, it wasn't that it was noisy, it was pervasive. 'Listen to me', it said, 'I'm soothing you and helping you re-affirm your oneness with the essence of your true self - I'm soothing your ass.' In addition there were clinking bits of pipey metal scattered all over the place; you couldn't see them but they emitted gentle tinkle -onkle -inkle - twing -twang- tongy sounds. Poor sod, she hadn't picked up on the fact that she was listening to... *musicians whose sense of devotion transcended technique and sound extending directly to the source that inspired them, and not only that they were exploring the terrain of their hearts through song plus a heightened connection to the sacred...* Well that's what it said in the blurb. She stood in the reception area now, feeling unusually calm but with uncertainty edging in, when a slender young person of the female gender, wearing a robe of white untreated linen, came along. Cop that, and the pictures on the wall - Susan Seddon Boulet, and a stargate in the foyer.

How dated can you get I wonder, thought Lucy with relief; this place was going to be a right doddle. Bunch of amateurs, if first impressions were anything to go by, I mean darling what are they trying to prove here I ask myself? And the young person of the f.g. said evenly, 'You are the one from the Home Counties who has been chosen to come to us, Lucy with a capital I shall I call you? I see you as a LucI somehow.' In your dreams you tiresome little cow thinks Lucy, and she smiles and says, 'Yes. That's me, but it's a fucking small 'y' by the way sweetie. L- u -c -y you got it?' And she continued, 'I expected to meet Mr Gould.' She let the remark find its own depth. No need to be too friendly.

The acolyte replies, 'Many persons exhibit negative attitudes on first entering the healing aura – it's a confrontational situation you see. And now, Mr Gould asks me to send you positive wishes and life-enhancing thoughts: at the moment he is in consultation.' Tell him he can kiss my ass thinks Lucy, and wanted to say so, but didn't. She could be quite stroppy now and again, as it happens. But the person droned on '... you see, Lucy we constantly go thru changes in our life styles; some are chosen. others are not. It is how we deal with life changes that determines how we develop. We can, like the seed, lie dormant, or we can blossom and thus endeavour to step out of our selves and our existence in order to deepen our self understanding. To create a safe sacred space to enable healing to take place and profound inner transformation of the other self, including zikr wazifas and meditations from the Sufi tradition, with births and life practice. Silence and group sharing chanting and story telling - we also offer year long training for experienced skydancers - new courses in shamanic Tantra, Tantra for women, Tantra for men and Tantra for gay and Lesbian Lovers...' The list must surely be endless. Lucy was tempted to say, 'Well bugger me. Is that right.'

A friendly voice broke in and said, 'Hi, I'm Purdue Gould. You must be Miz Creedmore.' Fortunately Purdue turned out to be much better she than had expected as he continued more or less without drawing breath. 'We are looking for someone who will improve the image here for Chrissake: that's what we hope you will achieve for us here,' he started cheerfully, 'Please don't get me wrong Lucy, or what should I call you?' She thought it not best to comment on that just yet, and he smiled anyway. 'Image?' said Lucy, 'I should have thought that...'

He smiled again, 'You see Miz Lucy, this is all new shi, I mean territory to me, I'm no health food nut or anything, I was brought in here to improve the fiscal viability of the whole operation of the goddam place, and I guess that I've done that in that we now show a profit, just about. It's that we need a better, more user friendly front here, if you hear what I'm saying? And that's where I'm hoping that someone like yourself will come in and re-furbish our image. Listen Miz

Lucy, half the people that come here are a bunch a crazy assholes for God's sake. We need someone to pull in a better type of person if you get my drift.' Lucy replied, 'I'm not sure that I entirely...' 'Aw c'mon honey,' says Purdue, 'Give it a shot.' And he smiled.

Unexpectedly, Lucy found herself warming to this man's line of talk. She remembered that Americans do speak out. He continued, 'Don't get me wrong sweetchips and I wouldn't want you to run off outa here thinking I'm not one hundred percent committed to life enhancement and stuff, but a guy has to eat. Hear what I'm saying?' This was getting even better. Purdue Gould was a lean looking guy; crew-cut military appearance and stuff, but more humour in him than you might have guessed at first sight. He wore a light blue seersucker suit. A pale yellow shirt with button down collar: in the shirt pocket was one of those things which Americans often possess: things that you hold pens in, made of black leather, and they look perfectly ridiculous.

On the wall of his office was a photo of him, a younger man then, in combat fatigues standing on some dusty battle-worn hillside anywhere, looking at the camera with the tired face of the exhausted soldier. Looks like a guy you could go to sea with, she remembered once having heard someone make that comment, and she wondering quite what they had meant, and who it was that had said it. Purdue's face gave her the answer. So she replied, 'Of course, I understand perfectly, it was just that I wasn't, if you see what I mean...' Christ she was slipping back into the apologetic I say, I'm awfully sorry to trouble you, but do you think that you could possibly, mode again, and now beginning to feel entirely foolish, but Purdue came to her rescue saying, 'You know what it is? You limeys really kill me.'

She reddened and Purdue, sensing her embarrassment, says, 'Come on honey, lets get a drink.' Lucy thought that was a great idea. Purdue said, 'It's a staff thing, know what I mean hon; some of the dudes don't like it, but I say what the heck?' And added, 'You seem like a good kid.' Lucy smiled and thought again, he's right, what the heck. And Purdue's thinking I feel horny, and she knows he is, and sighs. Does it ever get better? He continued, 'Here's the deal. First thing is you should take in one of the community meetings here. It'll give you an idea of the fruitcakes...- sorry, I mean clientele we cater for here. Know what I mean?'

She soon found out what Purdue meant at the first Community Meeting. The meeting was an 'awareness reappraisal' and 'whole giving re-entry encounter with apperception of the sustained realities.' Ho Hum. The general drift of the thing was that attendees should recount their experiences, well not so much their experiences as their sense of wonder, joy and revelation at the good that had been done them after a few days at the place, and the expenditure of a down payment of nine hundred pounds sterling before extras. Nice one.

After a period of silence someone said, 'The Tibetan bowls made all my bloody Chakras tingle and vibrate and I felt my bowels loosening: I broke wind and felt again the need the need for incense and smudge for my energy clearing crystals.' Immediately someone else then came on with, 'I feel now that I am unbelievably centred and at peace: I even had a past-future experience with my tingshaws and quartz crystal bowls.' In no time another goof was up on his feet, 'Just sublime and primal, the real stuff of the Universe in action- a real balancing and serene experience and I enjoyed the sacred quality of masturbation done quietly with reverence.'

And someone else chips in with, 'I transformed negative offload into positive divinity in ten beautiful minutes. And joy to repeat friends, I had a major evacuation of the bowels.' You get the picture.

Then the Presider said 'We thank you for sharing that moment with us, Now is the time to consider.' Everyone sighed agreement. This was going to be fun. The Presider, a brassy little piece from Runcorn called Lzye, said, 'Once in a Blue Moon, and we know what that means... ' an in-joke around here folks,'...The Blue Moon as we all know is a powerful rite de passage for all genders.' for she had the French and continued, 'We will explore our paths, current and future, looking at that which is resonant with the self, and that which is not. Vision quests and sound will raise our personal frequencies to higher levels, integrate the divine masculine and feminine within us, and close more subtly the precious contact with our higher selves, with guides and angels to find the true way towards self-healing and transformation. Feel free to get one off the wrist, it goes without saying.' She looked around confidently, 'Finally let us realise that it is imperative that we live in resonance with the earth and understand that by various exercises, we can change the vibrationary rate of our bodily cell structure, allowing our cellular memory to download information from past lives and enable the opening up of crucial lines of communication to higher levels of consciousness.' A ripple of appreciative smiles and sighs ran through the room. Yes yes they cried that's bloody it, I knew it, how true, yes oh yes.

And not only that, would you believe that the Presider was heavily into angels, in addition to all the resonance info. For she had been visited by an Angel during a serious personal life crisis of a fiscal nature with strong sexual overtones. Wow! She wore wall to wall designer kit and looked as if she just might bite anyone's dick off, thinks Lucy and then reproaches herself: she wondered just exactly where Purdue stood amidst all this torrent of crap. Would it be best to ask him, she wondered? Also she noticed that the Presider had undergone a tit and ass job. I'm not meant to think like that, she supposed.

From behind her, Lucy was startled to hear someone who said, 'I expect you're wondering what the hell you're doing here and why the place is full of loonies.' The unknown voice belonged to a cool looking young woman dressed in a linen caftan with the mandatory chakra and energy shield. 'Don't laugh,' she said 'we're not all charlatans you know.' Lucy replied, 'You could have fooled me darling.'

'Not so much of the darling,' said the calm young woman, 'I'm not a bloody dyke duckie and would it fucking matter if I was?' 'Well there's no need to use words like that.' said Lucy. Unabashed the young woman continued, 'I'm Gilli, you must be Lucy, our new head of public relations, you've been offered the meet and greet our wacky clients job and you're going to take it – am I right?'

'Well I'm not sure that ...'

'That's all right. take no notice –I'm joking – you could say.' Lucy felt unsure but let Gilli continue, 'Why don't you join me for a drink later, and I can fill you in on one or two things? I mean it wouldn't do for you to join us without knowing what's happening.' Lucy said Oh yes she would and was in mid-answer when she noticed that Gilli had slid away; she thought. What a funny place, but it was beginning to intrigue her. She was aware that someone had replaced Gilli as a presence beside her. It was the acolyte again: would she ever go away?

'My name is Seria. I wish to bring you to our midday refreshment.' Lucy replied, 'I'm sorry dear but I thought that it was Lyze.' The person glared at her and said disdainfully, 'Seria is my astral name you silly cow.' Lucy thinking this is definitely a right bunch of rather unpleasant loonies we've got here, smiled and said, 'I see.' And off they went to the refectory where, '... our organic, non genetically modified nutriment is specially chosen to revitalise your energy database and enhance your bodily and spiritual interchange systems.' This turned out to be a tasteless mess of indeterminate veggies which had Lucy gagging and longing for a real drink to drown the taste of the carrot juice and coriander whizzola cocktail.

Meanwhile Seria or whatever her bloody name was, chomped her way through the crunchy bits '... health giving and mind enhancing fibre to accelerate your spiritual empowerment in a stressed out age...' Would it never end thinks Lucy, thank Christ I've got some decent stuff in my bag as she hastily excused herself, and scooted to the bog to snort a reviving line, returning as pleased as you like, and ready to talk bullshit with this dopey young woman for as long as might be needed. But the cretinous Seria was warming to the task of spreading the word to the new recruit. 'You wait till you meet our newly appointed attending medico,' she said eargerly, 'I'm sure that he'll settle any doubts that you might have. He's a real whole person holistic doctor, you know. We believe that we need the assistance of those who are not blinded by so called science in the New Dawning Age.' Lucy said, 'Oh really.'

'Yes' said Seria, 'Dr Horatio Bargs, he's a very special person. He's from the New Alternative Therapy Institute which is part of a really forward looking institution in Southern California, and furthermore it's a drug free environment.' Lucy said, 'I'd really like that to meet him, I mean, you bet I will.' It was obvious that Seria didn't like Lucy's tone as she said, 'You'd better learn to button your lip sister if you want to get on in this place.'

And then her tone changed as Gilli appeared from nowhere and said sweetly, 'That's all right Seria dear, I'll take over from here and take Lucy through orientation.' Seria went off looking slightly miffed, she'd always had doubts about Gilli and didn't think she took things seriously enough a lot of the time. 'I suppose the silly girl has been telling you about Dr Bargs. Oh sod it, you look as if she has just been doing her being very important act on you. There's a lot of them like that in this place. Take my advice and ignore them. Most people here hardly know their own shit.'

She said that and smiled, 'Would you care to come and have a drink or something like I said? It's not all carrot juice and good karma you know.' She laughed and added 'I think we can take orientation for granted in your case. It's quite obvious that you aren't the usual new recruit here, fresh from treatment at some private loony bin.' and added, 'I'm sorry I had to bugger off like that but one of our people freaked out and I had to go and deal with her. We have more than our share of drama queens in this place, as you'll soon discover if you decide to stay.' She paused and said cautiously, but friendly enough, 'Just one thing Lucy, are you really sure that you'll be all right here? I'm getting uncertain vibes about you here.'

'I wouldn't worry too much Gilli. I can handle most things.'

'You'll need to,' said Gilli. 'Let's go then.'

Lucy wondered what she meant by that but reflected that she was perhaps a shade on the odd side and that she had a trace of an American accent which might explain things. Gilli now led her through a door marked 'Executive Level Personnel Only' which she opened with a smart card. 'It's OK dear, we'll get you one of these so that you may access the inner sanctum.' This turned out to be The Executive Dining Suite where Purdue was enjoying a large Jack Daniels. 'Come on in Lucy says Purdue. 'You need some solid food I reckon after listening to all that health stuff.' Gilli said, 'Purdue has a different dietary plan to most of us here. Feel free to choose whatever you fancy.' Lucy said cautiously that she rather fancied a plate of Steak and Kidney pud and a pint of Ireland's best. It went down a fair treat as things turned out and Lucy thought I think I could get to like it here, and it's a million miles from Tunbridge Wells. At lunch Gilli was helpful and not inquisitive. Lucy appreciated that. In her time she'd had far too much of people using personal questions as a way of getting their rocks off. Then Purdue said, out of the blue,

'Well. Lucy, do you think you might take the job?' She said 'Yes. I'd like to do that, but where would I live? I imagine it's not easy in an area like this?'

'We have accommodation facilities on site. You might want to start off using those until you get settled in.' replied Purdue, 'I'm sure Miz Gilli will show you around. Hey Gilli?' Here Gilli very nearly got frosty, and was all set to talk about not being a bloody orientation executive, and so forth, but there was something about Lucy that made her hold back. Lucy seemed like a decent person and a possible ally. Her concerns about the way things were going regarding the meetings with FX Sarno and Ted Blunger, and the rest of it, made her realise that it might be a good idea to have someone like Lucy on board as a buddy. Her guide agreed and spoke of Gilli's needs for stronger interpersonal bonding. Sometimes guides could be a right pain in the ass. No, she should not think like that.

As Lucy was on her way back to home that evening she had the idea that she might probably enjoy the new place much more than she had imagined. She would give it a go as it was certainly way outside anything in her previous experience. She had quite taken to Gilli and to Purdue, who seemed to be a good guy, and probably more honest than he'd like to let on. She felt vaguely embarrassed at the idea of all this. Did she fancy him? Was he married, she wondered and then she thought why did I ask myself that? Bugger it, tomorrow I'll move in and take my chances, I'm fed up with always going for the obviously safe option and keeping my family happy. The money was good too. Things might be looking up at last.

The staff accommodations were situated well behind the main building. They had been added on in the Seventies when the place had been used as a riding school. Some of the more whingey residents had wondered if the buildings were converted stables and murmured of horsey smells and sources of contamination. In fact the accommodations were much better than she had expected and well above most similar places. Lucy was amazed to discover that they were fully air conditioned plus a staff pool heated all year round.

The Shufi Center was making money, that much was obvious. Many parts of the place were really flash. And that's enough of that thought Lucy. All I need to do now is take a look around the area and find out where the fun is to be had. 'Who knows' she said aloud, 'I may have found my spiritual home or something.'

'There's no need to tell everyone dear.' said Gilli who once again had appeared out of the shadows. 'Save it for the Community meeting in the morning. They'll really love that shit.' Lucy was mildly choked at this. Was this bloody woman eavesdropping or what? 'Listen hon,' said Gilli, 'I think we need to talk. There are things going on here that bother me and I think that you should know about them, and I may add you're not the first person I've mentioned this to.'

'Tell me more.' said Lucy. 'This is a bit sudden isn't it.'

'You have a good aura, and are a trustworthy person. I can feel that' said Gilli, adding, 'OK Here's the deal. It's all to do with the way this place is run, and what I see as certain odd goings on here, I mean like some people are trying to take the whole place over, as far as I can see, and my intuition is that there's a good deal more to it than just a simple financial bid. The people involved are a bunch of weirdoes who give me the creeps. I'm taking a chance here Lucy, since I hardly know you, nor you me for that matter, but I'm asking your help in looking things over. Snooping around a bit. Are you up for it?' Lucy nodded her OK, and Gilli continued saying, 'The place is a properly run PLC. I know that it may not appear so at first sight, but it is. Purdue is a good guy but quite naïve in some ways. Know what I mean? Too often on the look out for a cute piece of ass; and that can cloud the judgement.' Lucy said 'I'd picked up on that. But he's a nice guy.'

Gilli smiled at that, perhaps too hastily, and went on, 'The guys that bother me are this bunch of weirdoes from downtown. What I had in mind was for you and me to smoke them out, maybe have a look around their place and see what we can find out.'

Lucy felt the stirrings of apprehension here; she had the idea that amateur spying activities involving these unknown people who Gilli had already categorized as weirdoes, might not necessarily be as simple and uncomplicated as all that. 'That's all right Lucy. You just told me what I had hoped to hear from you. I had no intention of blundering in just like that, but thought that I ought to test you out.' At this stage she thought it best not to mention FX and his advice as to what she might do about the crazy snoopers. Put it on hold for a while, maybe until she knew Lucy better. No point in Lucy getting hold of the idea that she had landed in a shower of loonies, which, to be honest, she had. And she didn't think that now was the time to reveal her connections with the secret world, such as they were. And she smiled at the thought. What would FX and Ted have to say if they knew the full s.p? She meant The Company. And smiled again as she thought of her meeting with Fizzer. Better to keep that on hold too. People might get the wrong idea. And she smiled again. So she said. 'OK Lucy. Listen honey social life in these parts isn't worth a, shit to be honest. But the nearest big town round here has a University so maybe we could go clubbing tonight. The guys are young but amusing. It's not up to what you're used to, but it's better than nothing so we might as well have a look at what's available. Why don't we meet at Reception tonight and take a look around.'

They had a great time that night drinking and fooling around downtown with a series of disposable young men who inhabit such Academic Centers in the pursuit of knowledge for its own sake. Later she thought, yes I will definitely give this place a shot; it's certainly a change from what's been happening so far. And she laughed and then she realised that laughing was something that hadn't figured much in her life for quite a while now. She could get to like this.

And that was the end of Lucy's first day at the Shufi Center.

CHAPTER SIX

From the beginning it was the religious overtones that had really got right up Gilli's nose; plus this bunch of intruders who had started infiltrating the Shufi Center and were snooping around the place. Not that she had anything against established religion as such, it was just having to avoid this creepy lot of bible-bashing wankers that came round wanting to have meetings at the place; and at late hours in the evening if you bloody please.

Gilli was always an interesting person, probably since birth. Gilli, former top Druid and doyenne of the healing arts and all that old shit, as she said in moments of irritable boredom, was drifting through the middle of a career crisis. It had been pure chance mixed with pique that had led to her having wandered into the healing life. Admittedly natural curiosity had played some part, even to the extent of a partial conversion to the whole belief system in the odd way that scientists like herself oftentimes have been known to undergo, usually to the dismay of their colleagues. So that your first impression might have been that she was just another of the weary procession of phonies and dickheads that trailed through the world of alternative healing, looking for a fast buck.

Big mistake - if you thought that way about Gilli, best to forget it, for it had been FX Sarno, who else, who had found out about her previous career in marine biology; her first in zoology at UCL, postdoc at UCLA and research post at The University of Southern California. Not what you might predict as a typical route to mystic wackiness and the world of crystals, Chakras and reflexology, but then there was nothing typical about Gilli.

Ms Gilli had always mistrusted people who regarded received wisdom as a matter of moral obligation. Also she needed to look around the world for a while, enjoy a few chemicals and hang out a bit. After the sort of life that she had enjoyed, it was no surprise that these local oddballs gave her the creeps and feelings of unease. At the same time she wondered if perhaps there was more to them, and if so, what might that be? They didn't half give you a pain she thought, turning up unannounced at the Center every other day, and looking as if they owned the place, or wanted to.

Their headquarters were downtown, about half an hour's drive away and they were patrons of the arts. OK, but it was all a bit too self-proclaimed for her, also this lot had too much attitude for her liking, tending to be pushy and secretive all at once. They never wanted to reveal anything of their inner selves, and she'd smile at her heretical thoughts, sometimes it's as if I believe all this crap about inner harmony and finding the inner essence and stuff. Perhaps she did, she reflected.

And what about their phoney names I mean, Messrs Y Spurlow, Jack Spudder and Ms Nansi Shafter? These had to be false names surely. And that was the next thing that annoyed her about the townies, if you could call them that, bloody bunch of hicks and hayseeds with ideas above their station. You could never find them if you looked for them, and if you didn't want them, they were on your doorstep first thing, Jesus. That was another thing. Why were they hiding something? Or were they yet just another bunch of dreamy nutters? In some way that she found hard to pin down, they seemed to be not one of us. She had even toyed with the idea that they might be aliens or something like that: as a rule she was surprisingly skeptical about parallel worlds, with the exception of crop circles. Another thing that bothered her was the name of their organization. Now that didn't encourage confidence at all.

The Religious Affairs Cultural Studies Group aka RACSG – that was all a bit too OTT, wasn't it surely? Every time any of their number visited the Center they just sort of hung around and half-smiled at each other more or less continuously, get up your wick it would. It was as if they were all snooping around and taking the piss out of the place and you, and everyone in the world; sometimes it even seemed that bad, at the same time. Not that she minded that all that much but it would be good to know what the hell all this was about.

And she remembered that dreadful night at the Booker thing when that crazy writer got taken out and Ted saw that she'd spotted what was really happening and how he'd been as reassuring as he was able and in no time it was action replay time... *And so they had dragged Iolo to the kitchens and everyone thought, these bloody drunks, or perhaps it's drugs; that's it of course it's bloody obvious when you think about it. They just make trouble, do people like that, and spoil it for everyone else. They were expecting him weren't they? Had to be if you noticed the way they took care of business. Someone set him up? Well, what can you say in this or any other case? For instance you could say that there might have been these five guys who appeared from nowhere, in black track suits and body armour. One of them said, ' Well that's all right, we take over from here, if you don't mind, 'and bundled Iolo down a corridor where they totaled him with silenced Glochs, and put him in a body bag. You could say that was what might have appeared to have happened, or could conceivably have happened, if you had seen it happen, so to speak, but then no one had, and so you wouldn't find anyone to testify as to whether it had or had not happened or whether it was all well, what do you think, asked someone? No one could say. And so it might have appeared that everything had been prepared for him, especially the special bag that was ready, the bag that was a new pattern of bag which was under evaluation for its leakproof capability, which was shown to be excellent, given the expected volume of fire in the firefight, had there been one. The one who had spoken was*

Fizzer. Well, it had to be, when you thought about it. It wasn't that he'd developed a taste for killing people. Or was it that once again he was driven to this by that impatience with the wastage of his life that made him blow Zeinab away? Was he losing the plot?

And that was the end of Iolo. The police said nothing much in the Press Conference, beyond noting that the unknown person whom they had been advised as being someone who could be deemed to be psychotic, had been found with a substantial quantity of Semtex strapped to his body, but that he had been discovered, after death, to have been someone who had presented at least the possibility of a serious threat, even allowing for the fact that he had no detonator. This proved, that is to say there being no detonator viz. the absence of an effective detonating apparatus, that it had not been apparent to the armed response unit which was in attendance and who had been obliged to open fire in the face of a potential threat, and in view of the threats already issued which could not have been discounted given the circumstances. All in all, a painful case. The cause of death was not touched on in the statement, and anyway no one asked. Those persons concerned, therefore, could not in any way be construed as having acted in any way that might be deemed to be inappropriate, given the exigencies of the occasion which had been construed as being possibly one of potential maximum danger. The Official Secrets Act had been signed by all parties...

And she'd said to Ted, 'My God Mr Blunger- your people are all people of violence, and I have to suppose that you are too, but I would have liked to think somehow that you were not that sort of person.' And he'd half smiled and said, 'Listen Gilli, it's all a load of heavy shit. My advice is to keep your head down: you weren't here: you saw nothing. You know what I mean?'

Remembering all that she had decided to contact Ted, as she knew that he was someone whom she could trust. Surely he'd have an idea about things like this. It was his bloody job was it not? There were other things about him and Mr Sarno which rather appealed to her though she would have found it hard to say exactly what they were. But it had been kind of him to mention an offer of help with any problems in the future. She would have been surprised had she known that it had been FX's idea. 'It mightn't hurt to keep in contact with that young woman,' he'd said that ever so casually, looking for Ted's reaction. 'I suspect that she is the sort of person who runs into all varieties of chance and coincidence is she not?' All this delivered, mind you with his own brand of well-bred disingenuousness.

And another thing was that the job at the Shufi Center was making her feel more unsettled every day. She had enjoyed meeting Luci the new meet and greeter, and hoped that she would stay. She came across as a humorous person who'd probably had a rougher time than she would let on, but who might be useful to have around if anything went wrong here. And then she began to wonder if she was becoming paranoid, I mean she thought "went wrong" I wonder what I'm thinking about what did I mean went wrong, but she knew that she was right and that something was going wrong and that it all smelt nasty.

Her guide was doubtful, sounding like a right bloody know it all, which when she thought about it, was probably what a guide was meant to be, and then she began to wonder did she really have a guide, or was it voices left behind from all those chemicals when she was at Stanford, and so it went on? Then the guide spoke loftily of auras. That did it. 'Stuff that,' said Gilli and switched her off Sometimes you have to, she said to the guide as she did so. 'It's a rational world that we live in, or so I've been told.' And she smiled as she now awaited the arrival of the great Dr Horatio, today's visiting lecturer. And a right wanker he turned out to be.

Dr Bargs had always wanted to be a doctor. His parents were keen on the idea too as it seemed such a nice thing for their son to be. He was a graduate of a mildly dodgy offshore American funded medical school, dedicated to the offspring of well to do families whose obnoxious sons were too thick to get into Harvard or The Hopkins. It had sprung up in response to the need to train doctors who were in search of a fast buck. He had failed to get a place in a good residency training program and so he drifted into alternative medicine where he did well in no time at all. He was a dim-witted fellow who meant well up to a point, but being unable to grasp the basics of scientific medicine, he found a haven in the waffly bullshit in the world of New Age and Alternative Medicine. This was easy stuff to learn about: the texts provided him with easy- to-assimilate garbage that you could pick up in an hour or two. And in a few weeks you could acquires a crap diploma in aromatherapy or reflexology awarded by a college in the basement of a whorehouse in Bayswater, and next thing you know, the big bucks are rolling in.

There is no doubt that it beats the crap out of being a registrar in the NHS and, working your ass off to pass the Membership: that's how he saw it, and it has the Royal Seal of Approval from the jug eared shagger, and anyway *The Guardian* thinks it's great and so it goes on. He could tell you how to align what you do with what you are, connect to your inner source of light, but he'd have been hard put to it to diagnose common ailments. In other words, to put it bluntly, he didn't know shit. There's more of them around than you might think.

And in no time he had rooms in Harley Street, a Roller and the occasional TV slot where he explained the essentially caring roles of Holistic Medicine and Homeopathy in controlling the AIDS epidemic in Africa. Seduced by success,

Horatio went even further than this: he became an expert on alien abduction, following the example of the loony shrink who turned the abduction story into a cosy little psychotherapy drama '...*These experiences are very real, not imaginary They collapse the distinction between inside and outside,*' as he babbled on about expansions of consciousness and that's why tales of alien abduction mean much more they appear: because it really happened folks. Trust me, I'm a Harvard man. Is that right? Horatio was on to all this stuff in no time at all. Even giving lectures and seminars. Wow! One of his accounts of witnessing an alien abduction went like this: '*... There on the side of the craft near the top of it, just above the protruding saucer ledge, I clearly saw horizontal rectangular-shaped windows around the object on the edge there were green rotating lights rotating while the spacecraft hovered...*' And guess what – all this happened in downtown Middlesborough.

'I could see three of the ugliest creatures I ever ... heads all out of proportion - no hair, very large eyes tending to be on the green side. they were escorting a woman into the craft: the woman was subsequently hypnotized by me and recalled the events in detail.' It gets better: for the first time ever, a UFO abduction had been witnessed and Horatio told it all. 'a housewife who lived on the lower east side of Manhattan (er Middlesborough?) was seen floating upwards from her apartment to a 'brightly glowing UFO', accompanied by aliens.

Chaos alert - with people honking horns, and shouting in dismay as the spectacle unfolded. Horatio had also seen 'two US Government officials and two foreign Statesmen, along with guards of their own. Either the man was lying or bonkers, but whichever the case it did not stop him from earning a pretty solid income along with Mr I and the reptoids. It made a change from Middlesborough, you'd better believe it, and in no time Horatio was on his way.

And telling the world about *my efforts in dealing with those who debunk anyone who dares to report alien abductions ...... ignorance and stupidity.. I am not referring here to diatribes against investigators like myself but to the abducted.: debunkers have chosen the abducted as persons who can be ridiculed: credibility denied to those who look into these extraordinary matters ... the abducted are "mentally ill nobodies mentally ill little nobodies" who are also mostly gay and lesbian. To me, they are heroes.'*

He was pretty hot on contemporary medicine too: 'drug and surgery-based medicine ensures that the human physical body operates at far less than its optimum potential. ... blatant misrepresentation and suppression of "alternative" forms of healing.' You get the picture. The audiences loved every word and didn't mind paying a few hundred big ones every time he addressed all-day meetings in Southend and Watford. Now he was really cooking on gas.

He had invited himself to lecture at The Shufi Center, where by chance it was Lucy's third day. 'Wait until you hear this guy,' said Purdue, 'They all say he's a genius, but from where I'm standing he sounds like a crook. I'll be interested on your opinion.' Gilli had made similar comments in less trenchant terms, but the rest of the Center was wet-knickered with excitement, not to say agog as the good doctor entered the lecture room or sharing centre as it was called.

Like most con artists, his appearance was unremarkable, if not pleasant and he was well turned out, with one exception, in that he always carried a pen, or even two in the outside top pocket of his jacket. That is never a good sign. The audience stood up in respectful silence.

'Friends,' he began 'I want to share with you some of my thoughts on various topics that I believe are of great relevance to us all ...' and then launched into a one hour talk about his personal experiences of alien abduction and how it was clearly part of a generalized conspiracy in that it was denied by the

Establishment, which ensured that well intentioned persons such as himself were slandered by them as it was all interwoven into the strands of an even more extensive conspiracy to keep people away from the truth, and unlimited access to aroma therapy, healing of every sort you could shake a stick at and multiple orgasms guaranteed for every person of the female gender on site.

As might be expected the, audience was enraptured and they lapped it up, as they always do. Question time was pandemonium. People were freaking out all over the lecture hall,having trances, seizures and pissing themselves with joy and new found enlightenment. Talk about snake oil. His new book, 'Towards Universal Health for All' was sold out in no time at all.

And then the good doctor startled the audience by inviting anyone who cared to join him to go on a trip to Southend to learn more about the conspiracy of giant lizards that was taking over the world. 'I think,' he said with phoney gravitas, 'that it will be most relevant if we can visit and sit at the feet of the person who, to my knowledge is the only one who can bring awareness to all of the great conspiracy of the evil slimy ones who are talking over all commercial enterprise, infiltrating our governmental offices, even our space research and medical research programs and...'

A voice from the back of the room said, 'I think Dr Bargs that's it's time that you left. We're not running a goddam political platform here. I suggest, respectfully, that you quit and maybe you can return when you're calmer. You read me?' It was Purdue Gould. The good Doctor knew that it was time to quit.Purdue was cool and unmistakably angry. 'Your car is waiting for you Dr Bargs.' he said.

The next morning Purdue was quite surprised when he received a phone call from Horatio Bargs, HB or, 'The Good Doctor,' as he had named him on the day after the 'Lecture' that HB had delivered at the Center. Apart from the wildly overenthusiastic reception displayed by the audience and most of the staff, the core people at the Center had remained quite unmoved by the performance. Gilli summed the man up as a phoney from the soles of this feet up, and Lucy, the newest member of the group, was even less pleased by the appearance of a man, obviously a chancer, who in her words, patronised a simply appalling tailor, and therefore could not be trusted. And now here was Purdue awaiting the visitation from the Doctor, wondering what the man might want of him.

His call had been a wearisome mixture of pomposity and bullshit.Purdue wondered why the really pompous have no insight and think that they are doing you a major favour as they make their suety demands, 'Oh look here, good, is that you Gould? Look here old man, I thought I'd give you a call as I felt you might be interested in some ideas I have that might be of mutual interest to us, if you hear what I'm saying. As you may imagine my diary is pretty full, but I could pencil you in a slot or twain, and pop in say at eleven on Friday. I take it that will be OK by you.' And without waiting for Purdue's reply, he hung up.

Purdue laughed at the idiocy of the man and wondered what the Good Doctor might have in mind. And then he called Gilli, 'Hey Gilli your guy Bargs is coming over on Friday to address me; that's almost what he said to me, can you believe that? So I guess you and Lucy might want to join me and we could find out exactly what this asshole wants. I think you mightn't want to miss out on such an experience.' Gilli said yes she and Lucy would come along and Purdue said 'Should be a bunch of laughs I guess.'

Sure enough Dr Bargs turned up on the bloody day, right on time at eleven o'clock. And not only that, the silly prat was wearing a black jacket and striped trousers. When he saw him in the car park getting out of his Roller, Purdue says to Gilli, 'He came straight from the funeral parlor by the look of things is that it? One of his patients didn't make it to the aromatherapy clinic?'

'No Purdue this is how Doctors used to dress about a hundred years ago or, it could be seventy. I'd say this tells us something about him.' All that could be said was that Dr Bargs appeared to be the very apotheosis of a dickhead. Although he was a young man he was beginning to flesh out as a result of too much good living: too many puddings and tasty bits of grub had gone down his greedy cat's arsehole of a mouth and the folds of fattiness were beginning to roll over the collar of the hand made shirts whose buttons were beginning to pull tightly over the belly. Small drops of sweat glistened on the shiny forehead, and his makeup was running ever so ever so slightly. He showed every sign of the likelihood that if he didn't get his ass straight he was just going to become a big old thing in no time at all. Worse still was that his attitude of superiority and omniscience was beginning to leak out of his asshole. Even his farts were patronising.

He came into the offices in a cloud of fatuous apologies for his having arrived late, speaking weightily of the pressures of overwork and of being in such demand. 'Where would it all end,' he asked, 'but no the work must go on, must it not?'

Purdue listened patiently to all this, offered the Doctor a seat and, having introduced him to the rest of the team, said, 'OK Doc, why don't you tell us all here what you had in mind.' Dr Bargs looked slightly miffed at this lack of ceremony and looked sort of haughtily at Purdue and disdainfully at Gilli and Luci, before leading off with, 'If you'll forgive me saying so, Mr Gould. I am, as you will probably know more au courant with the Groves of Academe than a place like this, if I may coin a phrase, and so I had anticipated something perhaps more formal in style at this first meeting. What I had in mind was the possible establishment of a department here, Chaired by myself of course, ideally with professorial status, which could be arranged with my alma mater with no trouble at all, with the object of developing a modest research facility based on your institution. And in addition, and perhaps more important, the establishment of a training facility on these premises in order to produce a cadre of certified therapists, who I can guarantee, could be assured of an income of at least 100K a year after completion of our accredited training program which will last approximately two weeks.' He paused and smiled at his hearers, 'What do you say to that?'

Purdue was a decent chap and was taken aback by this man who was making a bloody fool of himself in less than a minute of arrival. Barging in uninvited and appointing himself as a species of rinky dink professor funded by some diploma mill in the middle of the Caribbean or wherever. Was the guy crazy? Or drunk? Or both.

So Purdue said, as kindly as he could manage, 'I'm not sure that we are able to involve ourselves in such a high powered endeavour. I suggest that you might need contact with a larger facility than ours.' But the Good Doctor was not ready to be put off so easily, 'Au contraire Mr Gould. I find that the degree of karmic energy here is perfectly appropriate to our needs and can assure you that this offer is not being made lightly.I should perhaps add that our training program will include a fast track series of intensive seminars in contemporary marketing techniques.' He drew breath and continued, after asking for coffee and biscuits, 'The powers of the mind can be harnessed to create perfect health, as I am sure you will all know. But my techniques go further than that in that we can inspire our people to unleash the healing powers of their minds, to increase our clients immunity to illness and say good bye to pharmaceutical products, develop empowerment and enhancement of self esteem, and by using karmic Astrology, lead to angelic revelations,enhanced states of consciousness and well being. It's also useful in erectile failure I should add. And while we're at it, you might like to take a look at this: it's another idea of mine that I think we might want to incorporate in my plan.' Here he produced a document, more of a flyer than anything else.

It read: 'Our Four Day Courses can guarantee you earnings of 50 to 100 K per year after Certification in our Natural Healing Training Program, AND ALL FOR ONLY 1-2 days work a month.' He smiled at all of them. I'm a clever son of a bitch aren't I he said, without actually saying so.

Alarm bells now began to ring inside Gilli's head and, forestalling Purdue who was now looking apprehensive and uncomfortable, she said, 'I am sure that I speak for all of us, since we operate in a true spirit of parity and all that shit, when I say that maybe we would have appreciated some advance notice of your ideas before this meeting. In that case might I ask for an adjournment for say, forty minutes while we discuss your proposal amongst ourselves?' To everyone's surprise The Doctor accepted this without a murmur and went off happily to address a hastily assembled group of the karmic Community on the topic of 'Angels and their relationship to whole person healing.' The word travels fast among the seekers after the eternal verities when the likes of maestro Bargs are on site.

'Listen you guys,' said Purdue, 'This prick bothers me. He comes along here uninvited and next thing, he's wanting to introduce some wacky research and teaching program and for all I know wants my job. What do you say Gilli?'

Gilli replied, 'I think we should get him off the premises as soon as we decently can. Don't ask me why, but I just find him mildly sinister to be totally honest, quite apart from anything else.' She paused, looking at Lucy who appeared puzzled 'What's up Lucy?'

'It my be nothing, but I'm pretty sure I met this person Dr Bargs before. I need to check out a few people, make a few calls...' and she left the room hurriedly.

'What's was all that about honey?' said Gilli, 'She looked kind of sick for a minute there.' And she got up and ran after The Good Doctor.

'Dr Bargs,' said Lucy, 'I had the idea that we might have met before. Forgive me for asking just like that. Am I correct?' The good doctor looked straight through Lucy and said 'Good heavens no. I'm sure that we've not met before. Absolutely not.Whatever gave you that idea?'

'I'm sorry about that,' said Lucy,and she began to feel vaguely embarrassed, though why this should be she was not sure. Anyone can make a mistake. 'No no,' said the Good Doctor, 'I never forget a face: it's all apart of the medical training you see, I mean not forgetting a face.' Lucy didn't see at all but thought it best to drop the subject, but she was certain that she had met the guy before somewhere, and in the next instant was not so sure, wondering if the idea was entirely a reflection of the fact that she found him to be such a fearsome shit. 'And by the way, young woman,' said Dr Bargs, 'If you take my advice you'll not make remarks like that to those who are in a superior, and I may add, more powerful position than yourself. You see that sort of remark is the sort of thing that could be harmful, career wise.' Lucy suppressed the urge to burst out laughing at the pompous sod and wanted to say Listen you boring fart, you take my advice and stop being a pompous windbag. Stick to being a charlatan, it suits you better, but didn't think it would be the right thing. Purdue would be upset and she might lose a job that she was beginning to enjoy. The unspeakable Bargs was not about to let go, 'Stay out of my way you interfering bitch or you'll be out on the street. I'll see to that.'

'Listen buster,' said Lucy, 'Now I remember you very well. Have you forgotten Trinny Walters who died in your clinic? She was a good friend of mine.'

Dr Bargs looked as if he was about to puke up, and said, 'I have nothing to say. You would do well to hold your tongue young woman. And in any case her death was entirely due to misadventure.'

'Bullshit,' said Lucy, 'You were lucky to get away without a manslaughter rap there, or murder, and you bloody well know it.' And she started to storm out while Dr Bargs began to deflate as he realised that this time he might well have come a trifle unstuck. And he called out. 'How dare you. Any more of this nonsense and you'll hear from my lawyers.'

Lucy turned and said, 'I think Dr Bargs, that you might be wise if you were to get the hell out of here and stay out.'

CHAPTER SEVEN

Gilli often visited The Town situated a few miles down the road from the Shufi Center whose besotted visitors probably didn't know it existed. If they could have torn themselves away from the bells and tinkly bits they might have enjoyed a visit to an interesting small town protected from tourists by a motorway. Everyone was friendly in this little town that dreamed on happily in an indeterminate time warp when life was reckoned to have been all right as long as you were middle class and had a job. It was a sunnier place than Birmingham or Walsall, more welcoming than Pontypool and not only that, it seemed somehow as if it was meant to be that way. Probably it was related to the unashamed affluence of an area which was not too far away from a real University which knew nothing of degrees in Media Studies, hairdressing or football.

In the market square there was a library, all Victorian grandeur and librarian bodily smells. In the past it had been the Corn Exchange. There was a Town Hall with beams, half timbers and a wide staircase. In the recesses of the Town Hall there were commodious bogs and unexpected rooms where on Market days the sirens of The Womens Institute tempted you with tea, cake and unexpected blandishments hinting at God knows what. There was a Big Five Bank, once splendid and panelled: spacious but killed stone dead by the uniforms of its staff and the airport departure lounge furnishings. There was also an Are You Being Served department store which dominated the square. It was a rare find: formerly a large private residence, it had been converted into a store in the nineteen fifties. This had given it an impermanent theatrical appearance which made it look as if it was going to fall down. It was full of loyal staff and had the bustling air of a *souk,* with its unsteady displays and collapsing profusion. In order to promote sales on special occasions the staff were sometimes obliged to wear Victorian costume. Most of them did this uneasily and looked embarrassed unlike Members of The Local Operatic Society who swelled the ranks and preened and strutted, proclaiming we're better than professional actors in case you don't know: we care, and aren't in it for the money. They looked a right load of wankers. On the top floor was the skyline restaurant where homely persons served plates of stew, pies and scones. Surprisingly, the restaurant was perfectly air-conditioned. It was pleasant to sit there and look out at the gentle broken skyline. Off the square and in the narrow streets nearby there was an labyrinth of shops and cafes where you could buy all sorts of unsuspected gifts such as aliens, UFO's on key rings, also fairies, books on aromatherapy and tree worship, joss sticks and many herbs and books about bunnies: you get the picture. In the main square, every Saturday there was a market which, in its way, had much of the crowded bustle of a market in a similarly sized town in France, not the same, but not bad. The mobile stalls were much the same as in France and sold an unexpectedly Gallic assortment of merchandise.The main difference was the absence of stalls selling wines, good foods and firearms. It was all pretty much OK.

And then there was the downside, The Garden.Gilli had discovered the garden almost by accident. It's just as if nobody wanted you to find the bloody place, was what she thought, they had notices and references to it and all, but where was it when you tried to find it? OK so no one was saying and then just when you can't find it, there it is. That was what had annoyed, perplexed and worried her. Somehow it seemed to be all wrong, and not only that, it was made much worse when she arrived and had taken a look around. The atmosphere was deeply upsetting; she felt that quite strongly as did her Astral Guide. There were two ways of approaching this garden. The first was through a gateway that was set slightly back from the high street. It came off a narrow pavement on which you ducked away from the passing traffic as it roared up the hill. The second entrance was half-way up the road that was on the next corner up the hill. The road branched suddenly into a leafy mini- boulevard lined on both sides by a succession of well-maintained old buildings, mainly occupied by out-of-towners who glared imperiously at you as they drove by in spotless Four Wheel Drives. Half way up on the left there was an unexpected gap in the buildings.

You might pass it by, but if you cared to inspect this unexpected place you could go down a passage and visit a Gallery that displayed modernist art in faded rooms that had photographs of places that might make you feel uncertain: as if they might have seemed to change as you looked at them, or when you looked away and wondered if they might jump about and gibber or moan behind your back.

This is where it all started to give you the creeps. The entrance was arched and covered with stonework which bore uncertain convoluted and vaguely devilish patterns that made you wonder and look away again, and then you would think, 'Stuff this, I'll think I'll go down the pub,' to whoever was with you and you'd laugh it off and pass by.

God knows what Gilli must have thought when she first saw all this. Once inside the Gallery you might just have noticed a door that was never seen to be open, though you presumed it must be sometimes, since occasionally you might hear murmurs within. A notice on the door said 'Art Club Committee Rooms.' Underneath it said: 'Offices of the Religious Affairs Cultural Studies Group (RACSG). Enquiries about its activities were fruitless you would be told that the group was under the supervision of three recently appointed directors, Messrs Y Spurlow,Jack Spudder and Ms Nansi Shafter and that was all that anyone could tell you beyond saying that they had been recently appointed by the Trust after their predecessors had unexpectedly resigned en masse, for no reason. And if you asked if it were possible to contact them, you would be politely told that no, such a thing would be out of the question as certain matters were still under discussion, whatever that might mean.

Inside the Gallery you soon got the impression that the members of the Art Club had known each other since they had been born, and it was all almost incestuous, that summed it up. The Gallery was privately owned but it was difficult to establish any details of the ownership. The brochure referred to Articles of Association and the Management Trusts, but the details were unclear: distantly unhelpful, as were the replies you might receive in answer to direct enquiries.

This left you with an unsettled feeling, as if in some unstated way that you were not particularly welcome; it was as if visitors were to be tolerated as an intrusive necessity; nothing specific here, merely an uneasy feeling. You even had the feeling that someone might be laughing at you behind your back, or that they had something going there, something so secret and nasty that they wanted to keep to themselves, and anyway it was none of your fucking business. But you couldn't put your finger on it.

Another thing about the Club was that the members all seemed to be about the same age: perhaps this was why they all knew each other. It was as if they had their own code of everything, as if they read each other's minds as they nodded and smiled.In conversation they used archaic expressions, exchanged single words and looked away from you as they spoke.

At one level you might get the idea that everyone was polite and helpful; but behind the smiles you sensed a certain knowing self-containment that permitted no intrusion - that was wary of strangers and seemingly suspicious of questions about almost anything. That was another impression that had been picked up by Gilli's sensitive antennae: a feeling which had caused her to get in touch with FXS and with Ted Blunger, almost in desperation: it was that bad. The combination of this atmosphere and the ambience of the Gallery was cause for further unsettled feelings in herself and most others who visited there once and never felt like going back. It was amazing that the place managed to stay open.The rooms were well lit, the ceilings high: it was not a big place, and yet as you turned, you had the impression of doors silently closing and of the light unexpectedly changing. The works displayed were an interesting collection of the paintings and prints of unfamiliar artists of whom you thought you had probably heard, but when you looked at the names, they meant nothing at all, even the names seem to fade as you looked at them and tried to make them out.

As you came out the door of the Gallery you might turn to the right and reach the street. If you turned left you entered a passage with flower beds on each side and odd statues. Suddenly you entered a dank, overgrown archway of dripping trees: winter or summer, they dripped and rustled, glistening dully and offering no comfort. And it was precisely at this point in her first visit that Gilli started to get bothered as she walked along an earthy path that seemed as if it might never be dry, even in midsummer.

It led to a space that looked as if it might be open but wasn't, and then on towards a garden that seemed near impossible to find in that its boundaries seemed to shift. Worst of all was that no one seemed able to find out the location of, nor direct you to its central feature, a maze which no one was able to tell you about, beyond saying that there was a locked gate and that you could get the key, from someone, except that they couldn't say who, and that no they had never been there, and then they would change the subject as if what was the point in asking, it wasn't a very interesting place by all accounts, and no one could understand why it was that visitors always asked about the place.

All this resonated inside Gilli's head as she walked around the beastly place. She could have approached the garden by the first entrance but here the path, again remaining dank and sodden, led nowhere very much until suddenly she found herself near a small dark park which looked as if it might almost be an open space until she neared it and found that again it had eluded her, and she was once again faced by a wall of bushes that bore few signs of recent passage, but which shook, as if someone had just passed by.

There was something odd about all this: the maze was a place that no one seemed to know anything about. If you looked carefully, you might see more odd statuary here and there, and if you looked again, you couldn't see it, and when you did, if you looked away, when you looked back it looked somehow different and the faces looked as if they had changed, or you might feel that they were changing behind your back. If you were oversensitive you might even have felt a sense of furtive watchful hostility. And then if you happened to come upon the maze, you would find that it was locked and there seemed to be no way of looking beyond the wicket gate. Enquiries about opening times were greeted with surprised indifference bordering on evasion. As you left you might even hear the suppression of equivocal laughter.

All in all the place had an unsettling atmosphere which might momentarily remind you of Sadcake Park and the bloody man who wrote of it, and you might smile uneasily at the thought until you realised that there was nothing at all that was funny about this place. It was unsettling, the more so because it was entirely at variance with the welcoming atmosphere of this pleasant market town, unspoilt by the present and its fretful discontents.

That was what made the park more than slightly disturbing, intangible and unattainable. Sometimes, as if by mistake, you might come upon an open lawn. In the middle of this stood a small temple, or it could have been a summer house. What was odd about the summer house was that from a distance you might see figures inside it standing around as if waiting for something to happen. Were they watching or waiting? That was the thought that might flit through your mind. As you drew nearer you realised that you had been mistaken. There was no one there at all. Behind the summer house, or whatever it might have been, there was a broken column. It was hard to know if it was really broken or if it was a part of some quirkish folly. At the top of the column there were the remnants of a head; the features were hard to distinguish. You could not tell if it smiled or sneered at you, it was odd and unsettling. At its base it bore a Latin inscription that was hard to decipher; and in any case it was in a form of Latin that was unfamiliar. The unfamiliarity of its language and its odd setting gave to the whole thing a vaguely brooding, unsettling atmosphere. The words gave the impression, almost of an incantation. You might think that were so, if you were unduly sensitive or fanciful.

Here was a place that didn't seem to welcome visitors. The Latin read as follows:
DEVOMNODENT I
FLAV IVUSSENILISPOSSVIT
PROPTERNVPTIAS
QUASVIDITSUBUMBRA

And no one took a great deal of notice of it whatever it might mean, which was surprising as it referred to a marriage ceremony which gave every indication of being slightly on the creepy side. You might have supposed that the CSGIRA would have been interested in the origins of this arcane inscription. Most of their members claimed that it was a Victorian hoax or something like that, and tended to discourage further enquiries about what they claimed was a spurious artefact of unworthy provenance or spoke loftily of Teilhard de Chardin and the Piltdown Man, don't you know, as if anyone gave a toss about a phoney Jesuit nonce. They even got collectively huffy about it, as if interest in it was being drummed up by nosey parkers. One of their members even suggested removing it. The next morning, when you were leaving for home after an enjoyable visit, you would be unlikely to feel much bothered by the experience, all of this added up to you recalling a rather down -at- heel art gallery in a small country town, and the gallery had this derelict garden with a statue nearby and you forgot about it. Big deal. There was also a maze, or was it a labyrinth? The whole thing gave many people the creeps and this was probably why it was rarely visited.

When Gilli saw it, the inscription gave her a major attack of the creeps and it had her on the phone in no time to FX Sarno: the vibes were bad, and with her misgivings about the funnies at the Art Gallery, she thought, what else could she do? She told him, 'I'm working down in the country and there are odd things going on here that I can't quite be sure about, beyond they give me bad feelings, if you know what I mean. I know that it's not exactly your line of business, but my intuition tells me something is badly wrong here.'

FX said, 'I do know exactly what you mean and would wish to know, perhaps in more detail. I'm sorry to hear that, Ms Gilli.I think you should come and see me quite soon, and we can talk about it.' He knew that she'd been in touch with Ted and said, to no one in particular, 'How interesting. I always thought that we'd hear from her again. Ted Blunger will be pleased.'

And then he called Ted and told him about his conversation with Gilli and they agreed it was perhaps not exactly any concern of theirs, but perhaps maybe they should both have a look at things, to see what was happening. Which is another way of saying that they both rather fancied Gilli. For her part, after the phone call Gilli thought, how can he know what I mean, and then remembered that FX was no fool as she recalled her other meetings with himself and Ted; particularly the earlier ones.

She smiled at that and thought, maybe we'll get somewhere and thought, what can I be thinking? The other thing was that even though she wasn't mad about some of the people at the Center, she didn't like the idea that they might be undergoing a takeover or something like that. They deserved better than that, even if they were a bunch of idiots. What a strange world she thought. Her guide agreed and said that she was doing the right thing.

Gilli said, 'Well honey, you ought to bloody know.'

The funny thing was that when FXS saw the Latin inscription he remarked that it never ceased to amaze him how incurious some people were. 'Well you bloody would,' said Ted.

CHAPTER EIGHT

FX had this special meeting place which he reserved for meeting people whom he wanted to sus out, or for special occasions when he met people whom he disliked intensely, or for those people that he thought might find the place amusing. And this time he'd chosen it as the place to meet Gilli who he needed to interview since he was thinking of employing her. He'd taken a fancy to Gilli at their first meeting and, intrigued by what he had learned about her background, had remained ever curious to know more about this young person who, he was sure knew more than she let on about many things.

The Flamingo Café had long provided him with an island of safety on such occasions. It was situated in one of the maze of streets that lie behind Wimpole Street in a cluster of shops that people never notice in that mid-London village. Which is why he liked it. Also he was amused by the locals who appear to be marooned in a time warp where women wear out of date expensive clothes, heavy make up and speak in la-di-da accents and the men all look like old fashioned nancy boys in tight waisted suits and funny hats as used to be worn de rigueur in ancient black and white British movies. This is a part of London where you can't usually find the place you're looking for when you search for it, even though you discovered it six months previously. Worse still when you ask anyone about it, they never seem to know where it is and they look at you as if you were a visiting yokel from just outside Canterbury. 'Just the sort of bloody place you might expect that FXS would like.' Ted had said that, whilst conceding that it was an agreeable place where you could keep your head down if any shit happened to be getting into the air conditioning. At the same time, he still thought it a bit daft on FX's part, knowing his preference for certain of the flashier places in town and all. FX knew the owners pretty well and they had laid on all manner of special arrangements for his benefit. For instance there was an exit in the dining rooms in the basement. You went into the gents bog, formerly an old wine cellar, through which you could get out the back into the basement next door which lay underneath an upmarket bordel where the owner kept a spare shooter handy for FX should the need ever arise. FX was totally unmoved by Ted's ribald comments when he heard that.

The Café Flamingo was a surprise to anyone who encountered it for the first time. From the outside it was just another eatery: a few seats on the pavement and a traditionally indistinguishable-from–anywhere-else, nineteen- fifties interior. The staff were an interesting mix of people The owner, The Headmaster, looked and acted like the Head of a minor Public school and treated you as if you were a pupil. 'Take a pew,' he would say, 'We have some very fine lasagna today, and some excellent puds.' The others employed there included Ben, who looked like a promising member of the First Eleven, Julian an athletic young chap who was at times over friendly, and Jack, an amiable dried out drunk.

As you entered, Julian recited the menu and as you made your choices you were advised to take a seat and your dinner appeared in no time at all. There was also a rather anxious looking woman called Dolly who appeared every day at the counter looking slightly off balance with a strand of hair hanging over the left eyebrow. She had been educated at Benenden or somewhere and consequently she tended to recite the menu as if she was reading out a list of prizewinners on Founders Day.

All of the staff had read Dr Dog and dutifully washed their hands after voiding or defaecating: in consequence no one developed food poisoning and gases. Smokers were not segregated. The Headmaster often said languidly, 'We're pretty laid back about that sort of thing you know.' There was a large dining room downstairs, but FX, for security reasons, preferred to sit upstairs facing the door. He particularly enjoyed meeting MI5 people there,the chappies from that department that dares not speak its name,as he called them. He liked to watch them as they squirmed with distaste at the absence of good clarets and falter when he pointed out that the Flamingo could never be described as a drain on the taxpayer. 'I bet that cut a big load of ice with the tweedies and the poofters.' Ted would say, and FX would say, 'I don't know what you're saying Ted.' And added sympathetically, 'They mean well, you know: it's just that they made a few recruiting mistakes in the past, poor dears.'

So here he sat today enjoying a slivovic while awaiting the arrival of Gilli. The Headmaster came along and said loudly, 'Doctor Sarno,' - he always called FX Doctor, for some unexplained reason, 'a young person is asking if you are here. Shall I introduce her?' FX smiles inwardly. The Headmaster has funny ways,I mean introducing people. FX noted that Dolly had recognized Gilli and was making something of a fuss of her; it appeared that they had met before at Glastonbury. 'What an interesting coincidence,I mean our Dolly knowing the young person,' said the Headmaster coyly. 'Breeding tells you know,' replied FX. The Headmaster looked mildly huffy.

FXS had to admit that Gilli blended well with the place. There were no signs of her alternative interests; she appeared like an upwardly moving junior exec in the media world. He was impressed. If it had been Ted, he might well have come on with a spot of ironic comment. Not FX, he merely said, 'Welcome to our world Ms Gilli,may I offer you a glass of water from the St Estephe monastery.It's reputed to contain the faintest traces of aroma of the pine trees that line the fields in which it lies as I'm sure you will know, only too well. It's very healthy you know.' Not an easy one to follow.

And he added, 'I find that sort of thing strangely comforting in these troubled days. Oh and while we're about it, I really don't think it was necessary for you to have brought along what Mr Blunger will insist on calling a shooter, and a Makarov at that, in your cache pochette.' She replied, 'You can't be too careful: I've learnt a lot from your friend Mr Edwards.' FX preferred to take no notice: the idea of a meeting between Fizzer and Gilli being too incomprehensible to contemplate. 'It's all right,' she said cheerfully, 'OK I'm not one of his babes, if that's what you're thinking. It was entirely that when I saw him in action that time at the Booker thing, I realised that he might one day be a valuable person if ever I needed to learn anything about self protection.' FX replied, 'The world of alternative healing must be more dangerous than I'd imagined, is that what you're telling me? I'd no idea …' What was going on here? Was nothing sacred?

Gilli ducked round that and said 'I was rather hoping you'd tell me about that as it was yourself who arranged this meeting.' And added, 'Don't you think it's time we leveled with each other.' FX replied, 'It's always best to do that: it's quite simple really: I asked to meet you here, as I hoped that you might consider doing some work for us. Just a spot of fact finding you know.'

'Well,as it happens I had thought of looking in other directions away from the health industry.' she said as inconsequentially as you like. 'So what had you thought of doing if you contemplated a change of your field of fire; supposing that it were shall we say, a viable proposition given the right circumstances?' Another of his elliptical questions she thought and said, 'You don't half come to the point quickly don't you?'

'Not if I can help it: it's not in my job description that is if I have one, which in a way I must have. You should perhaps ask Ted.'

'Sorry Mr Sarno, but excuse me, I'm not sure that I know what we are talking about here.'

'It's simple I am merely asking you if you could help our people out a shade.'

'Your people?'

'No need to be so obtuse my dear. You know the people I work for,. Here is the full SP.How I relish these butch police words.Such frissons of distaste I assure you.' Trust FX to say relish.

'You will have heard of course about the Archbishop and all that banjo playing in the Cathedral and other distasteful matters. We have reason to believe, well hark at me, that these people may have links with the funny persons at this Art Gallery of yours: the people that have caused you such concerns.Why do they say concerns I wonder? Also there is the matter of the disappearance of Dear Stanni, one of our field people , though he may turn out to be involved in yet another pointless diversion, poor thing. I always wondered if he might just go off the rails one day. He has unsatisfied sexual urges of an extensively boring nature I suspect. They do that you know,go off the rails.'

'So what exactly had you in mind?' Thinking is he taking the piss or what? Ted did warn me he was like that.

'We believe that your tenuous familiarity with these people gives you the entrée, possibly, to their world – an "in"– as Ted would say. Also we could give you some techno help – I mean we could wire you up and all that sort of thing.'

'That wouldn't be necessary.I have a guide you know.'

'So I'd heard.' replied FX seriously, 'but this could be a spot of extra insurance for you. No?'

'You've certainly got a lot of balls,' said Gilli, 'I'll say that.I mean you asking me to carry surveillance. That's ridiculous.'

'Balls.Don't be vulgar my dear. It's really quite inappropriate you know.'

'All right.Suppose that I go ahead.What exactly are you looking for?'

'Anything and nothing. That's what we spend our lives doing. Looking for the anything in a world of nothing. What sort of things do they talk about amongst themselves might be a starter. You could help us out by planting a few interesting little toys that we use and so on. Our experts will be happy to show you the way we operate. You might keep an eye out for a chap called Dr Horatio Bargs while you're at it.' Gilli said, 'Ted said one of them hasn't washed under his arms for years. And I heard about Dr Bargs.He gave a talk at our place last week.A phoney, in a word,is my opinion..' FX said, 'I don't know that I am able to comment on that, but I imagine it's true.'

'I suppose I can manage. Let me ask you a question. It's something that I wanted to ask before.It's a bit personal.'

'I can handle that.'

'Is it really true that you played alto with Stan Getz.?'

'Baritone actually,and yes I did and also Zoot Simms if you want to know.'

'It's incredible. You must be quite old.'

'Most people are. I was always musical from childhood.' Replied FX, and left it at that. 'And now Ms Gilli. let's get on with it.Are you really prepared to help us out?'

'Of course.' she replied. 'I always enjoy a change of scene.' And then she said, 'Would we be using wall probes and all that stuff?' FXS acknowledged that remark as he smiled inwardly and merely said, 'Good, in that case. Lets do it shall we?' He had her on toast now.They all love the electronics.

And that was how Gilli was hired. FX had brought the paperwork along and she was put on the Payroll,Special Assistant Temporary Grade 2. When Ted heard about it, he said he thought that was a bit stingy and said so, but FXS said 'We don't want her getting ideas above her station.' And then he said, 'You know Ted I'm confident that there is far more to Ms Gilli than she lets on.'

'How's that,' said Ted, 'Well, as it happens so do I, but I'm not sure why. When I first met her I thought she was just another eccentric health nut and then I discovered I was wrong.'

FX agreed, 'Every now and then she gives hints of knowing more about matters that aren't in her areas of interest. I think I might just have a closer look at her background one of these days. Having said that I should admit that I have done so already and come up with nothing. I think we should be cautious lest we take everything she says at face value. I wonder if she has her own reasons for making things sound worse than they really are.' He didn't bother to mention her earlier indiscretion involving Fizzer and the possible uses of the shooter as an instrument of self protection. That would have made things unnecessarily complicated.

'It wouldn't hurt to go,' replied Ted 'If you like I could do that. Things are in a state of organized uncertainty at the moment; it would be no trouble at all and I could go down to the place for the day.' FX replied, 'Don't be in such an unseemly hurry Ted. What would Ms Sandra say to that one wonders?' Ted omitted to mention that he had already seen Gilli. In any case FX knew and Ted knew that he knew: everyone knows everything about everyone else and yet we are no further on with the present problem.Sometimes the secret world could be a right pain, you never knew exactly who knew what about whom most of the time and that's before you start including the suspects. Meanwhile FX couldn't resist saying, 'You mean you might go down to her place and see her again.'

'That's right,' said Ted. 'I could go down tomorrow.' Not wishing to sound too eager.

'Find out if she knows anything more about this chap Horatio Bargs. I have an idea that he may lead us somewhere.'

'What makes you think that Guv? From what I hear he's just another chancer who keeps airing his daft ideas about alien abduction on the Telly and at meetings in cinemas in Barking. And he's some sort of doctor.'

'It's Dagenham mainly, and Southend actually,' said FXS. 'And Romford.'

'Well it would be,' said Ted.

FX had called a second meeting with Gilli in order to 'clear things up.' Although he was prepared to hire her as a 'Technical Assistant' or something, he was concerned about his growing suspicions that she might know more that she let on about the world of the spooks in general and the CIA in particular. Did she in fact work for them? And he had said to Ted quite testily, 'You can imagine what a state the paymasters would be in if they discovered that Ms Gilli was a CIA employee. An acute panic attack of the fiscal department. The very idea would have most of the silly buggers calling for the smelling salts.'

'Amyl Nitrite more like,' said Ted, 'with that bloody shower of Hampstead Heath ass fisters.'

'No need to be quite so coarse,' said FX, 'but I know what you mean.In any case the thing that would really throw them is the idea that there was someone working for us who was on two separate payrolls. Imagine the consternation That would be the clincher.' And added, 'quite apart from the provision of health services; access to BUPA, pension rights,even parking and dry cleaning privileges – it hardly bears thinking of.'

So as soon as he meets Gilli the second time he comes straight on with, 'Ms Gilli, I think that it's time you levelled with me and told me exactly when it was that you were recruited by the Central Intelligence Agency and what this is all about.'

'I'm not sure that I understand what you're saying Mr Sarno. Me employed by the CIA, don't be ridiculous..'

'Next you'll be telling me you never heard of such a thing.'

'You're not far off the mark there.' FX knew that this tedious fencing might well now go on forever; that was after all what he was paid for, and Gilli too, if his hunch was correct. He wasn't sure whether or no he wanted this idea to be correct. The notion of Gilli being on the other side of the wire; was that bad or good he wondered, and, he thought, stuff the Special Relationship, as if it ever existed outside the imaginations of two Prime Ministers, one drunk, and the other on the downward slope. Perhaps he should let the idea go. Did it matter all that much whether or not they knew about Gilli and the cousins? What a bloody waste of time it all was.

He decided to assume that she was on the CIA payroll and take it no further. Gilli sensing that, smiled and said, 'Will that be all Mr Sarno?' FX replied wearily, for by now he was becoming pissed off with the whole matter, 'I thought you might like to have lunch. And then you could start telling me what you know about these people whom I call the funnies. After all that's what we're paying you for, with or without assistance from the CIA.'

At that point Gilli was looking a shade preoccupied, as she was in touch with her astral guide of whom little had been heard lately. The guide counselled her to display caution followed by frank in depth discussion at peer group level. 'Thanks a bunch buster.' said Gilli.

Fortunately FX missed that remark or he might have suffered a loss of confidence in the future performance of Gilli as a possible colleague. How could anyone explain to a fiscal department the necessity for an astral guide as a justifiable expense? Even FX might have been tested by that one.

Unaware of all this external dialogue that had been going on, he said, 'When you go to visit these people you should be careful. You might even want to try and get hold of them outside, say at the office they have in Town.'

CHAPTER NINE

The route that took Steve from Nowhere Ville South West Eleven to his new life in Bluegrass Green started with the assignment given him by Spiro Karbnis the Director of Operations and Termination Benefits. Steve had never liked what they called the contractual deconstruction operative role all that much, but then whenever it came up, it paid the rent, didn't it? He was designated as ' local casual hire.' Reliable and you could guarantee that he'd do a good job; no mess, no fuss sort of thing, yet at the same time Steve was classified as being potentially too unstable to be given substantive status. This way matters would be more easily negotiable for the settlement of his own final contract termination, if things worked out unsatisfactorily. Which is how such matters were set out in The Exit Visa Department job description. Never mind what they say about new images, when it comes to tidying things up, you can't beat the Civil Service.

In any case the consensus was that it was usually all pretty straightforward once you got used to the job, it really wasn't all that bad, except when they started crying and making a mess on the floor with the sick and that. Some of them even defaecated on the ground from the tendency to be very afraid of what was going to happen. Imagine that. Where had their coping mechanisms gone to?

And on the briefing day, (and what a balls up that turned out to have been you can imagine), things had started to go adrift when Steve had spoken to Karbnis, as he thought Karbnis, what sort of a bloody name is that for Christ's sake? He said, 'I don't exactly understand the instructions here.' Karbnis smiled his usual here I am being the tolerant – understanding- of -the- uncertainty -of -the –new- boy smile. 'I'm sure that we have nothing to worry about here.' We,that was nice. As if it he was taking part in the thing, not getting some other unfortunate schmuck to put his ass on the line. Trust bloody Karbnis to say something like that. So Karbnis says 'OK, here's the pitch. All we're asking you to do take care of things nicely for this guy who's leaving. I mean it's not the first time, now is it?'

Steve replies, 'That's right It isn't.'

'And there's another thing we need you to do.'

'What would that be then?' says Steve.

'Well it's a matter of the termination of someone's contract you see.' And Karbnis laughed heartily. Laughing wasn't Karbnis' best number. 'Oh well I thought that's what I was meant to be doing anyway,' said Steve, and he laughed too, 'What had you in mind, I mean anything like in particular?' Karbnis laughed again. 'You could say that. It's just that it's one of ours, not one of theirs. It's nothing personal but different. It's no one you would know. It's a matter of individual choice you see. We look on this sort of assignment as being a bit special you see.' And added, 'And while you're at it there's no need to be such an insolent prick, if you follow me.'

'That's nice,' said Steve. 'No hard feelings at this end either, I'm sure.' And wondered why it was that this guy Karbnis always had to make things seem so hard to follow.

'That's what we hoped you'd say,' said Karbnis. 'I'll fill you in on the details in the usual way. It's a routine thing.'

'They usually are, aren't they? I mean it's not as if it's a new enterprise for us.'

'I'm glad that's how you see it. Makes things easier, I always say.' And as Steve got up to depart, Karbnis said, 'As you know we do have strict house rules here about not stating the reasons for a person's contractual termination, but there are occasions when we feel that it's prudent to mention certain basic points as they may prove helpful to the operative. You hear what I'm saying?'

'I do.' Said Steve, now feeling a shade doubtful: He hoped that he wasn't being asked to deal with a former colleague.

'It's nothing very big. It's like this. This person is leaving us because he let the team down badly. A question of loyalty. I thought that might be helpful if you knew that. That's OK, you can go now. It sometimes helps to know these things.'

And that was more or less it. As per usual, as Karbnis would say. And by the way Steve is thinking what a lousy piece of overblown shit that bloody git Karbnis is and he was right. No one liked Spiro Karbnis. And so it was arranged, as was the custom of the organization, that as one person departs, then another is ready to fill the vacancy since the first one has left the club unexpectedly A financial settlement is arranged with the loved ones and it becomes a satisfactory arrangement for all concerned, and everyone is as happy a pig in shit.. All in the line of duty, as Karbnis carefully explained.

And so good ole Steve went off and, well, you could say that he did the job in the usual way. And it all seemed fine, and no one thought bugger all about it until Steve was sent on prolonged leave of absence, more or less immediately. He felt quite comfortable about that, but in a way he felt a bit, well odd, you could say.

For it was tactfully explained to him that he had made a particular error in his assignment in that it was possible that he might have 'arranged' the 'exit visa situation' for the wrong person, so perhaps he should make himself scarce, as someone else might have to go back and get things sorted. The trouble about all this was that it was never clearly established whether it was the full SP: they meant about it having been the wrong person, but then what the heck, you win a few, you lose a few, as George Jorgensen often said. And it was what Karbnis had arranged anyway. 'Talk about the left hand not knowing,' and 'Not the first time for Christ's sake.' as George J had also said.

In any case, by now Steve was fed up with the bloody business, and had said to a 'colleague' in a rare attempt at self revelation. 'I'm off to pastures new you see. I need a change:

it's for my health's sake.' In fairness to Steve it should be said, that it had been the right person and that someone had been giving him a load of old shit like that, in an attempt to destabilize him, as if he wasn't unstable enough already as George Jorgensen remarked.It was merely that someone had suggested that it might be it in everyone's interest to let Steve wonder if it had been the wrong person. Then he'd keep quiet without the possible need for his own termination at some unspecified date in the future. The Civil Service would take care of everything no matter how complicated it might seem.

'To be honest I was quite glad to see the back of him,' said Karbnis, and someone said, 'Where has he gone to then, the daft sod; if you ask me he looked as if he might be going round the bloody bend or something. He was beginning to worry me and we can't afford any more old rubbish after the last lot.' They would have been surprised if they had known what had happened. 'There's no real point in worrying about where he's gone,' said Karbnis, 'more likely dig his own grave sooner or later.' And they all laughed like the clappers at the thought. Old Steve digging his own grave that's a good one. It was all very accurate in that they were not far off course.

Unfortunately Good Ole Steve had been taking speed or something, and it had driven him into the wall. He always took large doses of speed whenever he had a special job to carry out. Those pills helped him to look on the bright side of life. On this occasion, he went on taking the stuff for too long and he developed drug induced madness, voices, delusions, the lot. And off he went, as people do when the voices tell them that is what they should do. Any other person but Steve would have probably ended up in the middle of total inner city decay, on a parking lot or under a flyover, totally out of his head: picked up and dumped in some A and E department in Homerton. But not Steve,he knew how to survive when he came down.

If Karbnis had managed find out where Steve had gone to when he flew the coop, he would have been really surprised, not too say bloody choked, the very idea.But he didn't know the guy well enough to understand that Steve was someone who was able to disappear into nothing.

For Steve had found this flash apartment home in a listed building opposite Bluegrass Green. What a nerve. What business had the likes of that bloody jerkoff going to live in a flash area, who does he think he is the bloody oik, would have been the departmental response. They liked their people to live in places that no one had ever heard of for Christ's sake, like Stevenage or Milton Keynes. What more could life offer, like everything nice and clean, and saves on the dusting too? But they were totally wrong this time.

Surely everyone must know that Bluegrass Green is the place where you should live in those parts if you're on the way to a better life style in a highly competitive and striving society of on the whole perfectly formed people, looking for better things for themselves and their children, and what's wrong with that? Nasty minded people might have muttered about islands of pretentiousness in a sea of shit: bloody ill informed tossers who don't have their fingers on the pulse of the essential nowness of what's happening here, leave it out Sunshine. No question.

Not that you can live on the Green itself, because that would be well against the law you stupid git, but around it:that's deffo the place to be where it's burgeoning, as the charming punters down there would say smiling over their Chardonnays and Perrier and coming on with, 'Well if you insist then I will, Oh but I'm not driving so maybe ...' The old-timers still called it The Village and agreed reluctantly that 'yes it's a great place to live in being handy for the railway, I mean what more could you? But it's not what it was.' And sigh.

And you might add that there's everything around like I mean all sorts of really fine architecture, twenty-six hairdressers; more than you could shake a tampon at as a local wit had once said. Jeez they didn't half laugh, isn't Roger delicious, and really, no end of really up and coming eateries that somehow always get roasted in Time Out, but what would they know, bloody jumped up petit bourgeois from nowhere, one would suppose? The restaurants never got it quite right though they could not be faulted for trying; they even put saucers of olive oil on the tables just like in bloody Hampstead where they put olive oil on everything it is said. Bloody bunch of shirtlifters probably. And yes there was a superior dress shop or two, including one where you could buy really hideous frocks that had been designed for scarecrows, or for those unfortunates doomed to spend their lives in loony bins, or go before the firing squad in the Gulag.

But it's the people who live there who actually that give it that very special flavour is it not, is what everyone said? Being on the whole persons of superior educational attainments, and tending to be of a professional sort like loads of doctors hanging from the trees, and barristers who said 'everyone knows the Birmingham Six and The Guildford Four were guilty, bloody Micks it's bloody obvious, anyone knows that one would suppose.' And double handy for many good schools of the private sector and opportunities for music and stuff, for instance a School where they are all very clever with eating disorders early on. And a primary school where you could learn all about how to live with each other, but not to read all that much.

The church had a Vicar who marketed the wares of the Almighty with talks about multiethnicity and caring, commonalities of purpose, shared values in a non-meaningful society and all sorts of soothing crap.He was pretty High, so High he wouldn't bury you if you were divorced said certain unkind critics. The locals talked in braying voices which got louder the nearer they approached The Dordogne or even Tuscany. There was a big private estate with unmade up roads and pools. Yes it was one hell of a place. Above all there was a Local Society for the Preservation of Everything We Hold Dear, which picked up condoms and dogshit, kept the place spruce and kept out the blacks and the poor. The local Society was quite a big deal and preserved local history and found artifacts of a bygone age, as if anyone gave a shit. It supported concerts and culture, and hated fish and chip shops with great fervour. And wasn't it a shame about the NHS, I mean it's like the Third World?

In general everyone thought that it outshone NW3 and places like that, but as it lacked a hard core of Jewish intellectuals, it really wasn't quite up to the standards of NW3. Though many did their best and read the right books, had psychotherapy, went to the NFT and to lectures and Glyndebourne, and there were some who even gave each other the high five when they won the parents relay at the school sports and so on, but it wasn't the same somehow, but it didn't really matter because everyone who lived on the Green was as happy as a pig in shit, though they wouldn't have put it quite like that probably.

Poor ole Steve, well he didn't know anything about this, and he'd say things like, 'I'd always wanted to live here.' That's what he kept saying to people as soon as he arrived. The neighbours thought that he seemed rather a decent chap and took little notice of him, beyond noticing that he seemed a bit uncommunicative, even for an English person, that was one thing. The other thing was that no one knew exactly who he was. That was bit of a worry, because Steve was starting to lose his bloody marbles, or become psychotic if that makes you feel happier. And he never told you his name, and any mail he received was addressed to a software company: what else?

The next thing was that after a few months they all began to realise that he was becoming a bit odd. The neighbours below him decided to call him Walkman and boy, they really laughed no end.Walkman? I should cocoa. That's all he bloody did. No way was it normal walking Seriously, this guy upstairs they said, for God's sake he walks around all the bloody night and most of the sodding day; it wasn't normal walking, you could tell that. They were right. It was the restless walking up and down of the seriously psychotic, of the card- carrying nutter, not just some poor son of a bitch who was worried about credit card payments, global warming and the collapse of the international banking system: this man was a real crazy. At first they all thought, OK so he's doing exercises and so he's a bit of a weirdo, but then you remembered the funny things he went on about, again that was OK at first, but the more they heard, the worse it got.

He'd always wanted to live in the house: he kept telling everyone that, when he first moved in there; but he would keep on about it and look at you in his odd way, as if asking you some unanswerable question. Some people who lived nearby, a right bunch of twits who lived in *The Guardian*; they couldn't see it. Just said, 'Oh he's got some problems, but he's a real sweetie, and I mean we've all got problems if it comes to that.' When anyone with half a brain could sus he was a nutter.I mean sod it, he went around answering the voices didn't he poor sod, but no, to them, he'd got a problem full stop.Some problem poor mad bugger.

He'd say 'I wanted to live here and see the green fields you see. It's the air. The air is good because there's no pollution from Satan and his demons you see,' and then he'd pause and he might say something like, 'Do you believe in thought transference?' and then he would ask your views on exorcism and demonic possession. 'There's something in it you know, despite what they say. Don't you think? I mean there's evidence isn't there?'

He'd say that, and then he'd smile at the side of your head and say, 'That's why I practice breathing exercises and yoga. Have you tried that?' Another time he said, smacking his lips noisily in a frightening excess of relish, for madmen can be bloody frightening and forget what the social workers bloody say. 'Tea,' he might say, 'That's good for you, that sort of a drink, isn't it?' seeking reassurance that it was, yet refusing it if you gave it to him, when he'd flinch and change the subject hastily. And then he'd drink it, saying, 'I never realised how refreshing it could be, I mean a drink like tea, you wouldn't think that would you?' And he'd smile to himself, then look suddenly at the corner of the room. 'Did you see that?'

And he'd look at his hearers intently and say, 'Do you know how it is that people become ghosts and angels?' He'd wait a while and say, 'I do, you see,' and laugh. 'Yes, I'm going to see my wife you see. Quite soon.' They asked, 'Your wife, I didn't know you were married. That a new thing then?' Almost jocularly, then cautious, as it didn't look as if he could take a joke, and anyway it wasn't exactly a joke. 'Well not entirely, in a way,' he said and smiled, and said, 'Yes I'd like some more of that tea.' After a long pause, he added, 'That's why I'm here; yes I'll be going to see her next week, you see. She lives in North West London you see. It's not very far from here in a way you see.' After a pause he said, 'Can you hear that noise?' and he smiled and hummed a few bars of a tune.

And then he'd speak of his childhood in a Home, and of his sister from whom he had been separated after they were taken into care when his parents lost the plot and went away. 'They went away, you see,' he'd say, and smile as if expecting you to offer some reason for their going, for having left himself and his sister in a semi-detached house in a place he didn't name. 'My sister is married now and she's in wherever.'

He often spoke of The Home and of his time there. And he'd tell how when he was sixteen he joined the Army where he learned about missile systems, got bored and found a job in computers in civvy street. At the moment he was between jobs and enjoying the fresh air, 'I really need exercise and the purification in the body fluids.' He lived mainly on zany diets, 'to purify the system and to rid it of toxins that they're poisoning us with.'

On cold days you might meet him exhausted and sweaty, running, his feet bleeding in his shoes and he'd say 'I need to keep fit you see.' And he'd smile and run on, 'I must have lunch soon you see.' But you knew that he wouldn't because you knew that he never did anything that he said he was going to do as he didn't want anyone to know what he did, and in any case, he didn't do anything. That was it, he did nothing. Mad people don't. That's what it does for you. Oh no, it's a mind expanding and enriching experience they say, if only we had the insights of the mad, and they get PhD's for this sort of crap.

Then as time went by, his windows remained open for longer periods until one freezing night, when they were all open on the coldest night of the year, open, wide open they were, with the lights blazing while the poor troubled sod hummed and chanted against fancied evils, burnt incense and gibbered. In his flat, the wide-open windows on that coldest night of the year, set off a call to the police from a neighbour who used to talk to him in the park. Even when he disappeared leaving the place empty and bedraggled with pools of urine on the carpet, bugger all happened: efforts to get help for him seemed to be useless in that no one came to visit nor gave a rat's ass anyway. Attempts at getting advice were met with disdainful indifference from statutory services hidden behind bureaucracy and committees.

And so he disappeared, returning briefly, gaunt and dishevelled, to face the humiliation of eviction and of being shunted into 'alternative accommodation.' He was seen perfunctorily, by a bored psychiatric registrar, when yet again, he spoke of his wife and of how he was going to see her. He refused to 'accept help' and said he was off to find his wife. 'Or did he say find a wife, or did he mean life? ' asked someone at the case conference regarding his disposal-planning-scheduling-in-a-non judgmental-setting, and they all laughed and said don't be so daft Roger, I mean him getting married.

If only he was gay, said someone. If only he was, such a big meaty thing like that, such a waste, and they all smiled: it was such a lovely in-joke and they were very clever people. Especially the newly appointed consultant who was a very remarkable person and quite stupid. As it happened he was the first consultant in the NHS to have been appointed wearing trainers at the job interview. Forward with the new NHS they all said, that will show them, no elitism here. His photograph was on the clinic wall. It showed him front of camera sticking out his studded tongue. A right prick. What a statement they all said, he will really wake the local psychiatric services up, bloody establishment. A stud in his tongue, imagine that. How they tittered at the case conference when they spoke of Steve. The consultant only said, 'He needs to do his thing. Probably abused in childhood know what I mean innit? OK?'

'Well, I mean, him having been a squaddie innit, and all that,' they said. It was a pity that no one took too much notice. In any case it was nearly lunch time, and the clinic was agog with excitement about a seminar that afternoon on 'New pathways in facilitating gay lifestyles.' A sure fire winner in the wastelands, I mean it brightens up the longueurs of the day, especially when it's raining.

So Steve slipped through the net. So what? Another boring psychotic what can you do? 'And don't give him any medication innit.' said the new consultant, 'I mean after all it's a chemical strait- jacket, know what I mean, innit?'

'Not exactly a triumph for community care or whatever they bloody call it these days.' said FXS, ' but it's important that we find out where this ghastly man is, I mean in view of his areas of special experience in the Service, wouldn't everyone agree that it's important that he is found, if you get my meaning?' He loved making a point and hammering it into the floorboards. It could be tiresome at times. He looked around plaintively, 'I mean he can't be allowed to wander all over the place and blow whistles now can he? I mean he did have access to sensitive areas.' Ted said, 'With his experience in encryption plus the fact that he's as paranoid as all get out, fat bloody chance.' and added, 'In any case it's nothing to do with us. It's ancient history. He's done no harm really.' And added, 'Sod the poor bugger - he probably needs a bit of peace; he's not going to harm anyone if you ask me. Leave him alone can't we?'

In any case Steve had already started moving along, pretty quick with it now what with him having chosen a bride-to -be. Not that she knew it as yet. She soon would. He'd seen her in a Lucky Eater or a Burgerama and knew immediately that she was destined to be his bride for the simple reason that he could tell from the angle of her Hermes scarf, and also from its colour, which quite clearly showed that he had been chosen to bring a message of peace and that she was to be his bride. He wondered what her name might be and then he overheard the person with her saying, 'Lucinda darling do look at this stupid little man over there; he can't take his bloody eyes off you.' All said in Upper Class tones you could hear in Cockfosters. Lucinda, yes that was a good name: it meant like lucidity, you might say truth you see, that's it.

The eternal truths and eternal was like maternal in a way, and yes she could bear him children of a greater godly nature in the field of the great ram and the paths of the ungod. The man was barking mad, but you wouldn't have known it, and if you'd raised doubts about his sanity, it's ten to one that one of his neighbours would have said hold on chum, we've all got a right to our beliefs. Until they'd got their throats cut that is, in order that he could liberate their souls for The Great Ram which is what he was actually considering doing at the particular moment when he knew that Lucinda, if that's what her name was, she was the one for him. Which was nice because it meant that he would not need to cut his neighbour's throats after all. Which was a relief. No need to bother about that any more since hers would do the trick and liberate the days of evil or someone like hers. He'd had misgivings about the job that Karbnis had given him mind you.

In any case by now it hardly mattered because next thing Steve disappeared as silently as he had arrived at the place. Nobody noticed a thing. They just thought that he'd moved on again and left it at that.

One morning this white van had come along and picked his things up, and they never saw him again. It all came about when he discovered that following his life long old ambition - to join a cult - was a no-hoper. The solution was to start his own personal cult to settle matters once and for all. That was it. This way he would get things straightened out. Everything seemed to be going wrong: her name wasn't Lucinda. He'd misheard what was being said or had he? Now he wasn't so sure and he became agitated. In any case he soon forgot her name as he was overtaken by events.

The point that no one seemed ever to have noticed was that OK so the van may have picked Steve's things up, but no one picked him up. So he'd done a nice little runner and gotten clean away from his persecutors. After this he began to think things out, he'd have probably told you that, and he calmed down after he had got hold of some tablets from his doctor and felt better; he forgot about his marriage plans and realised that it was now time to confront the conspirators once and for all since he had started thinking in capitals.

As soon as Steve reached this pass, he had thought, I'm out of here - so he went first to a Millets Store and then to a camping supermarket in preparation for the showdown; the Stand Off, the confrontation which he now knew was inevitable. The treatment had rid him of all his deeply crazy notions, and now that he could think more clearly, he knew that he was no longer ill, and knew too that he was the victim of a larger conspiracy perpetrated by forces outside his control. Days spent thinking in this fashion cloud one's judgement.Now that the effects of the speed had gone– he was no longer a mad person, merely a borderline madman getting ready to confront the world from his hideaway and prepare for the Big Stand-off that would clear the air once and for all.

CHAPTER TEN

Another boring day in South East London. What's new? It's been going down the tubes from the day they closed The Big Store: decline spreading like neglected sickness. This part of London lacks the trailer park chic of Romford or the pizzazz of gangsterland Essex; no designer T shirts, no Armani jackets, just guys with shaven heads, gold bracelets and no flash birds; it's strictly for assholes On this day in mid-May there was an icy drizzle in the air. *Bordelles de merde.* But hang about, for the likes of the Stanislaus Z Waxman tribe this was a truly sacred place: the intellectual powerhouse of suburban London. Imagine that. The Waxman family thought that it was heaven on earth and would talk to you about it all day if you let them. This was where everyone should live: it had all the high octane glamour of La La Land. Move here, they cried, live with us and enjoy. Why do people tell you where you should live and leave off living where you are content and well handy? Hurry on down to my house baby and you can kiss my ass among the vandalised cars in the wastelands of cul de sacs between Camberwell Grove and Coldharbour Lane.

On the corner near where Stanni lived there was a parade of shops, a corner store and sub post- office, a betting shop, a dry cleaner and a kebab house. The family home round the corner was large and rambling; one of a row of detached houses adjoining a well -kept park which, on good days displayed graffiti and lager cans, and on bad days, mountains of French letters and dogshit. The cabaret was provided by dossers retching and gobbing out all over the place, as they hurled curses at cruising gays. But Stanni's family said it was where it's really at, and that its charm lay in its meaningful squalor. The family was socially aware and of a caring disposition and read *The Guardian* and *The Independent* like a man with no arms The local pub, The Blaggers Arms, was on the opposite corner. Once it had been a Victorian boozer with a billiard room and loads of really quite cheery birds who'd laugh at you and take the piss as you went in. Now it was a dingy street level cavern with darkened windows advertising all day karaoke plus weekend live Country and Western. The patrons were punters who'd been barred from the worst pubs in Catford and Lewisham, and that's saying something. They fought all the time and occasionally tried to set the place on fire, that is when they weren't pissing in the doorways or worse. Outside a blackboard said, *all day breakfasts. Chicken pie and chips £3.75 Beef pie and chips £3.75. our Chip Butties and Burgers £1.75.* Not far away there was the poor relation of a teaching hospital that had dumped on it as sank beneath local protest and the Lib Dems. Sixty percent of the nurses had said that no way would they have their families cared for by the National Health Service if they could avoid it. UNISON didn't like that.

Most of his friends would tell you that Stanislaus Z. Waxman, self-proclaimed polymath, was a mystery man. No one knew exactly what he did for a living for he'd say 'how I earn a modest crust is my business- my needs are simple and predictable.'

Some said that he was a failed medical student who'd done a crash course in Sociology at Mickey Mouse University when the going was not so good, but since he never revealed much of the past, or where the money came from in the present, no one really knew. It was rumoured that he had a part time lectureship in Social Science at the University of Bexleyheath where he endured the platitudes of wet –arsed students in gloomy seminars, but that would barely keep Stanislaus in the style to which he wished to be accustomed. But I mean it wasn't just that nobody knows what he does with his life, everyone said, I wouldn't mind that, it's more that he hinted that he was a big shot -that he might be a nuclear scientist or a doctor, because that's what he believed that he should have been - he let you understand that he had some connection with the healing arts. He quite fancied himself as a doctor and could act the part pretty well too, except that he disapproved of doctors and their fantasies of omnipotence in a cloak of elitism.

If only he'd thought of getting a steady job it might have helped. But he didn't, and so he just behaved as if he was an unrecognized genius, 'if you see what I mean darling.' said most of his mystified friends, 'but he just will go on camping it up and talking a right load of old bollocks in the process.' To which he'd have replied, 'Outside the operating room, my real home is the Times Literary Supplement.'

And he'd add, 'I should have been a brain surgeon: I've got long sensitive fingers you see.' And talk of 'me old chums of yore.' And smile and tell how he dined with the President of the Royal College last night. 'Silly old me.' And then he'd say that well he didn't mind if he did, maybe just the teensiest little single malt before 'I gang awa.'

But he was charming, and so people let him get on with it, admiring his charm, and the flow of charming talk that came from his charming face. If the people had known how he really spent his working day they would have been astonished, disgusted, even outraged. For, cop this folks, Stanni was a full-time watcher in the secret world of FX Sarno and Ted Blunger, and quite well paid too. His family was partially to blame for this unlikely state of affairs. They had predicted too much for him and at the end of it all, no one knew what to do with him.

The Waxman family was a mutual admiration society that banged on about everything, telling the world how wonderful they were and repeating the family mantra 'Of course we're all so bright,' convinced of their shared genius, and Stanni the greatest of all. Talk about luvvies, these guys were major league. Going on about culture and stuff like there was no tomorrow. But, as someone said once and others frequently,

'You can't help liking such a bunch of harmless assholes.'
The deadly curse of charm had struck - that was the clincher.

And they all lived in the house where Stanni's parents held court. His father 'Big Daddy' Leo, *en secondes noces*, literary agent and claret sniffer, with step-mother Cynthia, overblown poet, wearer of flowing vestments and creator of uncertain dinners. At times Cynthia could be quite disgusting, wear hairy tracksuits and look like a shithouse, at others a podgy *poule de luxe* with a five-megaton libido of whom the malicious said 'I heard she screws like ten men.' Her grotesque appearance and Gothic horror was, for certain people, a massive turn on. She was a studious person who read books, took courses, attended discussion groups and lived in fluffy squalor despite a personal six figure income.

She took a patronising interest in Afro-Caribbean matters and ate palm oil chop, jerk chicken and appalling stews full of coconuts until Leo, engorged with this vile grub, put a stop to it and bought her a copy of Delia Smith. Despite her personal affluence, the wine was always Sangria until Leo put his foot down. Her house was, at times, quite exceptionally dirty. '*Nostalgie de la boue* incarnate my dears,' said another unkind friend. She liked serious literature and worthy causes no end. She was a passionate supporter of the United Nations and the banning of fox-hunting. She had been divorced many years from a most unwholesome person, and then one day she met Leo who had recently been deserted by a harmless wife who had endured bloody enough thank you: poor sod: she'd had it with her family. All she had wanted was that her son Stanni might get a steady job.

When Cynthia looked at you, she smiled through her mossy teeth as she asked the room, 'Where is my beautiful beloved?'

'Is that you I wonder my sweetest one?' Leo and she would say in chorus.

'Come let us kiss each others sweet faces.'

And they would too, all moistly, splish splash I was taking a bath, rockin' on a Saturday night or whatever it was, you'd better believe it. With people like that around him in his impressionable years that how could Stanislaus Z. have become anything else but a near wanker, poor bugger?

In his time Big Daddy Leo had been a star player in a prestigious literary agency, but he had blown it through his liking for good Clarets and cricket. One afternoon he had said that he was looking forward to the day when he could stay down the wine bar after lunch and get seriously pissed. Someone overheard him, and next morning his desk was cleared. He was also the Liberace of the Pianola. He had rebuilt a player piano and sometimes gave recitals at Pianola teas in a multi-gabled Gothic building,the Headquarters of the Pianola Society in Surrey. 'Our hosts in Tadworth were Len and Gladys and others of that ilk. After a recital of pot pourris from Wagner we had Ted on his duo playing selections from Lionel Monckton and dare I say it Schubert?'

From this establishment Leo sent out messages in *'Strings and Rolls,'* the Journal of the Pianola Players International: Leo would go to the guillotine rather than see the abolition of the player piano. But that did not diminish his passionate devotion to trivia. Strange world.

He was a lifelong friend of Portia Braithwaite – Jones, Principal of the Surbition Academy of Movement. She had dedicated to him,' Laban: perceptions and precepts: a collation in Sapphic modalities.' That was how high he stood. Portia had suggested his name to The Academy as someone who would *add lustre to their endeavours . . .(sic). His knowledge of the practicum of movement and its contribution to the empowerment process movement* would be totally shit hot,in an artistic sense. The other side to all this was that Leo was quite the domestic tyrant and a disagreeable shit. Everyone had to agree with his half-baked ideas, be they political, how to ride a bicycle or his loudly stated views on current affairs, using terms like affirmative action,, multiculturalism, ethnocentricty and politically correct as punctuation, in an endless torrent of bullshit. Once he got into overdrive he would bring in his big guns, *hegemony, empowerment, post-structuralism and deconstruction.* Fortunately he was cushioned by Cynthia fluttering around agreeing with everything: so his job loss hardly mattered. She said darling we can do without second rate people like that can't we, and he said yes of course we can angelic one. The family adored each other to bits, and likewise everyone adored Stanislaus Z.

It was a family that drifted through a world of smiling at each other - as an exasperated friend had said, 'secure in their overweening superiority in every aspect of the human condition.' It must have been nice for them. But they just kept on discussing vintages, the latest interesting little sauce and Feng Shui. And they really believed all this crap: one has to believe in something was what they said.

And people wondered what Stanislaus Z. did with his time; it wasn't as if he worked all that much, or did he? It was a hard one to answer for he gave you the impression of being hard at it all the time... but it was hard to pin him down. He had done *quite a bit on the classical side in me day,* whatever that meant but it hardly paid the rent. The curious would have been surprised if they'd known of his connections with the secret world. Even more surprised if they had known of his minor reputation as a dealer in bent gear. 'Possessed from early age of an abundance of striking good looks,' as he would have said, 'well I was just lucky darling.' And all this was reinforced by his adoring family.

And good old Stanislaus he'd come on real strong about all sorts of stuff. It might be the latest ten volume work by some Russian asshole on the history of mushrooms or next he'd shoot off unlikely questions such as, 'Have you ever had sexual congress with a prostitute: I can't abide that sort of thing, I mean what should be a sacramental act of physical union reduced to mere commerce, I mean what's that all about?' and he'd look at you accusingly. He had interesting and irritating but harmless linguistic affectations: he'd rather get a dose of the clap than get a foreign word wrong. Andaluthia, he'd say, and smile. He was fussy about his diet too; no vegetables out of season, and double choosy about wines, noses, growths and similar bosh.

When he was called to an interview by FX and Ted, he was delighted to accept their offer, much to the disgruntlement of his wife, a long suffering woman who had endured much in the tohu -bohu of their existence. All she wished was that he had found a steady job. Stanislaus must have been the most unlikely person ever to enter the secret world. You might think that his affectations would have deterred the Board.

But someone, could it have been FXS? spotted his reliability, plus a natural born cover that could never be blown, and the fact that Stannie came across as a harmless gossip to whom everyone confided everything: the sort of person to whom total strangers would divulge their plans to embezzle their employers, leave their wives, take up Morris dancing. You name it; they'd tell him. Underneath the unusual exterior, some said, maybe there was a truly honest man. And so in no time he was installed in a nice little gaff in Greenwich, a run down shop that sold bits and pieces with a cellar full of listening gear and God knows what else. So what with all this and his gossip and picking up bits here and there, old Stanni was kept well busy some might say.

'What a perfect cover it will be.' said FXS, and added, 'File him someone, but don't forget him until we need the poor sod.' And then, 'And when we do we should make it all sound as big as a bloody mountain - a major coup and all that; that will please him no end.'

'But we can't just leave him like that at the taxpayers expense.' said Ted. 'Of course we can,' said FX. 'Just feed him exciting bits of nonsense now and again until we find a use for him. I'm sure he'll deliver. You'll see.' Ted replied, 'I'm not so sure of that Guv.' FXS smiled, 'In an any case Ted, if he becomes a problem, I'm sure Fizzer would take care of him.' And he looked out of the window. Ted shuddered and said, 'I'm bloody sure he would.' And so it went on. Much of the time Stanislaus carried out meaningless assignments which nourished his sense of the dramatic and gave him additional monies in lean times; but every now and again he would bring in some brilliant stuff. His friends asked each other, 'How does he ever manage to keep going?' They'd have done their collective nuts if they'd known. Worse than that for God's sake, his family would have been aghast and wept and rent their *Guardians*. An Oi Veh situation. His honesty was a cruel but convenient paradox, and with his near perfect memory he could retain information without having to write anything down.

And then one day adventure struck unexpectedly when he went off and very nearly blew the whole thing. Stanni was having lunch in a wine bar; an unusual event for him, for, Normally he despised such 'manneristic contrivances of a tasteless age'. But this place had become a secret favourite place for him where he could do his thing and bugger off without paying the bill; another of his funny little ways. He'd never been sussed at le Bar Rossini - in one of those funky cul de sacs off anywhere in W1, all chrome bar top and smoked windows, leather topped seats and loads of booze: seventy different sorts of vodka, four varieties of vin ordinaire and seventeen vintage champagnes. The food was not too bad, mainly designed to act as blotting paper for the booze, but there were edible omelettes and steaks and frittes and stuff. The bar staff and waiters looked at you as if you was dead me old son; spoke in the bogus accents of Tuscany or somewhere and wore Millwall supporters badges under their tops.

Stanni toyed with a Salade Nicoise and an omelette, fretted at the smokiness of the champagne and was generally in something of a pet, and next thing he was no end surprised to be aware of the fact that this amazing wild-looking bird was giving him the come on.

Kick off with this - she had a deepest black vampire hairdo, near black lips, a skirt that was slit from ankle to crotch, no end of beads and bangly bits and from where he stood she looked a fair old hardon, not that he would have used so vulgar a phrase. He noted a near perfect ass that you could die for, and immediately choked on an olive. She would keep smiling at him as if she knew him from somewhere. That was the tantalising bit – as a matter of fact it worried him. How would she know him he wondered?

So she calls out, 'Fancy joining me for a drink darling, you look as if you could do with one, Oh yes, and another thing, don't think of walking out of here without paying, because I saw you do it last week. Why do you do that I wonder? I think you are a naughty boy and may need to be punished.' He blushed. Someone had rumbled him at last. It was bound to happen sooner or later but why did it have to be someone like this one for Christ's sake? She looked as if she'd eat you for breakfast or worse. He shuddered.

Next thing she's not only giving him the big come on, but she's talking to him, chatting him up, climbing all over him near enough and practically grabbing for his dick, or pretending to, which was bad enough. For the moment he thought it all looked good or at least worth a go. Next whoops folks, she's only inviting him to leave family and friends and go for it, go for what, he wondered? I mean leave it out. She soon made that much plainer. What a strange person, he's thinking, and acting as if he's scared, which in a way he was, but really wondering what happens next, and also he was feeling quite flattered at the attentions of this crazy young woman whoever she might be.

'Oh yes, and here's the deal big boy,' she said, 'why don't you cut loose from that goddam dumbshit wife and children of yours I keep hearing about all the time from everyone? I hear she's a big old thing and while you're at it get me a Margarita.' In no time at all, he'd ordered her a drink as if in a dream, and he's wondering where the hell all this might end and she's not letting up asking him daft questions and if he enjoys shagging women up the back and all sorts of stuff. I mean he thought, there are limits but said nothing. She paused and added, 'Why don't you take me for a ride in my car or yours?' To his horror, her motor was a double flash Ferrari. He could see it outside the gaff. It stood out in the street, bright red and shameless.

'I never said I had a wife did I? And you can drive me honey.' But it was too late to argue. Next thing she'd practically carried him outside, he'd not paid the bill and now they were in this bloody car with him driving like buggery down High Street Kensington or somewhere.

But she goes on with, 'Dont be such a schmuck. I bet you got a picture with you right now,' she said, as calm as you please, as if nothing much had happened, as if she dragged guys out of bars every day of her life, which she probably did, he realised.

'Well,' said Stanni, 'Well...'

'What did I tell you? Come on, lets see it Daddy.' And as cool as you like she opens his jacket and pulls out his wallet. Inside is a picture of a... 'No please don't do that..' says Stanni

So next she opens his fly. 'Keep your eyes on the road, for Christ's sake, or you'll kill us,' he says.

'Don't be so dumb, you're driving darling.'

'Oh yes,' says Stanni, 'Of course, how stupid of me, I quite forgot.' He never liked being called darling, he remembered that.

She didn't answer, since by now her mouth was full. Holy Christ alight she was only drinking greedily from a huge bottle of booze that was all. Sweat broke out on Stanni's forehead. Jesus God, where would this all bloody end? In a car with a drunken broad. What a strange woman he kept thinking. Well you would. Next thing she's opening his fly again and Oh Christ what next? When she'd finished and he'd driven back on to the road, she said, 'OK, let's go to the seaside for a few days. It's time you had a change of scenery. I'm sure your wife won't mind.' And added, 'From what I hear, she don't give a shit one way or the other. Why don't you have a little fun for once in your life and let the silly cow go finger diddle herself.'

She paused, 'Or me, if you prefer.'

'I don't think that's very nice,' said Stanni helplessly, 'You shouldn't talk like that.' Adding inconsequentially, 'You don't even know her.' She replied, 'How do you know?' And following it up with, 'It wasn't meant to be nice you dumbshit, don't you know anything?' She looked at him coolly and said quietly, 'I'm making you an excellent offer, in case you didn't know.' He had no answer. 'All I'm offering you is a bit of an adventure for once in your life. It's obvious surely, everyone needs a change now and again, or hadn't you heard?'

Some change, thinks Stanni, I'm going to puke, and that's it. This isn't happening. He wanted to ask her what this was all about, or something along those lines, but somehow he was sucked in at the idea that he might be up for something that might be more exciting than anything he'd ever experienced. He was sure of that. 'Oh yes,' she said, 'I know, why don't we go to a place I know. It's slightly down the M3, well after it in a way. In the New Forest. It's like a Club sort of thing, but you wouldn't know about that you prat. It's near a lake and it used to be a... never mind what it used to be' And laughed. 'You'll love it and we can have a great time.' Adding artlessly. 'If you like we could fool around too. You'd like that.'

By now they are driving past the Hospital for the Incurables, what a name, and heading towards the Kingston by- pass with her calling out directions all the time, and telling him to drive quicker. In no time they will be on the M3 and it'll be the point of no return. So Stanni is feeling a shade frantic, but less frantic as they edged further along the road and hurtled, for that was how she drove. He kept his eyes shut until she said 'Look honey. I need some money' All this as they drove off the M3 into a small town, or was it a big village? She pulled up in a mini shopping mall. 'OK let's stop here, this looks fine. I'm just going to get some drinks and cigarettes.' He said helplessly, 'but I don't approve of those who smoke.'

And then she got out. As she did so, as calm as you like, she pulls up the long skirt and next thing she's got a Browning automatic in her hand or it looked like one, he was so woozy he wasn't too sure. 'What are you worrying about I just need to get us a few things for the night.' She called that one back to him and laughed no end. For the night. Some message So she goes into this seven to eleven store and he can hear a hell of a bloody racket and everyone shouting and she's shouting, 'Calm down you stupid peasants, I'm only robbing the till.' That was really great, and he's thinking Christ she's not robbing the place. Oh my God what next?

In due course they had reached the place, a motel or a hotel or a club- it was hard to say what it was, which stood off the road in an upmarket area on the outskirts of a stockbroker golfy village in deepest Hampshire. Not all that far from a marina you could be sure of that. Stanni badly needed a rest and he crashed out thinking what the bloody hell's happening here, and what's going to happen, and you know the funny thing was that all of a sudden he didn't care all that much.

He woke up slowly, one eyelid at a time, just to be on the safe side. It was worse than a hangover this global uncertainty about what was happening beyond the certainty that there was dead weight on the lower half of his body. It turned out to be she of the car, astride him. He tried to lift his arms in protest but was unable to get far as she'd handcuffed him. 'Don't be such a bloody spoilsport, I thought we might have some real fun.' she said. Holy Christ he thought: this isn't happening at all, I'm dreaming it all, I know, she must have spiked my drink they do that, people like her... I read it in the *Weekend Guardian* '... shame of our new universities... I escaped from drugs hell after I was date raped.' Or was it the *Sun*? And she continued, 'Can't you see I'm enjoying myself.' He only said, 'That's it damn self, that's all you bloody lot think of, the bloody me generation, the self, that's all you lot know about.'

'Don't be such a petulant old fart.' 'That's great,' he said 'Call me a fart. You've committed bloody armed robbery for all I know and all you can think of is self-gratification. What a world. Have you no social conscience you dreadful young person?'

'Get lost asshole, you know you can't wait to get into my pants properly.' She looked at him, daring him to say something and he only could say, 'I don't know what you're talking about?' Ignoring him, she climbed off and said, 'Well it's about time you did.' And paused, 'What have you got to say to that?' Stanni found himself saying, 'I suppose a poke would now be right out of the question.' She came back with, 'Don't get ideas above your station sonny; you are definitely way out of your league.' Jesus he's thinking, you can't say anything right with this one. How did I get mixed up in this? And then she said, 'Come along, it's time we were moving.' and unlocked the handcuffs. 'What time do they serve breakfast?' said Stanni. She said, almost tenderly, 'You can fuck my ass if that's what you really want. Everyone else seems to.' And she slid out the door. Ignoring her invite

Stanni summoned up enough bottle to call out, 'Don't rob another bank.' She only laughed and ran out to the car and drove off.

When he had straightened himself out he discovered that it wasn't a motel, but a converted roadhouse of the sort that had been common in that part of England many years ago, after an period of popularity which disappeared as quickly as it had arrived. A few slightly raffish examples may be seen, usually displaying tired looking roadside ads offering bargain accommodation and book now for our holiday special attraction. If you like a mix of modern and kitsch they are definitely the place to go. This one was called 'The Captains Cabin.' There was a neon sign that said *Ahoy all me shipmates, all day breakfast, pool and Jacuzzi*. At one end a logo - a pirate with an eye patch. Enough said. Its clientele was varied; mainly transient holiday makers, but it had acquired a good reputation amongst certain villains who used it as a conference center: its appearance would never suggest to the police that any villain worth a shit would be seen dead in it.

The more he thought about it the more Stanni realised that he had to do something to get away from this woman. Suddenly he realised that the whole 'adventure' was a replay of a movie he'd seen some years ago. That was it. This wild young woman picks up a guy in a bar and takes him off on a ghastly trip. The whole thing was disturbingly like it -like she was a bloody *doppelganger* or whatever they were called, and he too for that matter, or was she replaying the movie for her own God knows what fearsome reasons? When she returned he really would ask her a few serious questions about this adventure or what ever she called it.

The whole thing was ridiculous and not to be tolerated. Things were getting out of hand. Time to straighten things out and get out of all this, back to normal, yes that was it, normal, but it didn't occur to him just to bugger off immediately and he knew that. And he knew that he'd been infected with something, something disturbing but somehow enjoyable in a way that he'd not experienced before.

But the more that he thought about it, the more absurd and plain bloody stupid the whole affair became even allowing for this seductive sense of fun, something which had never featured much in his life thus far... Was she really re-enacting that ridiculous movie as she appeared to be, and how could she possibly know that it had been an unexpected favourite of his, one that had puzzled and disturbed him to the extent that he sort of played out the lead in it by not paying his bill every time he went to that place, and hanging around there waiting for something unexpected to happen? And if this were so, why had and how had she picked on him or known anything about him? It made no sense any way that you looked at it.

He thought that surely it had nothing to do with the 'job' as he called it. Well it was a job wasn't it? Or was it connected in some way? And if it did, how and why? He was not so dumb as to think that his job was little more than monitoring and processing a load of crap. Hardly a prime target for counter intelligence, or could it be counter-counter intelligence? Where had the ghastly bloody woman gone to this time? As like as not holding up a bank...

So when she came in looking quite unexpectedly fizzed up, in a new, or at least another outfit, he came straight on with, 'OK Ms whoever you are, lets cut the crap shall we this time? What exactly is going on here? You've more or less kidnapped me and God knows what else.'

She replied, 'Well you're at liberty to go any time you silly bugger. No one's stopping you. I thought you might be beginning to enjoy yourself for once in your miserable little life, you pompous asshole.' And she poured herself out another bloody drink, saying 'Fancy one? For Christ's sake chill out. Enjoy yourself and take a risk for once in your pitiful life, dickbrain.' He pondered, 'Well perhaps just the one.'

She laughed, 'I suppose you think that this is all part of some larger conspiracy.Is that the deal?'

'The thought had crossed my mind. I mean perhaps you...'

'I what?'

'Never mind,Its nothing really.' Thinking Christ what am I saying, this bloody woman has my ass in her hand

'Well listen Stanni,' she replied, 'lets just call it a jeu d'esprit or something.' and she went on laughing.

He's now thinking this is a right bloody waste of time. She's unreal - that's it bloody unreal. Oddly enough though however once again, he did nothing more for the moment did he? Why didn't he just get up and bugger off? He wondered about that. And then she said, 'Well aren't you going to bang me? I mean people usually do you know. It's a bit bloody insulting not to under the circs don't you think?'

He said stiffly, 'Have none of you people ever heard of sexually transmitted disease or unwanted pregnancy?'

And then he found himself saying, 'What happens now then?' and leaving his enquiry in the air, not that she showed any sign of answering him. Still he's wondering wouldn't it somehow be best to try and disengage himself from all this thing, but somehow he knew that he couldn't do that. All that he had picked up from FX and the weirdoes in Building X, all that information and training seemed pretty useless at the moment. It was all slipping away through his fingers under the attentive and mocking scrutiny of this disturbing young woman. If only she would stop eyeballing him like that for God's sake. 'Well,' she said. 'That wasn't too bad now was it, you can't say you didn't enjoy yourself.'

And again he said 'What happens now?' and pretty lamely at that. 'What happens now?' she repeated, 'Well I had thought about that and wondered if you'd like to meet some people I know. They live round here and it seemed, well like kind of a pity not to call in on them and tell them the news and stuff; what with them being so near and all, you know what I mean.'

Jesus he thinks, it's the local vampire club or a coven of Satanists more like; she can't possibly have any normal people for friends.

She said, 'I know what you're thinking; you reckon as I'm so bloody ghastly, my friends must be too. Isn't that it?'

'Well not exactly like that,' he replied. giving way and his resolve liquefying. 'OK, I suppose it can't hurt.' I'll humour the tiresome cow and then maybe I can ease myself out somehow.

'There's no need to be totally ungracious, you little prick you know when someone like myself is trying to do you a favour.' She said that quite sharply.

'My word you do blow hot and cold. You're so fickle.'

And now, quite suddenly she does the chameleon bit again and she's looking affluent with a total change of kit, like Gucci and Prada. And not a trace of the graveyard and she's the Home Counties Successful upwardly mobile young media exec taking the boss home to meet the folks after all that plus his sperm trickling down one ankle, more of a trophy than anything.

'This is Giles, my boss, isn't he a sweetie?'

It's all too crazy; it's like she's a witch or something for Christ's sake Next thing she'll change into a pumpkin. And thought, and then where would we all be? Then he thought that if he tried acting normal with her that it might get him out of this ridiculous mess, but at the same time he was in a way, quite enjoying the whole experience, despite everything, realizing that perhaps he was enjoying all this much more that he wanted to admit to himself. At the same time he had a strong suspicion that it would all end in tears or worse.

'OK. I'll go along with you and meet your friends, but for Christ's sake you've got to admit, it's all a bit odd I mean isn't it?'

'That's for you to decide. It's your life not mine.' And then she said, 'Yes Love, and while we're at it it's time for you to freshen up a bit. Next thing she's brought a load of people on board, is it a dream or something and there's a hair stylist and a manicurist having a bash at him, and he's getting a nail job and a facial, that is after she'd supervised a general cleansing of his numerous smelly areas. Plus she's organized a new outfit. Smart casual sort of thing. Stanni had always been one for really bad clothes of the sort usually worn by actors. Say no more. He looked quite good. 'Yes,' she said, 'You'll do. You know what: I'd shag you if we had the time. At least you don't smell as bad as you did when I first met you, and that's saying a lot.' Then she laughed and said. 'OK Stanni, let's go meet the people.'

And in no time they were in the bloody Ferrari racing through the new Forest until they came to a large house, set back from the road. Quite grand with it, Stanni noticed appreciatively as they pulled up on the gravel outside an impressive front door. 'Here we go,' she said as she yanked him out the door and into a large entrance hall where stood two rather pleasant looking elderly people, obviously husband and wife. 'Home at last,' she cried, 'Mummy and Daddy, this is Stanni, we're getting married.'

At this stage it was all too much for Stanni, who keeled over and passed out cold.' Poor sweetie,' she said, 'he must be tired out. Here Daddy help me get him into bed poor dear. It's all the excitement. He's so in love with me, you know Mumsie, he can't think straight poor darling.'

As Stanni passed into what he hoped might be a deep and healing sleep, his final thoughts were, just so long as she hasn't got a murderous boy friend like in that bloody film, I suppose I might just survive all this. But it wasn't any sort of a sleep until he had remembered that he still had his mobile that is if the ghastly young woman hadn't sold it, but she hadn't, and he made a help call to the number. Then he slept. How interesting it all was, and what an adventure he had enjoyed and soon it would be over, and she wasn't so bad after all, poor soul. He might have reflected that at no stage in all this had he thought about trying to get help from his family. He had enough sense to know what a bloody waste of time that would be, and thought, Oh well some things are better left unsaid..

CHAPTER ELEVEN

Ted Blunger had been surprised when he received the letter from Gilli. He'd have been even more surprised if he'd known that FX had already seen it, and that FX had been in touch with her. Was he, or would he be surprised or was he kidding himself, that was the question he asked himself. He'd thought that he might hear from her again one day. Their last meeting had been atmospheric. Some atmosphere you might think if you want to talk about the awful night when the Booker Prize presentation had been hiccupped, for that was all that it had seemed like, by the casual execution of Iolo Morgannwg the crazy computer programmer, soi disant writer and paranoid windbag.

On that occasion when would you believe, no one noticed what was going on when the guy gets taken out and bloody shot to death, with all the guests thinking this noisy waiter who had freaked out was just another drunk who had to be got off the premises before he totally ruined things for the literati glitterati, I mean how dare he? And yes, how no one had even noticed nor heard the guys who had put more than a few rounds from their Glocks into him, just to be on the safe side, and taken him away in a nice new body bag to wherever it is they take the bodies off to, on such occasions.

Ted remembered how Gilli had been an unexpectedly agreeable companion on that occasion, and then he thought of their first meeting when he had walked with her beside the lime trees at The Rugforth Healing Centre, talking with her and learning of her eerie misgivings about what his life was all about, particularly her fears of the violence, the danger and the rest of it. He knew that she had recently been in touch with FXS; he'd heard a recording of her call. Good old FX, he likes to keep what's going on to himself now and again, well most of the time he does. Not all. Cards close to the chest. FX and Blackjack or Texas Hold'em? Perhaps not.

Her letter to Ted had gotten straight to the point.

'... *Some time ago you said to me that yourself and Mr Sarno would always be pleased to hear from me if ever I should come across something that might be of interest to you. Well I believe that I have – in my present job where it's all turning out to be dodgy, even sinister. I hope that I'm not being too melodramatic - I've torn this letter up a few times already in case I might be thought to be just another neurotic twit.I'm worried about certain things that are going on here. Perhaps you might call me on this number. Please remember me to Mr Sarno.I thought he was rather a dear, in case you didn't know as ever Gilli*'

And that was it. Just what you might expect from that particular young woman thought Ted.I'd probably better clear it with FXS before I do anything. He'll like that, the idea I mean. He always rather fancied her I reckon. That is if he fancies anyone. Best not to mention the dear bit. So he told FX about the letter, 'I had an idea that we might hear from that young person sooner rather than later,' said FX, 'She interested me as you may know.' He paused, 'Well there's no need to look at me quite like that Ted. She has an original mind and her work at the Woods Hole Institute, in particular what she did on communication with dolphins intrigued me. A pity she gave up on it.'

'I know,' said Ted, 'But it didn't pay the rent. Wasn't that it?'

'Something like that probably,' said FXS. He knew the score perfectly well, and even if her problem wasn't a matter that involved national security, what harm was there in helping someone out? Also it would be a change of scenery for Ted who had been getting a bit stale. In any case he'd checked her out from day one and had already been in touch with her. 'I suggest you get in touch with her and see.' And he said, 'Anything that might relieve the present ennui would be good news. It's all so tedious, would you not agree? The last time that I was forced to attend at the Central Criminal Court. I'm in the Magpie and Stump for a drink when two louts in blue suits barged in and one says, "the trouble with nowadays is there's no good villains around." I now know exactly what he meant.' He asked, almost plaintively. 'What's happening Ted? Has it ever struck you Ted, that ninety nine percent of what we do here is a load of pointless nonsense, and expensive at that?' Ted felt like saying why bloody ask me , you're meant to be the clever one around here, but came up with, 'I think we'll have to look into this one Guv.' What he really meant was that he wanted to see her again; to experience her cool appraising look and slightly mocking air until FX said, 'I suggest, if you could interrupt your daydreams about the delectable Ms Gilli,' said FXS, 'that it would be best practice not to confide in Mme Sandra on this occasion. She'd get entirely the wrong impression. Drift caught?'

'Jesus Christ Guv,' says Ted, 'You'll be calling her la belle dame sans merci next.'

'I can't think what you mean by that,' said FX tartly. 'But I wonder what she will come up with.'

He said, 'Well come along Ted, what are you waiting for? Don't tell me you that don't want to renew her acquaintance. Don't be such an old tease. Where is your sense of adventure?' Ted laughed, 'Don't worry about that Chief, I've arranged to see her tomorrow. She's in a slightly different line of country at the moment. I mean it's not alternative healing these days: it's more in the way of moral and spiritual regeneration, I mean, as far as I can make out. Well that's what it says in the brochures...' And he drifted off, feeling a bit of a prat. 'Good God Ted,' says FX. 'I knew it. I always said she'd make a convert of you.' And then he said, 'You could take up a totally different way of life I suppose. And why not? Sooner or later we all have to makes changes you know. Redundancies alert.'

When he arrived there on the next morning, Ted was oddly impressed by The Shufi Center. 'Bit flash isn't it, this place I mean?' said Ted, 'I'm sorry Ms Gilli but I had the idea that your interests lay somewhere on the less worldly side: this is more like Disneyland Home Counties than anything I'd imagined.' Gilli smiled and said coolly, 'The answers to many life problems come from many directions Mr Blunger.' He sidestepped and said, almost diffidently, 'Well it's a lot different from the last place isn't it?' And now he felt a bit ill at ease and thought I'm talking a load of old bollocks.? What a disconcerting person she is.

She continued, 'We have a different ethos in this place, but our goals are entirely similar. Replenishment and regeneration at the basic levels that meet the varied needs of our clients.' What Ted really wanted to say was OK yes, I'll buy that but what the bloody hell is an intelligent person like you doing hanging around with a load of tossers who are employed in the business of fleecing a bunch of gullible wankers? Dissolve to, *What in heck's a beautiful kid like you doing in a crummy joint like this- it's time I took you out of a place like this for something better, something cleaner ...* and realised that such a question was not likely to cut the mustard as she pre-empted him with, 'What you're thinking is what am I doing here? Am I right?'

He answered, 'Well it had crossed my mind Gilli. For Christ sake I've only been here five minutes and the whole place shrieks that this is a load of phoney crap from the moment you walk through the lobby.' He paused, thinking why can't I keep my mouth shut and remembered that she wouldn't have asked him to come along for no reason at all, and said, 'I'm sorry Gilli, I shouldn't have said that but you know what I mean.' She remained silent for a while and merely said, 'Be that as it may, there's something odd going on here. I believe you once commented on me as being an intuitive person. Well take it from me Ted, there really is:

there are people moving in here that are way outside my previous experience of this field and I'm suspicious of whatever it is they are doing even though I don't know what it is they are doing, as I can't put my finger on anything. It's the intuition you see' Ted smiled at that. 'That's why I ask for your help.' Ted really enjoyed the Ted bit.

She continued 'You see…' but was unable to continue as a calming voice, spoke above the tinkly tonkly Tibetan bells and those bloody flutes as Gilli had already called them. The voice went on, 'Listen people. At this point in time we have a crisis you good people within our community. One of our people is having an angel type revelatory experience in the sacred peace garden. All staff members are requested to attend and don't forget to bring your power shields and singing bowls.' Gilli said, 'That's us Ted, let's go.' Holy shit thinks Ted I never imagined that anything like this would be in the line of duty when I first met FX. What next I bloody wonder? I could do with some lunch and sod these bloody tossers, why can't they say ladies and gentlemen or folks?

'Don't worry,' said Gilli, 'It's probably some dumbshit bimbo who'd drying out, and now she's having a touch of the vapours. We get it most days.' She smiled, 'You see, the more they pay, the more they reckon that they can fuck the dog any time of the day. It's like The Priory you know.' And added, 'Just you wait until you get behind a Sloaney crackhead with premenstrual tension and Daddy won't buy her a Ferrari. Better still you wait till you meet Dr Horatio Bargs, that is if he is a Doctor. He's a total kill, believe me.'

Two hours later Ted was enjoying lunch at a pub well away from the health –giving, life –enhancing influences of the Shufi Center and he's thinking thank God as he wades into the steak and kidney pud, noting that Gilli had eschewed lentils in favour of a ham sandwich and a glass of claret. He was too polite to comment.

Sensing this, Gilli merely said, 'Come on Mr Blunger you know bloody well that we vegetarians need a holiday now and again.' And added, 'We all do it you know.' And then she said, 'I'm so pleased that you were able to come along and see what we are trying to achieve here, in terms of developing personal self- fulfillment and growth,' and smiled. Now she's taking the piss thinks Ted, but I don't mind. She always does have this effect on me even when she's at her worst. 'I got your letter Gilli,' said Ted, 'Why don't we just cut the crap.' Jesus that was a near one: next I'll be talking about the nitty gritty and the bottom line.

Gilli said, 'I came to this place about six months ago. The people here made me an offer that I couldn't refuse you see, and the executive head is quite a decent guy; doesn't take life all that seriously if you follow me. You'll probably meet him soon.' Gilli continued, 'It's quite simple really; it's just that I'm concerned that the place is becoming involved with these odd people who I suspect are trying to take it all over for what ends I don't know, but it stinks. I can't say exactly what I mean, and I'm now beginning to feel a right idiot.' Ted said quietly, 'Why don't you just go on.'

And thinking. Bloody FX, as usual, he was on to all this. I bet he's already getting ready to touch base with her; that is if he hasn't done so already. Reading his mind again, but then she did still have access to a Spiritual Guide, she said ' I must level with you Ted; Mr Sarno has asked me to meet him for lunch.' Ted smiled, 'At the Flamingo no doubt.' Ted thought, and I thought that I might be in there with a chance 'Yes, that's the place.'

'You'd better look out,' said Ted, 'He probably might want to hire you. And don't let them chisel you on the fiscal side.' And then he said, 'Who's Dr Horatio if you don't mind and why should I wait till I meet him?'

'Oh,' she replied, 'he's the new hotshot in our field, you know natural healing and all that. He's an odd man, and I suspect, a crook. Hadn't you heard?'

Ted actually found himself saying, 'I'm not hearing this, you're beginning to sound like one of our lot, I mean like we're all paranoid in Vauxhall Cross you know.'

She said, 'Well I know that. I'm worried about all this, and the problem is that I'm not sure exactly why. It's possible that my intuitive powers aren't what they were.'

'Or maybe you have come across an affair that is beyond them if you get my meaning. You may have stumbled into a dodgy area. This is what happens you know. We all have our off days.' I'm doing the patronising uncle bit again, she has that effect on me. 'Tell it all to Sarno. After all, he is the guvnor.' Gilli thought it best not to mention much about the call to FX, even if Ted did know. One thing at a time. And then she said 'And there's another matter. It's about this bloody art Gallery in the town. It's the headquarters of a loopy organization which is based there, The Religious Affairs Cultural Studies Group.'

'Oh yes,' said Ted, 'We've heard of them. Sarno will want to speak with you about them too.' Well, no need to tell her everything perhaps.

'And what is it about them that bothers you?'

'They really are an odd bunch of people who want to take us over or that's how it looks, though as far as I know there's nothing in writing; just a general impression of a group of people who drift in and out of the place looking like it's soon to be in their pockets sort of thing. It's hard to get a handle on it. They just give me the bloody creeps if you want to know. They disappear around corners and won't say exactly what they do. Also they're always on about building a connection with this place. I get the impression that they despise us but want to take us over. That's all I can say. It's a matter of hunches and poorly founded suspicions at this stage. And then there is the garden,'

'Which garden is that?'

'Well near the gallery there's this overgrown garden with a strange bit of statuary and an odd Latin inscription which somehow comes across as, well, Satanic and it's all...' And suddenly she started getting more disturbed than you might expect in someone like Gilli. 'You see Ted, I have a real sense of evil about all this. It's no good, I can't define it in the way yourself or Mr Sarno would like me to, but I know that there's something deeply wrong about it all and that's what I need to tell you about.'

'It's enough to be going on with I reckon.' Ted is thinking he didn't like all this, this is one frightened person, and all over a few odd punters hanging around. He didn't give a shit about demonology, but didn't like the idea of people in the twenty first century getting the breeze up about a load of crap that should have been buried centuries ago. If a bunch of dumb paysanos in Sicily wanted to succour the sexual fantasies of disturbed young dimwitted hysterics in shitty villages in Southern Italy, OK that was all right by him, but keep it off the mainland Guiliano. The whole story was getting odder. 'Tell about the garden,' he said. She paused and said, 'It's no good. You'd have to go there and pick up on the vibes yourself Ted. Then you'd see what I'm saying. You think I'm some silly hysteric that's it, isn't it?'

'Not so,' said Ted, 'For Christ's sake Gilli this isn't bloody Sicily, and in any case I respect your judgement. That's why I'm here. Let's get to meet these people.' He thought a bit more and said, 'Hang about, not just yet. Wait till you have a chance to speak to FX Sarno and let's not leave that too long. He'll probably want you to get into electronic surveillance, I suspect. We use it a lot, that's no secret: hope you won't mind that.'

'Well,' said Gilli, 'You never asked me that time in Rugforth when you got Sandra to put those bloody sensors on my Power Shield, and in my kit and you'd only met me a few hours before. Or had you forgotten? Why should I mind this time I wonder ?'

Ted had the grace to blush. And then he remembered, 'What's the word on this geezer Dr Bargs?'

'I bet Mr Sarno put you on to him.'

'We need to know the answer to one question. How seriously do we take him? Is he just another phoney, or is there some other agenda involving this guy. We wondered if you had any ideas.'

'I think it's the latter. There's more to him than just being the charlatan of the month.'

Ted thought for a while and said, 'Look, don't get too bothered about the garden and the statue with the Latin inscription and all that. If the atmosphere is weird, anyone can easily get all sorts of wrong impressions: there's usually a rational explanation for most creepy experiences.' And added,' Sarno thinks it's a whole load of crap set up to put us off.' And thought, at least I hope that's what he meant.

CHAPTER TWELVE

Fizzer Edwards looked out of the window of the apartment in Westminster. Was it now the time to move away from here, now that Sylvie had taken silk? Why did they call it that? Bloody briefs, it's all a bloody game to them he thought, what do they know about the real trip? Mind you he had to agree that Sylvie had come a long way since their first meeting all those years ago in Liverpool: the textbook feminist lawyer, political protest, save the bloody whale, and all the crap about the Kurdish women. That had near enough cost him his job for Christ's sake. And now she was all set to be right in there with the establishment. What a bloody laugh. Still, it might ease the pressure. Maybe now she could begin to get less paranoid about her skin colour, and less likely to accuse him of banging every female member of the Met, every hour, on the hour. Little chance of that.

After the last big blow up following the end of his relationship with Polly Zaftick, he had stayed pretty much out of the field in the legover stakes. Major blow ups, that was a nice one. And another thing this aggro with Hacker Tuke was a right pain. I mean what was that all about it? A prat like Hacker taking out a contract on Fizzer Edwards. I think not. Mr Blunger and you can leave it out Mr Sarno. He'd said that when FXS gave him the strength on it at that ridiculous bloody caff he goes to when he meets the MI5 arse bandits. Give you a right pain it would. Why couldn't he go to a proper caff like everyone else? Typical bloody Oxbridge git.

He turned at hearing Sylvie's footfall. 'So you're here,' she said, 'I didn't imagine you'd ...', and sounding pretty cool with it thinks Fizzer, 'I imagined that you'd be at the office.' He hadn't heard her come in the front door and as he turned to greet her, as always, her presence banished all thought. So he smiled and he said, 'Well yes, I thought we might go out to lunch or have a drink or something. That's why I came home on the offchance of seeing you. I mean that we should celebrate your promotion.'

Astonished at this she said, softening a bit, 'Well that's a great idea. Yes it is a promotion Fizz, isn't it? I hadn't seen it quite like that you see.' And she smiled right back. He felt that smile. And he believed her when she said about not seeing it as a promotion. That was her style. And thinking OK here goes, once again perhaps it's time to straighten out a few items that aren't on the agenda, he said. 'Sylvie, maybe this isn't the time, but sod it here it is, I'm saying it anyway, don't you think that things between us seem to be working better these days? Agreed?'

'I'd noticed that.'

'I'm not one for all this about working at relationships and all that shit.'

She laughed, 'I had noticed that too, despite your experience in the Therapy scene.'

He laughed 'I know OK, so in your book I'm a dumb cop. I can handle that Sylv, in case you hadn't realised.' She'd have to bring in a reference to the one I banged in NW3 what's that her name was again? He knew bloody well what.

'Not dumb, Fizz: it's the violence I don't like, you know that. Sooner or later you'll have to see that this is the thing that could destroy both of us.'

'For God's sake cut out the amateur dramatics Sylv, it's not like that at all and you know it. Violence is only a small part of what I do, always will and that's it, surely you know that: we do other things too as it happens.'

'But you and your pals don't have to like it quite so much – that's how it comes across to me.'

'I don't have all that much choice most of the time, and you know it.' How many times in her life had she experienced someone actually wanting not only to kill her, and not only that, actually having a bloody go he wondered? Bloody none and she knew it. Did she really think any of us like going in with a fair chance of our asses being blown inside out? We don't get into it all the time Too much TV, has to be that, that's what makes them bang on so much about violence. And she had this endless thing about him and all his pals being obsessed with violence. Shit scared more like it half the time.

'What about that Arab woman you killed on the plane in Damascus?'

'For God's sake Sylv, she was after my brains. She only shot a hole in the side of my head, that's all. What more do you want?' and then he added 'In any case Sylvie, you know the whole story. Remember how I graduated from hostage negotiation after the Embassy do, or had you forgotten?' Fizzer was already a promising young DI in the Crime Squad, the natural choice for the task of meeting Sylvie, the feared political activist, in order to chill her out. 'He's a good looking lad and you never know, she might fancy him,' an anonymous DCI was reputed to have said.

It was a more or less genuine attempt to establish some area of common ground during the mean- spirited aftermath of the Toxteth riots. Chronic insults and anger smouldered and flickered. His success was better than anything that anyone had dreamt of hitherto, and more-or -less overnight, he became an expert in chilling people out. From that day on, he was cast in the role of mediator. His success was taken up by his superiors, relieved to find someone who was willing to cope with difficult situations, get trouble off their backs and be dropped if he screwed up.

In time he graduated to siege negotiation: his first assignment was to deal with a group of incompetent bank robbers, borderline retardates in need of schooling for people with special needs, e.g., how to rob a bank properly. Next time round it was sharp-witted terrorists, a different proposition, but Fizzer did well once again. But it had not been easy, and anyway it was now centuries ago.

Sylvie chose to ignore the last bit of what he'd said. 'That's what you all say. You're trained to use violence – OK,' when the circumstanced dictate it, as I suppose it says in your manual but at the end of it all you really like it, brains on the deck and all that stuff, isn't that what you once said or something like that? You talk about these things as if they were nothing at all; as if human life was nothing. Where are you?' and then she said, 'Or is it that you pretend the hard man role more than you let on?'

He recalled Polly that had said something like that and he replied, ' Listen Hon a lot of the time we're trying to deal with shitty people who want to kill people, who want to impose their crap world on us by force, in case you hadn't noticed, amongst other things that you don't seem to want to notice Sylvie. Why don't you do-gooders get bloody real for once. Life isn't all a series of cosy meetings where problems and conflict are resolved in a setting of mutual understanding and caring concern. Isn't that what you guys call it?'

'This is what I mean Fizz. You never seem to even want to discuss things in any depth: it's knee jerks to everything.'

'What do you want me to discuss Sylv? I'm giving you a point of view here, but it's one that I find it near impossible to talk about with you: being on the wrong end of violent behaviour has to influence my opinion. In real terms my total exposure to violence has been quite small compared to most beat coppers in Liverpool, don't forget that. It's just that my experiences tend to get noticed more. Or is it that this is all another way of saying you want me to quit my job and join the good guys, is that it? Tired of being married to a copper, me being on the wrong side? Is that it? Or perhaps I should just piss off. You should have married a social worker.'

Now I'm being infantile, he thought. I did learn something from what was her name? Oh yes Polly. So much for the fifty megaton orgasm and its effect on memory enhancement. It was Polly that had been her name hadn't it? And he forced himself to have total recall of the moment when she'd said about him not being such a tough bastard as he made out. No doubt about it she was bloody good.

'I suppose it's a bit like that.' I don't mean that, she thought, and Fizzer said, 'In case you had forgotten, I only got into all this by accident for God's sake.' And thought of how it all had started when he was pitchforked into being a hostage negotiator with some bloody Mick in Liverpool and next thing he's a celeb at the big Embassy shoot out and all that followed. Sometimes he wished he was back at the coal face, that feeling never lasted for long. She said, 'In any case Fizz, it's quite obvious that you've got something big coming up at the moment, not that it's really any of my business, I can always tell when that's happening you know.'

'How's that?' he asked.

'Very simple, Quite out of the blue you start sounding off on serious topics in our life. It's as if you've suddenly become aware that you might just get killed quite soon and want to straighten things out. OK, so it's not really your style, but it tells me that there's something big going on in your world. I can handle that, you know. Just be careful and don't get carried away: and another thing, apart from your getting killed or injured, I really don't want to see you throwing your career down the tubes just because you got rougher than usual and some big shot in the Met finds out. I do know what goes on.' Not the half of it thank Christ thinks Fizzer.

And she continued, 'The point is that I do accept things much more easily than I used to. I think you know that. And I don't spend all the time wondering about your bits on the side. I suspect you've found better ways of dealing with all that.' Fizzer replied, 'Well, since you ask right at this moment Mr Sarno wants me to help him out on a case, and you're right about the other.'

'Do his some of his dirty work you mean. Why can't he bloody soil his nasty little hands too for once, bloody public school eunuch? I've never forgiven him for that "interrogation" he subjected me to.' And remembered that her complaints to legal high ups got absolutely nowhere. Polite dismissal of an overwrought hysterical woman. My Dear Mrs Edwards we are all of us perfectly satisfied that Mr, what was his name, Sarno and his colleagues were absolutely blameless in these matters if a trifle over zealous in the pursuit of justice, you wouldn't believe it unless you knew it was true.

'I'd wondered about that shit myself' said Fizzer, 'Well it's not quite like that this time. It's a matter of finding out who murdered someone. Calling the poor sod a eunuch doesn't help and that sort of remark isn't you Sylv. Cheap actually, if you ask me. And as to the questioning, OK so the guys went over the top. I thought we'd settled that.'

Ignoring that, she replied, 'Surely the CID can deal with it for once, or are they too busy picking up handouts and getting blow jobs from whores?'

'That's not worthy of you Sylv. This isn't New York. And as to the job in hand, not exactly is the answer. This one involves one of Sarno's former employees. I'm not meant to tell you this Sylvie, you know that.'

'It's that awful man Bill Poynton isn't it?'

'How would you know that? Yes he was pretty grim from what I'm hearing plus he was a card carrying traitor for years. Sounds old-fashioned.' She knows a bloody sight more than she lets on does our Sylv. Bloody lawyers, all the same.

'I'd heard he was dead and knew that he had more than a few unpleasant connections. These things get around even amongst we members of the legal profession. You'd be amazed at what we know,' and she laughed. 'Just stay cool that's all I ask. Stay cool isn't that what they say?'

'I will. Of course I will. And anyway what had you heard about him?'

'He mixed with some unlikely people, I mean for someone in his position?'

'Such as?'

'Well didn't he have some rather curious religious connections?'

'You know about that too. The Religious Affairs Cultural Studies Group, isn't that the name? It's got to be a front for something with a name like that.'

'Didn't I hear that they were paying him off? One of my tax lawyer pals heard that one.'

'Christ, you do hear about things. You might tell me sometime; there are people who need to know this.'

'Why don't you tell your friend Mr Bloody Sarno?'

'He probably knows anyway. He usually does.' Christ thinks Fizzer, this could go on all bloody night, is she getting paranoid or what?

'Oh yes,' she added, 'And you might want to look at this bugger Bargs.'

What doesn't she know, I wonder? And all the time he's thinking, and if all this wasn't enough I've got chummy Greg Dashper to deal with. My new pal as hell as like.

There was a real problem with this new colleague. Fizzer was worried by the new assistant; even when you made allowances for a cocky new boy. This guy smelt one load of trouble to Fizzer - like a major pain in the ass.. Too much of a smoothie. Fizzer liked a well dressed cop, always did, and dressed tidy himself, but this guy was just a bit too, well hard to say exactly, you couldn't put your finger on it. Fizzer had him down as, ' Lord Snooty' on account of his kit and his general style. What put Fizzer off on day one was the gold watch chain with a poncey gold ornament; a seal or a medal or something. At least it wasn't one of your fucking Masonic jewels. He hated that shower that crawled all over the Met like a bloody virus, and there was no way that Fizzer would have one of the members of the let's stick together - like –shit- to - a -blanket brigade in his manor, and you can tell that to the Commissioner and all the other apron wearing ass lickers. He had looked carefully at the new guy, taking in his immaculate suiting, his stiff cutaway collar and a tie that looked as if it might be O E but wasn't, and began to feel well leery about the man. It had been the first working meeting with him to put him in the picture, how we do things here you'll have to take us as you find us, we may not be what you expect but we piss barbed wire on waking if the need be, but whatever you do don't mess with us sort of thing. Routine stuff.

There had been a loud pushy knock on the door. 'Come on in,' says Fizzer who didn't reckon people who said, 'Come.' Your man waltzes in, sits down, just like that, and Fizzer thinking, I don't like the look of you me old son and then, sod it I mustn't be so bloody prejudiced, but he might at least show a bit of respect. 'Right,' said Fizzer, 'I hope you're settling in. Tell me before we get bogged down in the boring details. What are you looking for in this post? It's not an easy ride as you probably know.'

The oily git comes back with, 'Well I was hoping to take over from you eventually if you get my drift Guv, and by the way my name's Greg Dashper.'

Fizzer ignored that and went on, 'You see this department is not the most popular in the force. Everyone dislikes us in the upper end of the Met because they see us as an over privileged elite. The Media half know a little about us but not much; they all think we are neo-Nazis as far as I can make out.

Our remit is to feel the collars of punters that the Anti Terrorist Unit and Counter Intelligence are after, and occasionally we tend to find them for them before they know that they even exist. And that's what we do. We also give support to the Met and others in sorting out certain people who are getting out of line in the handling of sensitive areas in the field of Counter Intelligence. I'm referring to our own people, not just coppers. And while you're at it don't get lippy with me sonny or I'll crush your balls in a vice and I'm not whistling Dixie. This is the real world and you can forget bloody Bramshill you insolent bloody shithead.' Yes, he thought, this son of a bitch is going to give us a hard time if I don't nail him from the off.

But he let it go for the moment. Give the new lad a chance till he settles and we'll see how we go. That was OK until he overheard him saying to one of the WPC's, 'Is that right his wife's a nigger?' Fizzer thought I'll probably have to kill this bastard, except Sylvie really wouldn't like it: perhaps someone else might do it for me, you never know.

It wasn't long before Fizzer realised that he wasn't sure where the guy had come from. No one had asked for an extra body; they were team handed as it was, but when he'd queried this he was informed that it was all part of a New Direction Policy Mandate, and in any case this guy was on the way up and highly thought of so stay out of it chum because we know what we're doing.

That did it for Fizzer. Obviously this prat was another mummy's boy sent down from on high to keep an eye on Fizzer and the crew, and sus out whether they were doing things that they shouldn't be doing. The top brass had pulled this stroke on him before this. Fizzer knew how to deal with these punters. The last one ended up in a psychiatric clinic, and the one before that had a nasty road accident didn't he? And he's now in Stoke Mandeville. Say no more Squire. Problem solved. But it hadn't been a good start.

CHAPTER THIRTEEN

'That bloody shithouse of Bill Poynton's. I can't bloody stand the place.' That was what George Jorgensen had always called The Pink Lady. 'Give you pain in the arse if you ask me.What's such a big deal about it anyway?' But then George never really thought much of good old Bill. You might have predicted that Bill Poynton would bring up the subject of The Pink Lady whatever the weather. 'Just the sort of cheapo nasty place he would like, full of bloody nonces and whores.' said George Jorgensen, and he'd never let go with his banging on about Bill and the damn club. As if anyone gave a toss one way or the other.

It had always been a favourite of Bill's. ' It's getting late. Why don't we go down to the Lady?' He'd say that, right out of the blue he would: he called it The Lady, 'I mean just for a few drinks or whatever.' And next thing George would say irritably, 'And why does he always have to say " whatever." Beats me.' He'd always had it in for good old Bill, as he called him, he'd always hated his guts and it was George who eventually got him fired, everyone reckoned, 'Bloody crook if you ask me, that is when he's not selling us down the river. You mark my words.' And in any case no one could see what it was that Bill felt was so special about the place, but they all went along, more out of curiosity than anything else.

It had turned out to be a left -over from a past that no one remembered, perhaps something to do with Bill's past whenever that had been, an embarrassing anachronism that had survived in an age that couldn't understand it, at a time when club meant clubbing, Ecstasy and cocaine, not going to a schlocky dump where a three-piece band played ancient dance music and the membership was stuck in an age that meant nothing to anyone, but provided delights to anyone who might enjoy the company of people who belonged to a far distant age, like actors in Butcher Films of the nineteen fifties where the club owner was always called Ricky, and there were whores who spoke like they were fresh out of RADA, and you could see them at four in the morning on Carlton TV, if you were that desperate. The sort of people you can still find in mansion flats, say in Marylebone or the environs of Great Portland Street. What age were they all for Christ's sake and, if it came to that what age was Bill Poynton? You could never tell. Where did they come from, these dinosaurs, these oddball drunks and failed lechers from a Paleolithic Age where everyone had bad teeth and smoked all the time?

The Club was in a side street off Regent Street, in a mews that you couldn't locate in the A to Z, no matter how hard you tried. Cab drivers spoke knowingly of it, but could never find it, and you ended up discovering it almost by touch. Its familiars sometimes called it The Tacky Bugle, placing it in an age when students in duffel coats had invaded it on drunken rag nights and puked up in the bar.

You entered it through a garage full of decrepit cars which were in a state of perpetual overhaul. At the end of the oil-stained wall there was a door with a notice, ' Pink Lady Club - Private. Members Only,' then you went through another unmarked door guarded by a seedy looking geezer in a blazer. He had the air of the secretary of a down at heel golf club, and he'd call you squire almost contemptuously, half smiling, through brown teeth and make silly remarks using archaic slang, 'Some of the talent indoors is pretty good tonight,' or ' after a bit of skirt, are we Sir?'

Inside the door you went down a short staircase, took a sharp left turn and that was it, you were in. There was a small bar of the sort you might find in any crappy drinker, a small dance floor with tables around it, and a few desolate fruit machines. And all the while a three-piece band tinkled and moaned hopelessly, asking why the bloody hell are we here, we should be at Ronnie's, or something, and the drummer's brushes swished and tapped forlornly to some forgotten tune,

'I took one look at you, that's all I had to do and then my heart stood still.'

The main, the only attraction, was the singer, a blonde chanteuse from the days of torch songs. She was called Elizabeth Odalisque. She was the surprise package that gave the place far more oomph than it deserved, you might have thought that. Bill Poynton was always saying, 'Don't anyone try it on with her; she lives on her nerves.' No one knew what he meant by that, but then they weren't listening anyway, so entranced were they by her astonishing presence and husky promise.

She sang two sets a night, and when that happened the band came alive, and then she'd vanish as unexpectedly as she had appeared. That was the deal. You got what you saw. Occasionally if she deigned to stay on, you might get lucky and you might get to dance with her. This was near enough impossible since no one knew how to dance like that any more. And if you did, she talked animatedly to you of things you didn't understand; asked you flirtatious riddles, teased and provoked you. There was nothing explicit about this, but it intoxicated you with unsettling resonances and louche warmth. It was pretty good: the more so for being so unexpected in this depressing environment.

The membership was hard to identify: they all seemed to know each other and constantly reminisced about former members, as if striving to exclude outsiders from unspecified privileges and pleasures. 'Do you ever see Johnnie or Jon -Jon or Robert or Celia these days?' They'd say things like that across you, and laugh knowingly through you at their shared secrets, 'I heard he'd...' and laugh again, and say, 'yes well maybe just another one to settle the dust as it's Friday,' or some such fatuous bloody remark.

And next thing someone would come on with, 'Well it'll be a large gin I suppose, mother's ruin: hark at me.' as they coughed and spluttered through the next cigarette and looked around saying, 'Must give these up I suppose,' then snigger and shrug, and talk of having to go to the little girls room, and it's time to be shaking hands with the wife's best friend. Hangovers were a favourite topic. They gave a strong impression that they didn't welcome guests much, though since most of the visitors weren't members anyway, their continued presence saved the place from closure. If you asked for ice in your drinks the barman looked at you with homicidal indifference. It was that sort of place.

It was unappealing, but it was as if people were attracted to its tawdry presence in the hope of rediscovering some faded glamour, some awakening of lost excitements and stirrings within themselves. Perhaps it was the regular clientele with its echoes of shabby decadence: another roadside attraction.

The owner was called Freddie; a heavy faced man with the thick voice of the long-term chain-smoking drinker. Behind the bar there were one or two photographs of him standing beside aircraft at a flying club in Elstree or somewhere. His conversation was punctuated by occasional archaic slang: he'd speak of whizzoo popsies, prangs and types. If asked about these words he would change the subject and talk vaguely about it all being a long time ago now, as if anyone gave a shit one way or the other. In any case, said some, how could he have been alive then unless he's ninety or something? They were weak on dates.

If you'd asked him where you could get some good cocaine he'd have called the police. 'That's one thing I draw the line at: these kids nowadays, they're killing themselves with drugs.' His wife sometimes came and helped in the bar and looked at a few bottles, maybe rub a glass or two: she might even serve a drink to someone she favoured... one of my specials.

Mostly she sat with the clients as she called them. She was what you might call a real torn down piece from Memphis. Her handbag swung from the bar on a hinged hook that she unfolded and hung on the bar-top. She crossed and uncrossed her shapely legs scrupulously, daring you to make a comment on them as she hitched up the latest creazione from Fortellini and re-applied her lip liner. Beats me where she gets the money, I mean he doesn't look as if they're earning much does he surely? 'Beauty and the Beast that's what they call us isn't it Freddie?' she'd say as she sipped her Marigold's Special, for that was her name and she drank only this cocktail which had been named after her by the head barman in the Metropole in Brighton, Dear Old Reg. in the old days. Sometimes she would chat you up a bit and give you one of her famous looks, and Freddie would roll his eyes and smile tolerantly, 'My wife,' he'd say, 'I don't know, sometimes I wonder if she's.' and he'd glower as she reminisced of parties with forgotten people in forgotten places.

But she'd go on and tell of adventures and the gentlemen callers in the days when they ran the place outside Maidenhead, 'silly boys.' And then 'Take no notice of Freddie, you weren't jealous were you Darling' she'd say, 'I never went to bed with any of them, did I darling?' And she'd wink at one of the elite on whom I bestow my favours, and say, 'not half I didn't,' and again that no she didn't mind just a teensy Martini just for a change or did I mean an Alexander, silly me!'

And everyone would laugh and people like Martin and Hugh would say that they bet she was a right little goer, still is if you ask me. Not in front of Freddie's face mind you when they remembered what he did that time to the medic from Tommy's who did. Surgeon he was, isn't that correct Hugh?

And all the people who'd come along like that bloody prick Bill Poynton, who weren't members and all; they lapped all this up. ' It's a bloody cabaret for the Departmental Cretins from you know where.' Ted Blunger often said, and FX would say, 'No need to be so cruel Ted, they have their uses.' Not that he was a regular visitor. He only went there to pick up bits of information that might unlock the occasional puzzle. ' It's one of our research facilities you see,' said FXS. Or was it the other way around? It was believed that it was listed as such in Official Documentation. 'Don't knock places like this,' he'd say, 'you never know who is going to turn up here ready to sing all sorts of songs for our benefit. It's usually the ones who are really on the way out. Believe me, the ones who are so pissed off with everything that they want to tell the world what they know. They're the ones. That's why I like to keep an eye on the place.' It remained a decaying backwater that no one said much about nor visited. Occasionally fragments of information off the street turned up there to fulfill FX's faith in the place as an information source, as the Department supported it with surprisingly generous fundage. It might well have been let sink until Freddie found the body in the bar one morning. It was Bill Poynton, who else?

'Well it had to be, one might say.' said FX. And then he turned angry, 'Fancy someone leaving Poynton's body in the Pink Lady,' he said FX, indignantly, as if some sacrosanct rule had been broken about where disloyal employees' bodies should be left.. 'I mean it's a bit thick, wouldn't you say Ted?' Now he sounded as if he was referring to some misdemeanour in a prep school, like the astonished housemaster who, finding the blood spattered body of a housemaid, held back a gaggle of horrified boys, and exclaimed,' What dangerous clown has done this?' Of which FX used to say, 'Isn't it priceless and it happened at a school I went to, you know.' Not that anyone believed him.

Ted ignored that and continued, 'I don't know about that but they shoved a note on him, well to be honest it was in him, inside his anus in a plastic tube, but I didn't think you'd want to know that. The note said "Show this to his little pals in the Club". Makes you wonder.' FX said, 'It's definitely that bastard Karbnis, he always had a taste for the theatrical. We'll need to let him go. Get someone on to it Ted: we don't need this sort of thing. I'm sure that he can be found alternative employment.'

CHAPTER FOURTEEN

Hacker Tuke is now down the nick and already, as he would have told you he was now well comfortable in a material sense, and all things considered, he's as well as can be expected, taking into consideration his anger at having been sent down for fifteen stretch by that bastard Fizzer. In no time at all, by way of consolation, he'd already worked up a nice little line in creature comforts for the lads, not to mention one or two of the screws. He'd set up as a major dealer in white powders and pills, having bought out the on site opposition by means of the judicious use of a blade and a sock full of ball bearings. He had always been good at managing his life inside because he always had a product to sell.

Hacker was actually quite a dull person with the exception of one unusual characteristic: he said very little, took in everything that was said, watched everything that went on around him, and had the ability to act on it even though he was as thick as a plank. He never gave an opinion on anything, he'd sit there listening and making up his own mind. Imagination didn't come into it; he was just a single minded malevolent recording machine.

Apart from that one facet of his uninspiring personality, he was a typical boring and vicious criminal person with not an ounce of compassion or feeling in him. He'd kill you try or get someone to kill you, with as little feeling as he might experience in the act of opening a can of lager, or the stubbing out of one of his forty cigarettes a day. All his life had been lived in the process of breaking the law, thieving, extorting and bullying and the rest of it, for what reason he would not be able to tell you beyond the immediate gratification of his limited repertoire of personal needs. He wouldn't have been able to tell you more than that, as he had no pleasures in life beyond watching TV soaps, eating fatty dinners and drinking lager in certain ritzy gaffs in W1 that it wouldn't do to name for fear of embarrassing the owners.

Beyond this, and attending occasional race meetings with a twice a year bonus visit to a brothel in Nottingham,his life was about as stupefyingly boring as it is possible to imagine. Rather like the boneheads in Bonny and Clyde, like most villains who, despite contemporary mythology which assigns to them glittering life styles, orgiastic parties and yachts; in reality they usually live dull lives between being propositioned for anal sex and /or fellatio by thrill seeking MP's, appearing on TV chat shows hosted by narcissistic dickheads, or drinking cups of tea with their vile mothers in Plaistow or Thorpe Bay.

One thing that choked him was clothing.He didn't like prison gear one bit. The Hacker was quite fussy about his kit and always wore bespoke suits which he had made in a flash place in or around Savile Row.He'd never let on to anyone exactly where that was as the owners would not like it to be known. He always wore hand made shirts and he liked all his employees to look a bit flash in a quiet way. He thought that this sort of thing was good for the image of his Firm - a topic about which no one but Hacker gave a damn though they would be unlikely to express such an opinion in his presence or face the heavy duty mincer.

But these days inside Belmarsh, though he was doing quite well, Hacker was *well choked* about his having been nicked, and not just that but by that ' bleedin' sod Fizzer Edwards an all. 'He'd been sent down for fifteen stretch and he didn't reckon it one bit,'... no fuckin' way do I my son. Diabolical liberty I call it.' And he'd say that to anyone who 'd listen: he'd even said it to the Governor. He'd never reckoned the possibility of his having to do hard time again, but he was fairly well able to handle it, and once inside, he said little to anyone about anything beyond the placing of well chosen threats and their execution.

The weak link in the chain of his operations was Hacker's brother, but then he'd always been like that. Never one for being able to think very much was his brother, Tel - 'Bro' aka 'The Nose' Tuke. Now Tel could give you a bloody good whacking any day of the week, and he could nick anything you liked, but his abilities stopped pretty much right there. After that he remained completely empty. He was ten years younger than Hacker and when their old man had gone down for twenty five minimum, Hacker was left with his mother and Bro. to look after.

As proof of his lifelong devotion to his mum, long before she drank herself to death, he had bought this nice little gaff for her amongst all the villains near the Chislehurst golf course and the private loony bin from the Priory where all the rock chicks came down off the powders or puked up their meals, depending on what was wrong with them.

So when Mother drank herself into the loony bin after a lifetime of having had her face punched out on a daily basis by Hacker's father, an experience which had done little for her self- esteem, Hacker was obliged to keep an eye on the developing younger brother and supervise his further education and upbringing.

Fortunately for Hacker it mattered little what was done for him, since all Tel was good for was obeying simple orders and putting the boot in here and there. Independent action and decision making were not in his line of country. When Hacker went down for big time dealing and being an accessory to murder,Tel now felt that a great opportunity had come his way in which he might do his best to help his older brother out and prove himself as a man, you get the picture no doubt. 'I owe my brother he brought me up like when times was bad innit?'

On this occasion, as Hacker talked with brother Tel in the visiting suite at Belmarsh, he was angry with life in general and Fizzer in particular. Brother Tel always listened to his brother with respect for was not Hacker the family member who had done well, made a name for himself in the world and bought a Roller and a load of flash kit with it and all and whacked a few rivals. Tel loved that.

'Well Rog, what you reckon then?' asked Tel blinking 'Know what I fuckin' reckon? I mean an that.' Tel always called Hacker 'Rog'. This had never been satisfactorily explained. One theory was that he'd picked it up from Television in some sitcom about minicabs, not that it mattered. Hacker had tried everything to stop him talking bollocks like that but had long given up.

Since early childhood, brother Tel was definitely the weak link in the Hacker's chain of command: half the villains in London used to laugh their collective heads off at it most of the time. Not in front of the Hacker, it goes without saying. One guy did and he didn't do at all well, they all said, half daring to laugh and ended up well, like being eaten half alive by pigs in Swanley it was said, not that anything was ever proved, but you never know. Curiously enough it never interfered with Hacker's business affairs, him having a dumbshit brother. Hacker was devoted to brother Tel and did his best to look out for him, and so on. Tel was equally devoted and did his best so to speak.

'I'll tell you what I mean you soft headed berk,' says Hacker, 'You need to get that fucker sorted.'

'Who's that then Rog?' asked Tel happily.

'Fuckin' Edwards.' One of Hacker's linguistic problems was his restricted vocabulary. And this afternoon brother Tel was beginning to wear him down. But he was a loyal brother was he not?

'Well that's no problem with you like knowin' him and all innit Rog?'

'Are you stupid Tel or something. I'm in here doing fifteen stretch?'

This was obviously going to take quite a while as Tel was not on his best form.

'Got you me old son. Got you in one Rog.' He blinked, 'What d'you reckon then, you mean like I should blag him?' Hacker sighed ' Forget it, just work something out for us. I mean you could start off by finding where he goes regular, and getting like someone like Big Ron or Tosher to have a go with a shooter. Put the frighteners on, anything to put the breeze up him but have a go at him. Least you could try.'

'Just fuckin' do 'im that's all I'm saying, know what I mean.'

'That it then Rog?'

There the conversation languished.

'In any case, I don't know why I'm in here anyway. It was that little sod Kev who done the lad in the Park when you come down to it. I mean he put your actual fuckin' boot in?'

'Funny that, I always thought he done it with a blade. Who's the man then? Like what you just said.'

'Forget it just work something out.' and thought, what's the bloody use with this deadhead? Maybe I'm wasting me time.

If Fizzer had been aware of the plans that Hacker had in mind for him it is doubtful that he would have been too worried. He didn't reckon Hacker as being more than a dealer who had got lucky up to now and was doing time: it was possible that he underrated him, for Hacker had many friends that owed him, and Tel could easy enough find someone to do him a favour by having a go at Fizzer. Hacker said, 'Well that's it then. If you don't fancy it,I'll get someone else, know what I mean? You can bugger off now and stop wasting my time.' He had never run his business enterprises by committee. The other side was that Fizzer knew that all Hacker's friends were hardly worth considering as seriously dangerous, being on the whole too stupid, so this operated in Fizzer's favour.

Meanwhile Hacker sat looking glumly at Bro and thinking why the hell did I ever let this dummy do anything but clean out the shithouse at the club until he was near enough desperate, when he had a blinding inspiration which astonished him by its originality. He said to Bro ' Why don't we have a go at his bleedin' wife? That should do it for the bastard.'

'I don't know about that, she's a brief isn't she?'

The Hacker was one of those people to whom people talk and that's it. Besides he had already near enough set up payback for that sod Fizzer who wasn't half going to be double pissed off when Bro had a dig at his wife, the brief, and a black with it, bloody cheek. What next? All he had to do was to sit back and wait for some news about the bloody cow.

This could be Big Mistake Number One coming into the Frame Hacker me old son, said Fizzer when he had picked up the word from Turk the night previous in the Twenty Nine. It might be thought odd that Fizzer was in no hurry to get things moving until he had a clearer idea what was going on.

A lesser person than Fizzer would have warned Sylvie immediately, rushed in and made a dogs bollocks of the whole thing, but that, as we know, was never Fizzer's style. OK, so Fizzer had a short fuse and so on, but all the noise was a part of his persona that he had skillfully cultivated, to ensure that his adversaries become overconfident, be they villains or colleagues, either way, so that they might think, at last we've got the drop on that sod Fizzer. Big mistake chum.

He had decided that it was time that Hacker was asked a few questions about his future plans regarding Sylvie. He should clarify things so that everyone knew where they stood. He started in a quiet way, his usual approach and decided to set things up for a surprise medical consultation for Hacker, whose health had hitherto been normal, except for a weight problem and who was therefore surprised when Mr Jackson, one of the screws whom he had befriended, comes in and tells him,' You're up for a hospital check up then Mr Tuke. That 'll be nice. Bit of a change like.'

Hacker said, 'What's that about. I don't have any health problems do I?'

'Well it says here you're down for a routine visit to Guys Hospital tomorrow in the Cardiac Dept for special investigations on account of you used to smoke too much.'

'Suits me.' said Hacker, thinking, stupid bastards what do they know? And replied as polite and amiable as anything, 'Right on Mr Jackson. It's a change any road.' And he slept well that night thinking, you never know I might even get a chance to do a runner. He quite enjoyed his breakfast in the morning, and sure enough Mr Jackson said, 'You must be a right bloody VIP Mr Tuke, they sent a special escort to take you there and all.'

And so Hacker goes off dead chuffed with the Prison Officers who came to collect him, and seemed real friendly for bleedin' screws: kept making jokes. And they took him away in a special police car with darkened windows no less. 'They reckon I'm a VIP' said Hacker. 'Oh yes' said one of the officers who came to pick him up, ' definitely one of the VIP's you are. That's it.' and they both laughed again, and made more jokes about him being a VIP, and Hacker laughed at the idea too, what a joke he thought me being a VIP and all.

It never occurred to him that it was a bit odd that no one from the nick came with him, but then they were short handed in the Prison service nowadays: everyone knew that. He quite enjoyed the drive up the Old Kent Road, noting some of his old spheres of influence as he they drove along. He was a bit surprised to find when the route changed and couldn't understand why they went past the Oval cricket ground, that is until they arrived at their destination, and then he realised that they weren't going to a hospital at all.

It was this funny looking place near Vauxhall. They had him out the car sharpish as you might say, without laying a finger on him, and there to greet him was that bastard Fizzer, who bloody else? 'Right, you large piece of shit,' said Fizzer all smiling and evidently in one of his, I don't give a shit if I have to nail your head to the ground, moods. 'Don't piss around with me fat man, we've got work to do.' Next thing he was indoors in the basement and someone had strapped him into a seat. And then Fizzer started talking surprisingly calmly, as one of the others said afterwards, considering everything.

'Now the thing is Mr Hacker or whatever your bloody name is, my needs here are extremely simple and I know that you will be able to help us. All I need to know is what's happening to my wife, and where she's likely to be located so we can deal with things. It will be in your best interest to level with us as soon as you know how. Understand?'

'I got rights. You got no right to keep me here and you fuckin' know it Mr fuckin' Edwards. I ain't been cautioned nor nothing and furthermore I ain't saying fuck all.'

'As thing stand you have no rights Mr Hacker. To be perfectly frank it's for question whether you even have the right to live, but that's not my concern. Being cautioned doesn't come in to it. You are now in what we shall call, for the purposes of argument, no mans land, so I suggest you get on with it, and we can all go home. Do I make myself perfectly clear or is there anything else before we start?'

'What's this then a police state, is that it?'

'Not exactly. Let's just say that you are in the care of a special department that is designated for the purpose of the establishment of, and verification of matters of national concern, and the clarification of grey areas, and that you are here to assist us in illuminating them to the best of your ability.'

'You think I give a toss about that. You think I give a fuck about a copper's coon wife and what happens to her That it?'

'This sort of thing won't help you, so I would suggest to you that you get on with it before I start tearing your bollocks off, fat man. You talking about my wife sunshine remember, we haven't got too much time.' By now Fizzer and the others could hardly keep straight faces as urine started to leak down the legs of Hacker's pants, and he said quietly. 'We've got your ass, so get fuckin' on with it, you boring fat prick.'

He paused. 'No hard feelings you fat sod. Here's some medicine for you,' says Fizzer, 'It will help your memory. And now I have to leave you with my friends. They'll take care of you very well. I'm sure you'll be able to fill in the details that we need to know. I'll be back in an hour or two when you're feeling a bit better'

And then they started on things. Quite soon Hacker was more than ready to tell what was to happen. When it was over someone said, 'Are we going to keep him here or lose him?' Fizzer said, 'We're not bloody savages. He can stay here until we've picked up Sylvie: then he can go back. We need some insurance in case he's given us a bum steer. Otherwise he can go in the M20 extension, or the M2 widening bit. I don't care too much either way.' He laughed and said, 'I wonder if he could sign his name better than the late Mr Guido Fawkes. We must do it by the book. I want a signed statement and everything kosher.'

Hacker wondered whether they were taking the piss, but knew they weren't, so he coughed pretty soon, I mean, why not? People usually do, at least that's what he'd heard about that sod Fizzer and his crew. There was only one deficiency in the information that he had coughed. He had been unable to tell them when this was to take place. He didn't know, since he had left it to Bro to decide.

And he fell into a dreamless sleep from which he awoke in his cell where the screw said, 'That visit to the hospital must have done you good Hacker. Slept like a baby you did.'

'Did I?' says Hacker. 'Well that's handy then.'

He'd have felt different if he'd known about Fizzer's meeting in The Twenty Nine the night before.

CHAPTER FIFTEEN

You wouldn't expect to meet the likes of Fizzer Edwards in a place like The Twenty Nine. In the first place he wasn't a gambler and he wasn't particularly attracted to the high life, or even to middle of the road clubbing. And he'd never been one of those coppers who hung around with villains on the quiet buying drinks in search of information. And that extended into his social life in the Force where one of the things that had made him unpopular in the old days was that he rarely went out and got hammered with the lads.

Tonight was different, and this time he was on his way to the Twenty Nine to have a look around and ask a favour of the proprietor. He knew that it was a favourite place of Ted Blunger's, but he'd made sure that Ted wouldn't be there that night. It was his business to know about the jealousies and bad feelings that could screw up the management of a case like this one, and Fizzer getting his leg over with the girl friend of one of the top spooks in town wasn't likely to score too many points with the suits in Vauxhall Cross. And in any case he was here on business, so where's the problem? Yes, you can't be too careful, he thought that.

As he crossed Berkeley Square and looked at all the serious money that was hanging around the place, he felt resentful and angered at it all. The big Grande Luxe motors in Jack Barclays were too much to handle, and the sight of all the sleek sharp suited punters and their bimbos out on the town made him feel unsettled. He usually felt like that when he was confronted with too much of anything.

And then, next thing, he was interrupted by one of his favourite people, a total stranger in the street who wants to have a bloody good shot at kicking your ass. This one was a belligerent 'street person', blanket over the left shoulder, rings through the lips and a neck with barbed wire tattoos round it. ' Give us a pound you rich fuck.', the man said winningly through the encrusted saliva on his lips. 'Too much fucking speed that's your problem you bloody jerkoff,' said Fizzer; and as Fizzer's hand closed around his genitalia your man realised that this evening was the one when he had made a major error of judgement. 'Next time you should say please you stupid prick,' said Fizzer, 'The best things in life are free in case you didn't know,' he added while the guy puked up.

And then he walked over towards the door of The Twenty Nine where he took in the refurbishments. A new paint job inside and out, and chrome all over the place: that's a nice one for Mr Turk, that means business must be better than good, he thought and contrasted the flash geezers going through the doors with the poor sod who'd asked him for money and called him a rich fuck. Straight up, as soon as he's in the door, Ben Shiner the heavy man immediately lamped him as a member of the filth, so he calls Turk and says ' Listen Mr Turk we got that man in blue, the one you know, that Mr Edwards indoors.'

Turk was not bothered about the news. As far as he was concerned Members of the Force were always welcome, well up to a point. He knew all about Fizzer and knew that Mr Edwards wasn't after him, no way was he, him having been clean for years now, and so he ordered a bottle of Krug to be sent to Mr Edwards, compliments of the house and all, knowing that Fizzer would like as not tell him to shove it up his ass. It's always a good idea to be in with the law was how Turk looked at it. You can't be too careful, and if they need something give it to them as long as no one gets too embarrassed like.

He quite enjoyed meeting the Fizzers of this world. Other side of the coin: all brothers under the skin sort of thing. He smiled at the thought. He'd had some good times with the boys in blue in the good old days. However it was no time for a stroll down memory lane, he was curious to know what Fizzer wanted, so he calls Sandra and asks her to sus him out a bit. Not the brightest of moves it might be thought, as Sandra was still at least a part of Ted Blunger's life, but it wouldn't hurt to find out. In any case it's nice to have someone around who's on both sides of the fence, just to be on the safe side. Also did Ted know that Fizzer was there? He worried about things like that. That sort of regard for certain fancied proprieties of conduct concerned him.

Hard men are often prudes, like those Generals who marry ice maidens of the Hunt and live to regret it. Turk liked everything to be above board, up to a point. Now Sandra didn't know Fizzer at all, that is beyond odd remarks dropped by Ted, but Fizzer knew all about her, which was handy. It might be supposed that Ted wouldn't have been best pleased had he known what was going on. Not one bit. It was not that he was a jealous person, more that he tended to be a bit over protective about someone who, to tell the truth hadn't been too well treated by Ted who was aware of his own shortcomings and of his, frequently commented on by Sandra, lack of a sense of commitment.

Matters which had prompted FX to say, 'Isn't it a pity that you can't settle things *more definitely* with Miss Sandra, not that it's any of my business. She's a very *suitable* person for someone in your position Ted. At your time of life you really need to establish a more *bonding* relationship, and it would look good for the people in personnel, and our paymasters who like that sort of thing.' All said with mock gravitas and guaranteed to drive Ted straight up the wall for a moment or two. But Ted knew that FX had a point, though he wasn't too sure of the idea of settling. It was the commitment part that bothered him.

That evening at the Twenty Nine the atmosphere was edgy and, to be honest it was bordering on the about to get bloody nasty. A group of drunken Japanese bankers was threatening to disturb things, complaining that they'd been cheated, the very idea, and coming the acid like there'd never been

Hiroshima. Turk kept a tidy ship and didn't like this sort of crap one bit. He didn't like bother, but if necessary he was quite ready to dump the sodding lot in Epping Forest in the small hours after a good seeing to with it. Fizzer's presence didn't exactly encourage his instituting the public whacking of a load of the slit eyed brigade, though from what he knew, he suspected that Fizzer might not be totally unsympathetic to such a course of action, that is if he didn't personally lend a hand.

So that he was pleasantly surprised when Fizzer came along as cool as ice and says, 'A word with you Mr Turk if you have no objection?'

Turk liked his style, no fucking around with copspeak, thought carefully and said, 'That would be fine. Did you want to come to my office where it's a bit more private like?'

Fizzer was impressed with Turk's office. All black leather and chrome furniture and tasteful with it. Impressive selection of booze and a bloody great bowl of best Colombian, the cheeky sod, he might have hidden that with the Force on a site visit. First class surveillance gear, a well concealed weapons store and a neatly sited escape door. Fizzer approved of the man's appointments. Turk offered him a drink, and Fizzer accepted a single malt. This is how they live thought Fizzer. He knew anyway, but it was correct to appear impressed, and to date he knew that maestro Turk had stayed out of trouble for several years. Agreed it didn't make everything right, but it helped. 'OK Mr Turk,' he said, ' I don't need to piss around, so here's the deal. You're a busy guy. I have a favour to ask of you. If it doesn't appeal to you, we can forget it. If it does that's fine, and we can come to an arrangement.'

'You asking me to break the law Mr Edwards maybe, is that it?'

'Not exactly Mr Turk: it's mainly a question of getting some information. Let's go back to the Booker prize thing.'

Turk replied, 'You mean when your lot topped the Welsh nutter and said it was down to him having a bomb. I like it.'

'Something like that: I can't say any more.'

'So what you need ?'

'Hacker Tuke, the dealer, you remember him, he went down.'

'Dealing Class A: he was fairly big time, and that little ponce Clancy went down for topping some prick?' Ignoring the last bit Fizzer replied, 'Well he's doing big time now and doesn't like it: more important is he doesn't like me, and the word I'm hearing is that he wants my ass. I need the full SP on this one if you can get it for me as I believe you can.'

'You might need to give me a few hours Mr Edwards. Meantime you could relax here for an hour or two. Have some fun.' The conversation was over: Fizzer didn't care much about that. Turk was known for his brevity. He laughed, 'You never know you might meet someone you know.' So Fizzer took a wander around the place watching the players. Funny thing but Fizzer found gambling a risk that did nothing for him, and it was reinforced by the sight of the punters. Nice little gaff, he's thinking when a voice that he recognized says, 'Well Mr Edwards, I didn't know you were one of ours. Ted never told me.' It was Sandra, looking quite tasty, Fizzer noted, 'I'm here on business Ms Sandra.'

'Suits me, so am I,' says Sandra as chirpy and cheeky as you please. 'You can buy me drink if you like,' she added, quick as a flash, bit too quick thinks Fizz, and he's wondering what's her caper then, I thought she was on the straight, 'I'm sure you realise that you're not really meant to buy drinks for dealers but Mr Turk wouldn't mind.' In any case Turk had already called her and told her to look after Mr F. please and to be nice to him, a valuable client sort of thing, and perhaps it would be best not to mention it to Ted. Well she knew that didn't she? What did he think she was going to do, give him a blow job or something? Some people; you wouldn't believe it.

'That's fine by me,' said Fizzer, 'I'm not on duty.' Sandra said, 'I thought you were always on duty when you're a copper.' Fizzer laughed and said. 'It depends: it's all down to being discreet.'

'I often wondered how you were getting on; good looking boy like you. Do you ever have any fun I wonder,' she said and laughed, 'Ted never talks about his work you know.' She laughed again, 'In any case he's far too busy when he's here.' Fizzer had heard all about Ted Blunger's gambling. That aspect of his life made him seem more human, what with him being one of the spook; to be honest, most of them gave him the creeps.

He knew about Sandra too: she had a bit more form than she might let on and he wondered how it was that FX turned a blind eye to it, not that Fizzer gave a toss, but some of FX's enemies might, but then with that bugger FX, interesting, crafty sod, you never knew what he could get away with, or had done in all probability. Another thing that concerned him was that Sandra was one of those people who laugh a bit too much for the likes of Fizzer.

Sandra had reached a crisis in her life. She knew that she couldn't go along forever as a blackjack dealer. It was no route to a happy retirement and not exactly fulfilling. Her relationship with Ted was uncertain and she was often distressed by his unwillingness to firm things up. She knew he was a good man but knew also that his job was the real partner and driving force, and that inevitably she would never be a front runner in his world. She had a great deal of respect for what he did and stood for, but knew that she would never compete with the pull of the secret world.

For the Sarnos and Teds of this world it seemed to hold a magnetism that she could never compete with. It went beyond merely earning a living in an interesting, arcane and dangerous way, or having some schoolboy urge to serve the nation and all that old crap. It was a powerful motivator which she could never share, nor would she wish to. You either accepted that or you got out. Ted had never made a secret of the fact that this was what came first in his life. Not that he said so in histrionic terms. Whatever he did with FX and those people was what he did, and that was his job about which she could care little, despite the help she had given FX in the past. Up to a point she did accept this and was prepared to do so for a limited period, but she wanted something beyond hanging around while Ted made up his mind: no more tagging along waiting for a commitment. And so when she ran into Fizzer at the Twenty Nine she was ready to run around a bit. For the moment Ted could kiss her ass.

As he was about to leave, Sandra said, 'Actually I quite fancy you, if you really want to know. You want to come back to my place for some more, I mean a drink or whatever?' Fizzer said, 'We'll have to see about that one of these days possibly.' She came back with, 'Well don't hang about. You coming or not?'

She enjoyed a challenge now and again. So did Fizzer, but fooling around with Ted Blunger's piece of ass wasn't on his agenda at the moment, and anyway what would Turk have to say? Also he remembered that Sylvie wouldn't give three hearty cheers if it came to that. So he made the right decision for about ten minutes and then he changed his mind. It's amazing what some people can come out with in moments of excitement, he'd forgotten that. Who knows what she might say. Any excuse being better than none. He said, 'Hang on I need to talk to Mr Turk.It might be best if I followed you to your address. It's...' she said. 'That's all right says Fizzer, 'I know where you live, and another thing let's leave Mr Blunger out of all this. You read me?'

'In one,' says Sandra, and Fizzer went back to talk to Turk. 'What's happening Turk?' said Fizzer. 'Not good,' said Turk, 'The word I'm getting is that some of Hacker's people might be planning to snatch your wife, and that Mr Edwards, is the full SP.' Fizzer never moved a muscle. He replied, 'Any idea when this might be planned for then? That's important. If they haven't fixed a date, it doesn't mean so much and we can move in, know what I mean?' Turk knew very well what he meant ' No idea Mr Edwards. All we got is the story.'

'Right then,' said Fizzer, 'That's it then.'

'Talk about the Death of Romantic Love', said Sandra later, 'I reckon I've seen the lot now.' Fizzer only said, 'Well what did you expect tuberoses and Tiger skins?' and continued, 'or did you expect me to say that my wife no longer understands me?' He paused, 'Listen honey, if you really want to be a big help you might like to pick up a real influential person for me. It's someone I need to talk to and sort a few bits out. Mr Blunger doesn't know and there's no need that he should although I know that it would get his full approval; it's just that we haven't the time to ask him right now , but if you feel able to help me out on this one it could be, lets say important.' Sandra said, 'That's great, all you guys do is ask me to help you out with your dirty tricks activities.' Fizzer said, 'Well, will you? I mean someone has to and I'd prefer it to be someone I know.'

'All you have to do is meet this guy and entertain him for about half an hour Then you leave the rest to my crew. It's a doddle.' Sandra replied, 'Nice one Fizzer. What do you call entertain?'

'I leave that to you.'

'OK well before we get to that, may I ask what all this about?'

'It's a highly important matter of national security. I want you to sus this guy out. He writes crazy letters to the papers and they reckon he's probably involved with a terrorist group. I shouldn't be telling you this.'

'Thanks a bunch Fizzer. You really know how to please a woman, real old fashioned charm don't you. My word.'

'It's bloody H.E. isn't it?'

Fizzer thinks she does know what's going on, how about that then.

Sandra said 'I've heard Ted mention him when I haven't been meant to, and in any case quite few of the girls around town know him. He's got unusual tastes in entertainment is what I heard.'

'Is that right?' said Fizzer. 'In a bloody word, all we want you to do is compromise him, I mean so that his employers get to know and the media get a whiff.'

'Does Ted know about this?'

'I'm not at liberty to say.'

'That means he doesn't. He wouldn't like it you know.'

Fizzer said, ' Maybe not, but the way I see it we'd be better off asking someone like yourself to do this for us, someone with an in to the whole spooky thing with FXS and Ted' And he added piously, 'I'm sure Ted would see it my way if we put that to him.'

'OK then I'll do it,' said Sandra, 'I don't mind. It couldn't be more boring than being a blackjack dealer.' Fizzer added, 'In any case there'll be back up in case he gets nasty.'

'I should bloody well hope so.'

'It's what these bloody spooks call a honey trap, I prefer to call it getting a tosser with his pants down with a bird. It's OK Sandra we wont need you to get quite that far: all we want is to have him ready to be photographed and stuff. It's all arranged. You'll be picked up and driven there and he'll be brought along - just give him a drink or something and leave the rest to us and we'll stitch the bugger up,'

'Who is he really –I mean HE?'

'Just say he's a VIP. He'll like that. Mr Sarno is in on it, but he thought it best to leave Mr Blunger out if you get my drift.'

Don't I just thought Sandra and said nothing, the crafty bastards this lot, I don't know why I'm doing this.

CHAPTER SIXTEEN

Mr FX Sarno sat gloomily behind a long table in one of the lesser conference suites in the riverside spookhouse, flanked by Ted Blunger and one of the regulation Civil Service suits, brought along to pounce on any financial or procedural misdemeanors which might compromise HMG.

'Let me introduce myself,' said FX as smooth as anything, 'My name is FX Sarno and this is my colleague, Mr Ted Blunger, formerly of the Aircraft Research Establishment. We pride ourselves on being rather broadly based people here you know and all of us take a lively interest in the Arts just in case you might feel that we are too narrow and so on.' There was no reply from the trio sitting on the other side of the table who stared ahead, unsmiling and giving every indication of massive non-cooperation. 'You could smell it as soon as they came in,' Ted later remarked. 'This blooming lot weren't going to admit to anything that went beyond the requirements of The Geneva Convention or the possession of a bus pass, quite apart from them all looking like a deputation from Buffy the Vampire Slayer.'

'And in case they give us a load of old rubbish about Civil Rights you'd better tell them that we aren't playing that game,' said FX rather pettishly, ' in any case such concepts have no relevance for anyone on these premises. These people aren't prisoners, merely people who we want to talk to, for God's sake, about the goings on in an Art gallery in an obscure country town. Hardly front page stuff now is it?' Ted only said, 'I really wonder if we should be doing this at all; it isn't as if we have anything much to go on beyond a hunch, and some not so verifiable information from someone who, let's be honest we don't really know too well. I mean Gilli. What I'm saying is we shouldn't get too carried way.' But he didn't mean it; he knew bloody well that this shower of creeps had to be involved in something, and said, 'Well I guess someone is going to have to explain to them what we want from them. As long as it's not me that's all.' As it happened the funnies had filed in to the office in the Box apparently as calm as anything, but looking more than mildly pissed off. What was disagreeable about them was that they shared an extremely nerdy air which was more sinister than contemptible. They were definitely not nice people.

And so it was that Ted in a state of complete disbelief, heard FX saying, 'Good afternoon and welcome Mr Spudder, Mr Spurlow and Ms Shafter. You may have wondered why it is that we have asked you to meet us here. It's all perfectly straightforward. We are all of us, at one time or another likely to become victims of the search for truth and justice, and therefore we are all here in order to establish and clarify certain matters that concern our department, which I must remind you is concerned with matters that relate to the maintenance of National Security at the highest level. We are curious about certain aspects of your fiscal concerns and problems that may have or may be about to arise or may have arisen from them if you follow me.'

At this point any one in the room might have overheard the stifled noises of Ted trying not to burst into laughter. As usual he was sitting to one side of FX, not entirely in the light, and thanking God that he was. Whenever FX did this act. he always claimed that there was nothing to beat a ponderous start to any interrogation, 'It makes it sound as if it's all going to be a great bore, harmless fun almost, and offer apologies for having to follow the dictates of administrative necessity and so on: believe me it never fails. Next thing they're offering you their grandmothers' life, at least that's been my experience and I know it's been Ted's.'

Messrs Y Spurlow, Jack Spudder and Ms Nansi Shafter continued to look straight ahead and then Jack Spudder said, 'Stuff that for a game of soldiers chum. I act as the spokesperson and you should address all questions to me. I that is we wish to know what this is all about.'

FX said, 'Listen up here; bollocks to you sunshine or do I have to get heavy and bring in some muscle? We already told you, so let me lay it on the line Fatso. Lately, there have occurred a number of incidents of an embarrassing and ridiculous nature which have involved certain important public figures. Let's get one or two things straight, you overweight goombah. Like I just bloody said, my colleagues and I are attached to a Government department which has been asked to look into these matters, since they may affect national security. We believe that your organization may have some connection with all this and we need to find out if this is the case, and that's it. You are free to leave here at any time and are under no form of duress. I would remind you that you are not under arrest.'

If they believe that they'll believe anything thought Ted as he thought of the mob downstairs waiting to get cranked up, and said 'My colleague Mr Sarno has been under something of a strain of late. It's all down to stress you know.' and laughed inwardly as he remembered he'd just used FX's favourite lines.

'I don't think that I know what you are talking about chum,' said Mr Spudder. 'If you have any comment about our organization, and I presume that are you referring to the Religious Affairs Cultural Studies Group, I suggest you get in touch with our lawyer who is waiting outside these rooms.' Ted then jumped in again and said, 'I really don't think that will be necessary. We have good enough evidence which links your people to fraud, so, as far as you and your buddies are concerned, it's shit or get off the pot time, and you should start talking before I start to get nervous, and when I get nervous, let me assure you that myself and my people can get quite unpleasant. I refer first of all to a number of financial matters which are now in the hands of the Serious Fraud Squad.'

At this point the trio got up as one person and made to leave the room as Mr Spudder said, 'Don't suppose Mr Sarno and by the way, that's a bloody stupid name if ever I heard one: don't suppose that you and your colleagues are the only ones who can get nasty round here, you stupid bastard.' Ted looked as if he was about to get even more hard-nosed but FX said calmly, 'That's all right Mr Blunger; if they wish to go, let them go. We know where to reach these good people.' And off they went smiling amongst themselves at having gotten off so lightly. After they had left, Ted said, 'Well that was a right fiasco, we look a right bunch of idiots. What went wrong with you Guv? I've never seen you screw up like that. A bloody waste of time.' And thought again, it's no good, he's really losing it. They must have thought we were a right bloody shower of idiots.

FX said, 'Did you notice Ted that they all seemed to be barely alive. I mean their calmness was beyond normality.' Holy Christ thinks Ted, we're not back to bloody aliens again. 'No Ted, it's all right, I'm not talking aliens here, if that's what you're thinking as it's pretty obvious you are. All I'm saying is that this lot are out of the ordinary in a way that I don't understand. Let's trawl some more and find out more about where they're coming from. We seem to have fallen down on that so far. I wonder why? It's almost as if they've got the drop on us without us knowing. Don't you think it's time we did more homework? Another thing about them is that Mr Spudder appears to be unable to pronounce a simple word like bastard. He stressed the last syllable so that it came out as "bastARD". Now there's an odd thing, wouldn't you agree?' Ted ignored the remark and said almost hopelessly, an odd way for Ted to behave, 'We know their addresses and company details but little else. There's nothing from the CRO. Anyway, at least our technical people got a few sensors on them when they used the bog. Christ knows how.' After a period of silence FX said, 'Listen Ted, has it occurred to you that so far we're getting nowhere. These people are playing games with us.'

'That had occurred to me.' replied Ted.

'Well I suggest we do something more active about it, or is it proactive I never know these days? It's a stupid word.'

'Two days ago I started some old fashioned police work: you cant beat it you know.'

'No need to sound like a recruitment ad – next thing you'll be saying it's quite like old times and humming Dixon of Dock Green.'

But Ted was not giving up on this one, 'Plus Fizzer's people have been on their backs round the clock for the last forty eight hours. Also we have full visual surveillance on the place where they live - a rented house just a few doors along from this gallery in High Faldon, twenty minutes from the Shufi Center. With any luck Ms Gilli will be paying them a visit in the next twenty four hours. It's totally kosher, since they know that she's a staff member from the place they want to take over. I think soon we'll get to know more about them. And when we really get down to asking them a few questions, it is a case of whatever it takes to get at the truth, is it not? And the other point about all this is that this is rapidly becoming the most boring affair we've ever had a hand in; I wonder if we are wasting our time.'

'As always, we must act with circumspection,' said FX primly, 'and in any case, all good investigative work is boring.'

'OK, just one question.' said Ted, 'What exactly are we hoping to find?'

'I believe that Ms Gilli may provide us with the answer to that. My hunch is that already she knows more than she is letting on. I'm usually right you know Ted. Any ideas yet as to what their internet hits are showing. At least it won't be porn.'

'Now here is something. So far over eighty percent of their hits are on Medline. Almost entirely on genetics, virology and similar topics.'

'That's it,' said FX, ' we need red alert here now. And I think I'd like to have a close look at the place where they are living: myself that is.' He paused, 'And another thing Ted: Am I losing my grip, at least I'd begun to think I had until about two nanoseconds ago? Like I said earlier, we spent all this last meeting with the nutters with me talking balls and you thinking the old man is losing his marbles and not wanting to say so. Right?'

'Well, you could say something like that.' said Ted.

'The reason we can't communicate properly with these buggers Ted could be almost exactly as I suggested. I believe that they *are* playing mind games with us I'm convinced of that. Could it be that they have some way of interfering with our thinking. What about that Ted?'

Ted nodded agreement but recalled having read somewhere that what FX had just said was a sign of psychosis or something. 'It's OK Ted, I am not bloody bonkers. If you can put microchips inside peoples' heads which is what they are already doing at MIT, and influence their choice of underarm deodorant or whatever it is, why can't these mysterious buggers do something like that to us if their motives are strong enough? Also it could account for the funny goings on with the Archbish. You have to admit Ted, it all adds up, or nearly.'

'From where I am Guv, it's a case of go with the flow. What have we got to lose. So far we know so little about these people worth a damn. We don't even know how they got here beyond the record of their arrival at Heathrow six months ago.'

'And what about the place where they hang out? What do we make of that?'

'No exactly fun city from what I hear from the experts,' said Ted 'another run down old house, ready for re-development and situated in a quiet market town about sums it up.' He paused, 'Actually Guv I wouldn't mind pulling them in and sweating them.'

'It might come to that. Providing Fizzer hasn't beaten us to it. I believe he's had a go at Hacker Tuke, and did someone said His Ex?'

'Search me Guv. How would I know?'

The house where the Funnies stayed was a substantial Nineteenth Century building which opened right on to the street. It had a large walled garden which proclaimed 'keep out' to the world without saying as much. The main entrance stood beside an arched open hallway which had a door at its far end beneath which you could see daylight coming from the garden behind. The main entrance had a Doctor's brass plate at the side of the door. The Doctor concerned must have been long dead and the plate hadn't been cleaned for years. On the inside of the open hallway there was another door with a small dirty window beside it.

And on the front of the main entrance, beneath the brass plate, there was a rather grubby notice that warned that you should not deliver any letters nor packages that might be addressed to the 'lady of the house', to this address, and directing you to another doorway around the corner where the odious goods might be deposited. The consequences of such an appalling misdemeanour were not stated, but you got a strong whiff of the retribution that might be visited on any poor sod who got it wrong and delivered the groceries by mistake.

The garden wall was over twelve foot high and at one end it had a tiny door situated at knee level. There was a strong general impression that visitors were not welcome. The technical crew which had been sent down by FX and Ted had a wonderful time scattering sensors and probes everywhere; they were so excited that they could hardly be dragged back to London to talk things over. When FX saw the place he almost went into a trance of delighted surprise; he was so intrigued by the appearance of this *'ramshackle bordelle de merde.'* It's just like a fourth class whorehouse in Angouleme, I mean like a place that has known better days and now struggles with recession. All the employees have the clap and it's all going seriously down the tubes. Even the Mayor has stopped visiting A collector's item if ever I saw one, wouldn't you agree Ted? Messrs Spudder and Co must be a stranger bunch than we had realised if they can't see that.' Ted agreed, 'Seems like a poor choice. Look Guv when I see all this I can't help feeling that maybe we overreacted to these people. I mean what are they beyond a bunch of oddballs who have somehow nearly panicked us? That's rubbish Guv and we know that.'

FX said, 'A chap I knew years ago,' and he said it in the irritating way that people have of making 'years ago' sound like Holy Writ and say no more. Ted said wearily 'What did he say then?' FX looked slightly miffed and said ' He said if you watch something carefully you see it for the first time after you watch it a thousand times..' Ted replied, 'thanks a bunch Chief. I'll remember that.' And thought, no doubt about it, he's losing his marbles, poor old sod.

And so the watchers were not surprised when they found that nothing much ever seemed to happen in the house. Such findings never surprised them. It was something that went with the job. They were interested to discover that the funnies, as everyone now called them, seemed to be aware of what was going on, but appeared to be unaffected by it. As FX had observed this lot didn't seem to be one of us as you might say, not, he added, that they were *out of this world,* and laughed even a little sheepishly at the recollection of his *faux pas* concerning aliens.

By now Ted had become fed up with the whole affair and again said that they ought to go in and pull the tiresome buggers in, causing FX get all dignified and comment that he was beginning to sound like Fizzer and where was his spirit of enquiry? Down the bloody tubes, like as not was Ted's disgruntled reply and he muttered something about ' roll on my five.'

'Come along Ted,' said FX, 'those days are long past.' And said, 'and of course yes it's nearly time for closure of this affair Ted; my problem is that we still haven't established the connection of these people with anything very much, beyond the fact that they appear to be a rather offensive group of tiresome oddballs who live in a half run down house that looks like it's straight from the Munsters. I'm not convinced that we have a case.'

Ted replied, 'Not according to Gilli. She thinks they're Satanists as far as I can make out.'

'No doubt,' said FX, 'but that doesn't get anyone of us any further. Look what have we got so far about these people apart from a few hunches? Gilli had the idea they were trying to take over the Shufi Center. OK? That's not a crime. What's so wrong with wanting to develop a wacky health farm into a more profitable enterprise?'

'OK Guv, I'll buy that but don't forget our interview with them where you and I ended up talking bollocks and wondering if they were interfering with our brains for Christ's sake. At the very least, that can't be right.'

'Litotes alert.' said FX, 'that's another matter altogether.'

CHAPTER SEVENTEEN

Sylvie Edwards QC walked straight out of the Law Courts, crossed the road and, ignoring the lubricious temptations of the Wig and Pen, she walked along the Strand towards Charing Cross Station. Despite her enhanced status she was feeling pretty much pissed off with the way things were going. Back home indoors, as Fizzer called their domestic life, the usual range of problems were unsettling and persistent. Was there any real point in carrying on with a relationship that carried too many question marks about the present, let alone the future or were both of them making much too heavy weather of the life?

After all, the majority of people have trouble with relationships, at least that was what she'd picked up from Polly Zaftick, big deal psychotherapist and guru to the beautiful people, that is before she had discovered that Fizzer was shagging her cute little ass off. At the same time she worried about Fizzer's life, his attitudes to far too many matters, and although she worried much less about his sexual misbehaviors, these days she was better able to handle her feelings about all this crap. Was this acceptable or was it plain bloody stupid as all her friends kept telling her? Was it right, or was it merely an act of self-betrayal as defined by her friends? It seemed that this was how their lives must continue and Oh sod it she'd think, why can't I do something decisive about my life, our life?

Worse still, was that every day she found that it became more difficult for her to cope with the violence that seemed to perfuse his whole existence as surely as the blood pumping through his coronary arteries. She often felt guilty that she might be making too much fuss over all of this, but knew that she wasn't: Catching villains was one thing - killing them was another. Fizzer was a hard man who did his thief taking , as he called it, seriously, *'at the end of the bloody day what's a good copper but a good old fashioned thieftaker, I'd like bloody know that* ' He'd say that to you and mean it. OK, so he did it all in a hard, even ruthless fashion, but even Sylvie would concede to you, if she knew you well enough, that mostly the life of a copper was tougher and more ghastly than they usually might care to let on, and that people like Fizzer were well able to deal effectively with the maintenance of public order and make things safer for us, and that most of us never knew much about that aspect of life most of the time, nor gave near enough a monkeys one way or another nor cared too much about law and order, taking it all wearily for granted until some bloody toerag came in to our houses, nicked all our gear and pissed on the carpet, that is if they didn't shit on it with fear or anger, as if it mattered, for shit is shit however you look at it, or kick our bollocks in, or bloody kill us in the course of it all. When all of a sudden, the whole problem looked quite different when it became that personal.

So today she was pretty much relieved to be up for a change of scene; a special occasion that got her away from this constant turning over these problems all the time, or so it seemed. This day she was invited as the guest of honour to meet the celebrated Xanthia Clambake for lunch at her double flash penthouse apartment overlooking the river.

Xanthia was best known for her opinions and writings on many matters for was she not an aging *enfant terrible* of a band of sisters that banged on about everything, and sniffed out the politically incorrect like there was no tomorrow, as one spiteful ex member of the sisterhood had described her after a loud disagreement over the significance of Lacan, Barth and a few other French intellectuals, and all that shower of chain smoking gits, as Fizzer would no doubt have called them, and she smiled at the thought.

Xanthia was another of those many persons who admired Sylvie, who were in love with her, and who had become enchanted with her, depending on which way you viewed it.

Why don't we all join the club, as Fizzer often asked, as he dismissed them all as a shower of bloody dykes who hadn't enough bollocks to admit to themselves that they bloody are? Sylvie had to laugh at that. Were the differing views of the world that separated Sylvie and Fizzer now becoming intolerable for both of them, or was it plain ridiculous to go on like this with common ground between them shrinking and fought over all the bloody time? If only she could stop reiterating these thoughts in her head so frequently.

Another problem, which Fizzer understood perfectly well, was that Sylvie was one of those fortunate or unfortunate people who everyone found attractive. It's not always a happy thing to be like that any more than it is to be permanently beautiful. More important than all that and, leaving aside her intellectual qualities, physical presence and the possession of *the power to banish thought,* as Fizzer experienced it , one of the features that held them together was that Sylvie was one of those rare persons, someone for whom truth was not a negotiable commodity. A gift that hit you right between the eyes and put her well ahead of the sisterhood.

Her hostess, Xanthia was a well –heeled *patronne* of the beautiful people of the town. She admired Sylvie's achievements in the pursuit of justice and so on, but most of all, Sylvie was someone whom she desired as a possible addition to her collection of the famous and the up and coming, as a sort of personal award for her having selected Sylvie as a member of an elite of those who knew better than most people as a matter of course, if not of divine right.

Sylvie knew all this perfectly well and was ready to humour her up to a point, and that was why she was on her way to have lunch in her penthouse, and it was no ordinary one, built on the roof of a warehouse on the South Bank, and well handy for Tate Modern and that sort of cultural amenity, far from the bloody proles, I mean one can't be too democratic can one darling and all...

The place was quite a surprise; described by Max Desmoulins as being, 'rather like one of those magnificent old houses that hide behind high walls in The Seventh Arrondissement my dears' and as, 'an amazing jewel of incorruptible perfection,' by another of her more adulatory buddies in a rush of meaninglessness to the head. It was, in short a shit hot conversion job in which a warehouse interior had become *Belle Époque* without the cake shop bits. I mean there were gilded consoles decorated with medallions, *Regence* armchairs covered in silk, celadon and string – carved gold painted wooden chandeliers and a marble statue by Bertula Throvald. A dining room with Louis XVI panelling, a Venetian bedroom with silk covers all over the place. How could you live without that? You name it, Xanthia had it or would get it as soon as she discovered that she was meant to have it.

As soon as she had arrived, Sylvie wished she hadn't accepted the invite as she heard all these people, all the beautiful guests chattering their way in with a chorus of oohs and aahs like a load of bloody pigeons. Fizzer might have commented, and worse no doubt. She knew now bloody well that she had been set up as the star guest for one of Xanthia's lunchtime exhibitions and she didn't like it. Darlings, I know this gifted young silk who is going very far darlings, except she's married to this ghastly policeman who as far as can I gather simply *fucks* everyone's *brains out*. Xanthia liked to use a spot of profanity now and again to impress her pals. Hinting at the dodgy pleasures of rough trade might make some of them squirm no end.

'And so what's the latest with you and that ghastly man, what's his name Fizzer isn't that it. Poor you?' says la bloody Xanthia, handing her guest a Martini straight up with a twist. You got what you were given at Xanthia's and liked it, or you weren't asked again. House rules were abundant And another thing was that Sylvie never entirely liked the way in which her friends automatically put Fizzer down whatever the weather. Ignoring the hostile undercurrents, she said, 'Not so bright at the moment, you could say.' And sort of made to laugh, but failed.

'Why don't you get shot of him darling? I mean he's a bit too …'

Sylvie replied, 'It's come to that, almost It's not an easy thing. In so many ways he's a brave man, kind and decent and everything. It's the violent potential of his way of life and everything that gets to me.' Sometimes you felt that Sylvie went on too much about this violence thing. She didn't seem to have caught up with the fact that coppers are less violent than they used to be: it's just that they appear to kill people more often than they used to, because the media gets hold of it and never bloody let go, that's what Fizzer would have said and did.

'Well it would.' smiled Xanthia in her best, I'm really understanding how you must be suffering, way. And Sylvie is thinking. Why is it that too many of my friends always talk like idiots? This woman is patronizing me again. They all do whenever Fizzer is being talked about. They just can't handle the idea of anyone being married to a copper and liking it. 'You obviously aren't listening to what I'm saying so I'll have to repeat it. It's a clash of views of the world sort of thing you see.' She smiled at the bloody woman thinking why did I ever come to this stupid affair?

And she said, 'It's a case of remaining calm at all times.' And she as near as damn it called her a stupid cow. But by now Xanthia had drifted off to welcome another of the gang, and soon they were all talking animatedly about *important topics of the day*, thinks Sylvie, whose misgivings about the occasion were now hardening into something uncomfortably like resentment, and she was thinking why am I feeling like this these people are all here because they admire me and like what I'm doing, at least that's what Xanthia keeps telling me why, and is always saying that now is the time to honour Sylvie? The girl done well sort of thing, well perhaps not.

One of the crew, Rebecca Piker, the highly regarded philosopher and novelist, never the happiest of combos, came swanning up to Sylvie, full of gushy poison and had the bloody nerve to greet her with 'Yo Sylvie!' whilst trying a slosh at a high five. What bloody next thinks Sylvie as she smiled and said, 'Well I don't think we need that old shit, do we love? You think?' Rebecca had the grace to look embarrassed as Sylvie thought it's amazing how even the brightest of people just don't know to handle meeting blacks: they just go to pieces and piss around. She's probably as well meaning as anyone and probably doesn't mean any harm, or do you duckie? And at that moment Xanthia came by and said all sweet and wholesome, yes about as wholesome as a cyanide filled mint, thinks Sylvie, 'I've been dying for you two wonderful persons to meet, you have so much in common and I'm sure that you'll have so much to say to each other.' And Sylvie just said, 'We met already.' Last time I had a stupid conversation like all this Fizzer was hijacked, she thought that, and almost smiled..

'Lunch is served in la Dining Room,' said the manservant and added, 'Heavens knows how much it cost but I'm not paying thank God.' A couple more Vodkas and he knew he'd be all right and get shot of this crowd ruining the bloody carpets.

'Isn't he priceless?' asked Xanthia. And they all went into Xanthia's dining room no doubt taking on board the Louis XVI panelling, and sat around the table –laid with an air of confidence as one of the more sycophantic guests said - combining fine porcelain with bouquets of ivy and roses as another noted in a little book that she carried around everywhere just for that very purpose.

The lunch was minuscule but exquisite. Blinis, caviar and many other tasty and low calorie, non-fatty nutritious minced up twiddly bits figured quite a lot on the menu and the place was falling down with tiny dishes of olive oil and Italian bread with dead tomatoes and brown things that looked like dried shit as Fizzer would no doubt have thought, and probably said, as Sylvie smiled to herself and thought what a bloody laugh he would have if he could see me now, and then she thought how awful it would be if ever anything should happen to him and knew that happened to him really meant if he was killed by some bastard he was trying to take down, and how full of anger at herself she would be, and how it would be that she would bloody die of beastly unremitting grief. She really did love him most fondly, the sod. What about going on a holiday she wondered, almost in despair? There's nothing like a party in the middle of the day with people that really get up your bollocks to really piss you totally off, she knew that, but the thought was not particularly consoling. And on it went.

At lunch, Rebecca got back on her favourite target, namely the deficiencies of the legal system, 'You understand that I tend to see the law very much in existential terms, if you follow me: I suppose you could say that I regard all this law enforcement and peoples rights, and all that sort of thing as being non existent - not that I am assigning it a " thingy" quality in an existential sense, you realise, I see it essentially as being little more than a bourgeois *cave des folles* if you hear what I'm saying to you.' The drink was really doing its work on Rebecca, a few more of Xanthia's big ones and she'd be pissing on the ground. Jesus thought Sylvie, I really do wish I hadn't come to this thing.

Undeterred by the silence which she took for assent, Rebecca notched up one gear and started on about her belief in an ultimately anarchic society as being probably the best way to arrange things in the quest for sanity in a truly working together world so as to achieve an *intellectually relevant life modality*. Perhaps she'd thought of moving house and going to live in a sink estate. Was that where she had in mind to test this out, Sylvie wondered, as her eyes glazed over and she did her best to keep up with the homily that Rebecca was delivering, 'You see I find the whole concept of legal constraints totally alien to my experience in the sense that it all seems counterproductive in any truly societal and economic-political sense.' Sylvie nodded and wanted to ask her where the hell she had been living all these years. In a bunker possibly, but what was the point? And so it went on all the way from soup to nuts until Sylvie faced with the prospect of toasts being drunk and tears shed, felt that she might have to plead an urgent consultation in chambers. 'But not before we make a little presentation darling,' said Xanthia as she tapped her glass. and called everyone to order. Xanthia must have sensed that something was amiss, for she made only a brief as it turned out, rather touching tribute to Sylvie, and they toasted her and smiled and Xanthia gave her a present to take away.

Sylvie was able to leave, feeling guilty that she'd been hard on all these people. They meant well and she was a paranoid old bat like Fizzer would rightly say. She knew that. And so up and away and out the door into the afternoon sunshine she now went unsuspectingly into the land of the stuffed eel skin, or in her case as it turned out, a very much worse sort of world.

Brother Tel sat in the back of the motor keeping an eye out for Sylvie. Hacker had set up a complete snatch scenario in which Sylvie would be picked up and taken out of town for a while in order to put the frighteners on Fizzer who he figured would go totally to pieces if someone took his wife away and gave her a hard time. 'Dead simple Rog ' said Bro, 'from now on it'll be a right doddle, a fuckin' breeze, know what I mean Rog.'

Hacker had to suppress his doubts at this stage, for it was now all down to Bro. who had hired two gorillas from Kentish Town, Thicko Jackson and Tosher Moon, a right pair of dimwits except for their capacity to intimidate and, in Tosher's case, to drive any powerful motor he could nick. It ended there. Whether Hacker really knew anything about their range of limitations is uncertain. So here they sat in their BMW 735 with the engine running, waiting for the prize as Tel fidgeted and picked his nose more or less incessantly.

'Ere,' says Thicko, 'You mind packing that in, picking your fuckin' 'ooter like that. It's disgusting. Ain't you got a handkerchief or sunnink?'

'What's a handkerchief?' says Bro.

'Ignorant git,' says Thicko, 'It's like a bit of cloth you blow your fuckin' nose in.'

'Hold on' says Bro, 'This is her innit?'

When they saw Sylvie coming out of the apartment block, even this shower of head banging misfits became aware that Sylvie wasn't just any brass who they had to snatch for the money and that. This woman was something way outside their experience. 'Bit flash isn't she?' said Tosher, 'I mean d'you reckon?'

'Fuckin' don't be stupid, she no different than anyone know what I mean? Plus she's a coon.' That seemed to settle it: she was black and a brief, and it didn't matter what they did next. All they had to do was get her into the car, move her down to the chicken farm and work out what to do next. Hacker would come up with the answer to that one, no sweat, Hacker was the boy. A diabolical liberty him being inside and all because of nothing really when you came down to it wasn't that it? What he done then? Took out some little tosser who screwed up and whacked the wrong guy or somethink wannit. He was doing the law a favour, couldn't anyone see that. Must be dead stupid that lot. Stands to reason.

And so the car edged forward and drew alongside Sylvie.

Tosher said, 'Excuse me Miss, could you by any chance direct us to The Cut. We was looking for like an art gallery me and my mates.' As Sylvie bent towards the window and started saying or wanted to say, 'I suppose you mean Llewellyn Alexander don't you?' she failed to notice Thicko behind her or if she did, it was now far too late, and in a second she was in back seat of the car and out cold with a needle hanging out of her neck. For you see, Thicko was a dried out junkie and knew what to do. Foot on the floor and the BM is right down the Embankment going East. Who would have guessed that the smartly dressed woman in the back was an unconscious QC.Bro was wearing a dark suit and could have been her clerk, while the other two wore chauffeurs' kit and caps.

That was a mistake. You don't often see a car with two chauffeurs wearing caps. For once and the only time in his life Tosher showed a glimmer of prescience, 'I 'ope no one fuckin' notices us,' he said, I mean you don't see two guys in flash gear like we got on driving a motor much these days now do you?'

He was dead right on this occasion because a young Police Constable and his mate had noticed them go by in the BM and thought, that's a bit funny two guys in caps in the front seat like that, and the younger of the two, being keen and on his feet, phoned in and had it copied plus the reg. Even if it was a bent number it would be better than nothing. Next thing there's a call out to look out for this possibly suspicious motor, and fortunately for Sylvie it was given a lower degree of priority, so that there was no likelihood of a noisy chase, just monitor the motor when you see it and sus it out. The car was tailed as far as Exit Three on the M20 and then it just disappeared.

CHAPTER EIGHTEEN

Gilli felt slightly apprehensive as she and Lucy approached the house. The mouldy looking old place looked worse than ever. Whoever had compared it with the Munsters hadn't been far wrong. At first Lucy was inclined to giggle as she'd inhaled some of the white stuff to keep her spirits up. When Gilli had spotted her at this practice she had spoken firmly of the need for inner peace and that such strengths and rewards should not be sought from the outside by means of chemicals, adding that self discovery was the better road to go down and that Lucy should try and get her shit together, a comment which lowered the tone of a homily that started well, and then lost its way, but then Lucy had told her to mind her own sodding business and that was it. In any case Gilli had done her bit for psychopharmacology in her time.

To Gilli's astonishment Lucy shouted through the letter box, 'Open the door you bunch of bloody wankers.' Gilli commented, 'that must have been good stuff, dear, that you just snorted.' With this the door opened and an agitated Mr Spudder stood angrily there and said loudly, 'Who are you calling a wanker, you whore of Babylon?' Gilli had to laugh and thought that things can only go downhill from now on, and wondered where all this might finish when to her surprise, Mr Spudder lunged at her as if about to strike her. She thought sod this for a game of soldiers and deciding that attack was the best form of defence, she carelessly grabbed Spudder's crotch as he groaned and sank to his knees, and she said as sprightly as you like, 'Why it's you Mr Spudder, and that great dykey piece that works with you what's her name Doris Clunt isn't that right?'

'Not so,' said the aforenamed woman of Sapphic tendencies, 'get in here you two bitches before I get cross.' Since she was carrying a shooter there seemed little point in arguing. As they were bundled through the door Lucy said, 'I really don't like the way things are going so far.' She of the butch haircut said, 'Shut your face, female doormat and slave of the male organ of rape and penetration.' Gilli replied 'Listen duckie and mind your lip before I stick one on you.' And she decked the amazed woman in one with a brisk kick in the mons pubis. Lucy was astounded at all this. What in the name of God have I let myself in for she wondered?

Things were never like this in Tunbridge Wells, she thought, as Gilli briskly set about Spudder and laid him out absolutely cold. She laughed and said, 'OK Lucy let's have a look around this gaff.' And she smiled at her and said, 'don't worry dear, we were taught self defence on the campus when I was at Johns Hopkins. They have at least one rape attempt every month, so you need to learn a few things.' Feeling slightly foolish Lucy said. 'What on earth were you doing at Johns Hopkins?' Gilli replied 'Well, I'm not sure that we have time to go into that. Let's say it was to do with dolphin embryo brain cells and regeneration in the human nervous system...do we have to go into it at this stage?'

With that she produced a syringe from her bag and gave Spudder and the woman something to keep them quiet, 'I always carry some jungle juice to calm some of our wilder clients at the Center.'

At this point her guide cut in with a few comments on her use of violence, the general drift being comments about bad karma. Gilli had been becoming increasingly more impatient with the guide and said, 'Give it a rest, these people are enemies of the State.' Sometimes it was reassuring to remember that the guide was probably a chemical hangover from the bad old days, and that possibly the time had come to acknowledge that much and send the bugger away. Gilli remembered that these happenings were being monitored by the sensors and God knows whatever surveillance equipment was planted in the place. She wondered what the reaction would be from Ted and FXS. As it happened FX's only comment was, 'What did I tell you Ted, she is not what she purports to be. Just as I thought. She's on loan from the cousins and there's nothing we can do about that.' At that moment Lucy was saying, 'Well that was pretty stupid darling. What's going to happen when they wake up?'

Gilli said, 'Don't be so dumb sweetheart, they'll be amnesic for the whole thing. We now have thirty minutes to have a look around. Let's go.' Lucy stifled her astonishment at all this, but in fact she knew that she was beginning to take it all in her stride, when she pulled open a few filing cabinets in the main office on the ground floor. Gilli said 'Leave the computers to me, I'll see what I can find and hack into in the encrypted files and stuff and download it.' Naturally thought Lucy as Gilli hooked in her Desktop.

It certainly was even further from Tunbridge Wells, and a refreshing change from looking hopelessly through *The Stage*. Gilli was into the system in no time, 'OK,' she said, 'so far everything is in code, just as well, so I can take it home and work it all out.' And she laughed, 'If the punters back in the Center could see us now.' Her guide didn't like that. Lucy's search of the filing cabinets was unhelpful. A series of slim files with virtually nothing inside beyond meaningless invoices and acknowledgements to 'of all things catering firms darling' she called out.

After ten minutes she said, 'There really is nothing here Gilli.' Gilli said ' maybe this is the paperless office they talk about. It's all a front isn't it? They just order stationery and office equipment and muck about as far as I can make out, that is until we decode the answers. Anyway let's keep at it. The catering firms might be worth glance I suppose.' Lucy thought, if my brothers could see me now the stupid bastards. There's no doubt about it I'm improving. I could get to like this life. In no time Gilli suddenly announced, 'Now we tidy up and scarper and they wake to a tidy office and wonder what we're doing here. I think we should go now. Let's do it.'

Not so much later, over a drink Gilli said 'We allow alcohol in moderate quantities for special celebrations,' and laughed, 'and Purdue says we earn it spending our time living with the shower of misfits and wankers that we guide to The Right Way.' Then she became serious, 'I've trolled through enough of the decrypted material on the disks to know that there's more to all this than fun and games Lucy. I need you to cover this end while I get in touch with some people in London.'

'You mean Sarno and his mates,' said Lucy as cheerful as you like.

'You catch on quick, don't you.'

'That's what they pay me for,' said Lucy, 'I'm not just some dumb broad you know darling.'

'Hark at her,' said Gilli, 'Just keep an eye on this place. I'm sure Purdue will act as back up.' Gilli said to Lucy, 'Listen honey, I think that it wouldn't hurt if we were to make contact with Doctor Bargs and find out where he fits into all this shit.'

'What shit would that be?' said Lucy.

'You wouldn't believe it Dear so I'll spare you the details till the debrief. I'm concerned for Purdue. I think Dr Bargs is involved in all of this in some way and I don't want him taking Purdue down with him when the endgame comes. It's just the sort of thing bastards like Horatio do.'

'I don't follow,' said Lucy and thinking that this was all a bit too much really, not at all what she'd been looking for, and she'd thought it was some bloody stupid clinic. Well that's what her friends had told her. Lucy knew that whenever all this shit was over and done with, that she would have come through yet another experience which had led nowhere. And still she wondered what whatever next might be down the line. A line that had seemed to lead nowhere. There had to be more to life than a series of blind alleys. As to the man Bargs, he was merely an appalling con artist who had killed one of her friends through negligence. Otherwise, she suspected, he was little more than a tiresome red herring in the story.

CHAPTER NINETEEN

It's three in the morning and Ted picks up the hotline and whispers, 'OK What's happening?'

'You'd better get right on down to the firehouse. This is now what Fizzer calls the big one. 'Save it till you get here. And copy.'

'Nice one Chiefy,' replied Ted

Code of Practice Regulation Number One was that FX never said Firehouse unless it was a matter of topmost priority: an unbroken house rule. Only FX was permitted to say it. And in the same way FX knew bloody well that if Ted said Chiefy in response, that he was probably ten jumps ahead of him already. Ted knew, now they both knew that the phoney war had to be over fairly soon. 'You can't go on wasting public money on rubbish,' as FX had often said, 'and sooner or later it all comes out,' and added near enough lugubriously, 'and if it doesn't come out soon, we're all out of a job and that can't be right, now can it?' So Ted moved double bloody sharp and, as he raced through the glistening black streets he thought, why is it always on a wet night this lark, I mean it's just like a bloody film noir job, *haul your ass over to the Ramona House, there's a broad in the lobby with half her head blown away: somewhere in downtown LA sirens wailed as a roscoe barked a gutful of lead into the small guys quivering body this is for you shorty you son of a bitch ...* Ted had a pretty good idea of what FX might have in the frame. It had to be biological. All this pissing around with chemicals that made you act like an asshole and play the banjo: this was for laughs. The next instalment would be no laugh: that was certain.

'You look pretty much done in Chief.' says Ted on arrival. FX replied ' So do we all and a bloody sight worse we'll all look soon enough Ted when you take this lot on board.'

'Let me guess, it's bacteriologic right? OK. If I'm right, my money is on smallpox or mutant Type A Influenza. Don't tell me someone got at the Russian store of Venezuelan Equine Encephalomyelitis.'

'The way it looks at present like it could be a bit of everything.'

'And now we come to the difficult bit,' said FX, 'it's not just a threat, it's the terms and conditions of service as you might say, that's what alarms, what makes me concerned as to whether we'll be able to hold on to these people till we get hold of them. The way they talk here suggests that they're going to do it regardless of whether their demands are met or not. That suggests dangerous amateurs to me. I say that we can throw our standard procedures straight out the window. Calling in the muscle men that don't exist and all the rest of it isn't going to cut the mustard with people who aren't easily wasted in a fire fight with men in black overalls in an underground car park.'

'You're not suggesting a ride 'em cowboy sideways approach are you Guv?' said Ted.

'Well I think it's going to have to be something along those lines. These buggers are so well concealed at the moment you could send in our own gallant lads, quite apart from the US bloody marines and the green berets, and they'd be roaring with laughter at what a load of bloody idiots we all are.'

Ted said, 'So what do you reckon Chiefy?'

'I think that we are now up against a totally new group. They have none of the trademarks of anyone that we know. We cleared that in no time. I'm always on my guard plus when this type of situation comes on line. We have no idea how far they will go, though my gut feeling is they might just turn out to be lightweights, since they've been too slow in drawing blood and their asking price is too high. They'd bloody well better be or we're all sunk; of course the final possibility is that these people are in it entirely for the money, and they are using for instance, His Ex or whoever as a front. Oh yes, and as to the Jokemaster and all that crap. These people have corralled a group of eccentrics and minor religious fanatics to front up for them in order to frighten the horses. They can be pulled in after this is all over and put away somewhere.'

'So you're saying?' Ted's now thinking is he rattled? Or is he so cool that I'm getting lost here, and then he recalled the database inside FX's head; I always overlook that he had to remind himself. We switch on our computers - he carries it inside his head. How does he do that?

'First let us have an appreciation of a situation which has entirely developed within the last few hours. First we get a message to myself, I ask you, using the Provisional IRA code saying quite simply that we could expect delivery of smallpox virus via airborne aerosol delivery over a major City in England, to be followed by a similar dose of *yersinia pestis* on another city and then within twenty four hours, two droppings of aerosols containing fifty kilograms of Anthrax spores and a similar scenario in mainland America - all within the same time frame, unless someone meets their demands.'

'Which are?'

'Well this is it and what makes it all slightly absurd. It's nothing political, like releasing terrorists and a thirst for justice; it's old fashioned money. They want a down payment of one hundred million dollars to specified bank accounts in South America within forty eight hours, and that's to start off.' He paused, 'And then they threw in a bit about redressing the balance of anti-Islamic prejudice just to make it sound kosher.'

'This sounds like old fashioned villains. Anything else on the frame?'

'The use of a nuclear device is mentioned. I discount that as the technologic side is far too difficult for this lot, that's my guess. There's a distinct smell of amateur night about these people on the one hand, and a total sense of bloody doom on the other. Look Ted I'm not saying this to anyone else but you.'

'I wish I felt as confident as you do Chief.'

'I'm saying amateur night because they've given us too much time. That means they can't be all that good. They've been reading too much pulp fiction and watching disaster movies. Their demands are far too trivial.'

'All we have to do now is nail the buggers, is that it?'

'I thought you'd say something like that and I'll come to it later. In the meantime, how much do we know about smallpox availability? I thought it had all been eradicated and there were only two stores left.'

'Not as simple as that apparently. The last estimate was that unofficial stores were three definite and seven possibles. This from defector Ken Alibek. The problem is that no one really knows for certain. The only thing that is certain is that after September Eleventh, no possibility can be ruled out.'

'So what are we being asked to do? I mean for Christ's sake, it's hardly our job is it?'

'I think that those above us are clutching at anything.Good intelligence predicates good security, isn't that what we were taught at school?'

'You still haven't said what you expect us to do Guv.'

'I was coming to that. I suggest Fizzer and his best handpicked crew should be our personal action men kit: I want to avoid Special Forces taking things over and killing off all the intelligence in the act of surrender. This way gets us an in the door at source, so the villains could be collected without endless meetings with the PM and the Services. And then all we have to do is pull in the villains. I ask you what could be simpler? This is what they are asking Ted. We really haven't much time, Ted if we are to avert the deaths of millions. Such drama. ' He laughed, 'Would you believe that my immediate task is to run all this past the suits upstairs?' He paused, 'I'm not sure of anything at the moment. All I have is a rough idea.'

'It couldn't be any other way Chief. It never is.' Don't say he's forgotten that already.

FX said, 'I'll feel happier when I've spoken to the Committee in the knowledge that they don't really want to know the full SP. They feel that they have to go through the motions. Their main concern, as you will know, is that fiscal constraints are in no way to be compromised, but at the same time that we must be seen to be doing everything that is needed to be done under the circumstances, and given the exigencies of the service and all that.'

'I still can't believe it,' said Ted, 'I mean that they can behave in that way with a Mega death scenario staring us all in the bloody face.'

FX smiled and said, 'Well they've been looking at things in this way for so long that they don't really know any other.' He paused, 'When I first started in this place I didn't think that I could ever get used to these people, until I realised that they are not in fact the real power base. They control the money bags and it ends there; that's how I see it. They all went to the same to the same schools, were at Cambridge together, all members of the same clubs and so on, but at the end of it all, I don't think that they really know what is happening, nor do they want to. It's all too bloody ridiculous: you couldn't explain it to the French, I've tried: and it's not worth trying it on the cousins. The Soviets always thought it was all a terrific joke actually. It seems hard to believe but it's the only way to encompass it. I always think that the administrative, not wanting to know what's happening thing, is like the Nazis who spent all day at Wahnsee finalizing genocide, and at the last minute one lawyer gets angry because correct legal procedures might not be correctly followed. That behaviour gives me a clue as to what those people were all about - and their descendants are now no doubt running hospitals.'

And then he said carefully, 'You know it is all going to be all right Ted.'

With that he left the room to get the elevator to the suits on the top floor. Jesus thinks Ted, what a guy. All this going down and not a bead of sweat on him. FX was away for an hour, and all he told Ted was that the suits were no better and no worse than usual, and that they had expressed the hope that things would be brought to a satisfactory conclusion and that too much money would not be spent on transportation, if at all possible, and incidental expense kept to a minimum.'

Ted said, 'In the meantime I have to tell you Guv we have a problem with Fizzer and his crew.'

'That sounds normal.'

'No one can raise them, I've been trying all the time you were with them upstairs and I'm getting nothing.'

'He's out trying to find his wife isn't that it? She's been hostaged, you knew?'

'Well of course I knew, but it's unlike Fizzer to break contact.'

'No doubt he has his reasons. I wouldn't worry about Fizzer.'

'OK so what next? Suppose that somehow we pull everyone in. What are we going to do with them when we find them Guv?'

'We can discount trials and due process. We really don't need Civil Liberties and the wet knickered brigade giving us a hard time. And we can discount losing them. Waste of time. No Ted, my advice, which I gave them upstairs, is to keep them on deposit against future events. They can be kept in places that don't exist until they are no longer useful and then they can fade out.' He paused, 'Now we come to the big one. What shall we do with His Excellency? Any views Ted?'

'For God's sake Chief. He's untouchable.'

'I don't think so. In any case he's under surveillance and has been for a few weeks.'

'If this gets out Chief, we are finished, Every single one of us and you know it, his people have too much clout.'

'I think not Ted. The man has made a colossal mistake and I know all about it. And his superiors are not going to stand for that: for God's sake imagine what the penalty for treason is in his hometown. It's very simple. We already have incontrovertible evidence that he knows all about the smallpox deal in advance, and that he has it in his power to stop it whenever he likes but has chosen not to. When that gets out, he's fucked Ted. OK, so I'll tell you what my current appreciation of the situation is. This group is nothing to do with freeing Islam or anything near it. They are hiding behind the likes of HE and they are in it for the money and bugger all else.'

At his juncture FX's red phone rang. He picked it up, 'Yes.'

'Mr Sarno,' said the voice, 'I understand that you have been saying the bad things about me, and that I have it one mental illness, and that I take one tablet for that. This is a vicious slander and I am warning you that I am under immunity from that, and that if you persist in this one I cannot be responsible for anything that might possibly ensue. We have a Ministry...'

FXS cut short the conversation, 'I know what you are talking about, you tiresome idiot, you refer to the Ministry of Investigation and Control in your benighted capital.' The caller continued, 'These are very hard men who could do bad things for you, be assured of that my friend, and I mean in your own country.'

FX said, 'If that's all your Excellency, I think we can terminate this call.' And he hung up and laughed, as Ted said, like a bloody drain. And then he said, 'At least Ted we are spared having to attend the Emergency Committee which they have set up. First we're not clean and tidy enough, and secondly we don't exist. Isn't that a shame? I was really looking forward to hearing some of the top brass explaining why their bloody guns jam, why they can't get sand out of the tanks and why the radios don't work.'

Ted said, 'Well that's a relief.'

'I know,' said FX, 'but I have it on the highest authority that you and I will receive the minutes in less than a week.'

'These guys really know how to move fast when they need to.'

' And as to Messrs Spudder, Spurlow and La Shafter let me say this. We are about to bark up the wrong bloody tree Ted.'

'How so?'

'You see Ted, we've fallen right into it. Whoever is running the whole affair, and my money is still on His Excellency, is using them as a diversion. I'm sure that they are just a bunch of eccentrics who have blundered into all this and made fools of all of us. OK so they orchestrated the Archbishop, the banjo and the PM's bottie, but that was a smoke screen - the real thing is happening right now. Thank God we didn't get sucked into the other. And by the way had you noticed that the Bish, the Prime Minister and the CEO of the Stock Exchange had one thing in common? They were all at the reception at Lancaster Gate the night before. My guess is that the funnies spiked their food with a long acting mind bender. God knows there's enough of them to choose from. In any case it's academic now.'

'What do you suggest?'

'Let that part go until Stannie gets back. It would be the ideal affair for him to look into. God knows it's camp enough for the poor chap and he'd adore the Archbishop's kit I'm sure. For God's sake get someone to go bring him in, that is if he hasn't married this bloody tart whoever she is.'

'That's a quaint word to use Chief, I think it went out in the last Century.'

While this was going on, His Excellency was in his apartment fuming with rage and planning to make an official complaint in the morning regarding this man Sarno who he would have put in his place, or perhaps the group who had taken him on might get rid of him. Now there was an idea. The type of daft idea that only His E could have come up with.

The important point about HE that no one thus far had picked up on was that he was a king size phoney who had sweet talked someone into giving him a bogus title in return for his services in the Ministry Of Social Investigation and Interrogation. He had a bogus Doctorate awarded by The Mickey Mouse University of Disneyland, where his Doctoral thesis in Social Psychology as applied to the study of Female Circumcision, and what a jolly thing it was to be a woman in Islam, had really wowed every wacko in sight. If he'd stuck to that and stayed at home collecting new cars, smoking Marlboros and pretending to work in an office, like all his useless wealthy compatriots did, all would have been well, but the poor guy developed ideas above his station and started meddling in things that were none of his business. Writing letters to papers and joining in seminars in third rate universities in England where any ass would be kissed as long as it disgorged money.

Next thing he was approached by a bunch of heavies who were on the lookout for bigger things. They were only too pleased to take him on board and appoint him their mouthpiece without him ever knowing what was happening. Now they were home and dry with a tame dickhead up front: better still one with good credentials who would always be guaranteed a slot on BBC TV and the earnest wankers' discussion group.

How was it that this man ever got involved with a terrorist group? The answer is simple enough. He had been spotted as being as a possible contact in a powerful position and easily flattered into involvement with them. A few meetings for lunch, a few expensive whores, some good quality powders and they had his ass forever, and he loved it. He had a good job, security and so on, but these people offered him something that his well paid sinecure could never offer, adventure and secrecy and all that shit. It really does sound crazy when you say it like that, him being a well educated bright enough guy, OK a phoney as well, but the trouble was, he's never had anything nearly exciting, even hint like it might happen to him in his entire life, and here he was being given lessons in how to load and fire an AK47 in a cellar in Bayswater. Which beat the living crap out of diplomatic trade sessions and meetings with suits who talk about balances of payments and fiscal liquidity, the need for harmony and all that crap.

And so in no time, he was bought, signed, sealed and ready to be delivered to an ultimate death sentence whatever might happen. Some people never learn. In no time at all, when they put the heat on, and asked for sensitive information, he at first demurred, but they made it sound pretty good, and a quick death should the shit ever hit the fan, which they assured him it wouldn't since they had the man on their side. Devotion to the cause and stuff the Americans, it all made sense. He now felt great, and even felt that he was beyond being sussed by anyone.

He also knew that if the folks back home got to know of this the best he could hope for was getting his head taken off in the main square on a Friday morning at noon. That was the downside, but the powders and the sense of new adventure helped to keep him going. He was confident that the FX person would call him back and beg forgiveness or something like that. By the time it reached six in the morning he realised that he must have made a mistake and so he started to develop slight misgivings and a sense of concern. By nine o'clock he was unsure what he should do. Perhaps something had gone wrong. However, after a bath and a rest, he felt better.

As the day went on everything seemed to settle down and he was inclined to feel that perhaps he had worried about nothing. The agreed plans would proceed to unfold and everything would be fine: the infidels would tremble in their boots by the next morning, he was sure of that. By the evening he was positively brimming with confidence after a few reassuring meetings with his superiors. And now His Excellency was feeling pretty good. His recent comments in *The Guardian* had been well received by every intellectual in Town from Hampstead to Homerton; the Archbish had warmly commended his attempts to build bridges between East and West, and even The Primate of All Ireland, The Venerable Tamas O Faoilan had said that, though technically an infidel, His Excellency was on the whole, not a bad chap. His Excellency smiled at that. He could afford to, for had he not the infidels asses in a sling right now? In no time the wrath of Allah would be visited upon them, *'woe to the infidel, Allah shall defend the righteous,'* he intoned as he called up his mates in Beirut to discuss the latest move.

The word from that end was that everything was very fine, and not to keep ringing up, just wait for the word, and maybe he should go and take some rest. That made him feel even better, and he looked forward to a light supper in his apartment, maybe a glass or two of a good claret and a video. His new Personal Assistant would be waiting for him, and drive him home, or possibly out for some fun. To his surprise, his new PA was not waiting for him. It was a new person. His Excellency was put out at this, but the man's ID was kosher, so why worry? And then to his surprise, the driver said, 'Your Excellency you are invited to a Special Function tonight and I am to drive you there. You follow me?'

His Excellency positively glowed, as this was most likely to be the special treat that he'd been promised as a surprise by the Group, as a reward in kind for services rendered, and how thoughtful and discreet it was the way they were doing it, so as not to offend any religious susceptibilities. How very civilized. After all, if one could not indulge oneself now and again in a harmless fleshly way, at the expense of the infidel where would one be? And in any case it was a way of punishing the godless for their sinfulness. Plus they'd said the girl could be got rid of without any fuss...That was it. Now for some fun with a western whore. Big mistake pal.

CHAPTER TWENTY

They had taken Sylvie to a disused farm in a marshy wasteland near Folkestone racecourse. Here the dopey brother Tel had imprisoned her and had dumped her, locked in this ridiculously sinister farm. It was in that part of the Kentish countryside where the roadsides are bordered by ditches full of old prams and chicken netting; pools of stinking rain water where the locals cultivate discarded condoms, bloody tampons and Sainsburys carrier bags. And at the bottom of a small lane, that no one ever ventured to drive along, here was this chicken farm where certain villains had carried out the detention of people who had failed to pay up for a diversity of services, or the execution of those who had betrayed them.

The executions were carried out in a featureless concrete hut, previously used for slaughtering pigs. It had guttering to drain away the blood. There were also facilities for hosing down the walls and disposal of bodies. It was all very efficient. Hire facilities were available for the use of this transit camp of the doomed. One of Hacker's former associates had renovated it, and provided a wider range of facilities, without bothering to seek Planning Permission for Change of Use, and while leaving the outside looking derelict, he had made the place habitable for the captives and their attendants.

Hacker's plan had been that they should spirit Sylvie across the water through ' that French bloody tunnel' so that they could get shot of her somewhere in Normandy. He was so full of venom that he hadn't really worked out what he would do once she'd been snatched. He hated Fizzer so much that he could hardly think beyond the snatch, so it was probably just as well that he didn't know how things were going down on the farm.

That's what came of leaving things to his brother Tel who had brought Sylvie some pizzas and a portable TV. Sylvie's prison was clean and, while not Grande Luxe, it was at least warm. And there was this tiresome bloody telly which Tel watched as he tried to think of anything to say to Sylvie. She had refused the first pizza, but when he offered a second, she accepted one and a can of Coke. And Tel said, 'Well this is it.' Which was a remark that he frequently made as a form of commentary on life in general, in the same way as minicab drivers do when confronted by difficult traffic conditions. Sylvie was now attached to the wall by the aluminium chain links of the type used to shackle those who are about to be beheaded in law- abiding countries such as Saudi Arabia where people can walk the streets in peace, and women are shown real respect for Christ's sake, not like here, it's not like you think, it really isn't, and we really aren't here for the money, it's the culture, as any ex-pat Brit in that benighted country would tell you.

The owner had bought a few sets of these exquisite items from a company that specialized in the supply of similar equipment, including execution chambers complete with gallows and torture machinery, all regularly sold by benevolent English entrepreneurs to God fearing Arabs and black African dictators.

Meanwhile, despite her awful situation Sylvie was not as terrified as she had oftentimes expected that she might be, if ever she should end up this way.Fizzer had briefed her about the possibility many times, and outlined the approach that his people would use in order to extract her. She knew very well that Fizzer and his pals were unlikely to be sitting around playing poker or downing cans of lager at this moment, and while she didn't expect him and his cohorts to arrive on the scene like the US Fifth Cavalry, she was reasonably optimistic, for she was a courageous determined person with a great capacity for remaining calm.

She had immediately spotted that brother Tel was a mentally retarded psychopath who was way out of his depth and likely to be the weak link in the organizational chain of this bunch of felons. Tosher and his pal had legged it soon after arrival: their work was done since Sylvie's fate was none of their concern.Demarcation disputes are unusual in the world of these people.

It was also obvious to Sylvie that Tel had never been alone in the company of a black woman, or for that matter any woman, in his entire life.

This might possibly work to her advantage, though she was unsure beyond the fact that he was probably equally insecure in the company of any strange woman if it came to that. She had worked out that he was a member of Hacker's family from the scattered remarks in the rambling phone conversations which the dumb asshole made little or no attempt to conceal from her. From these words, she surmised that he was probably doing this to impress her, and make her feel afraid. She even felt slightly sorry for him, though she knew that her feelings of sympathy were inappropriate in regard to this vicious little creep.

She hoped that Nemesis was not too far away. It might be hoped that Tel might suddenly pick up on a few events that might be in the pipeline. He had heard that this guy Fizzer had a reputation for being hardnosed; Hacker had said so. So without realizing it, Bro was witnessing a brisk fall in his Hubris count in the run up to his asshole being reamed out with a chain saw by Fizzer, that is after he'd done with Hacker. Possibilities like that never crossed his mind.

And now, oozing charm Tel says, 'You fancy a cup tea did you darling?' There the conversation languished, as Sylvie pondered on what might be next on the dullard's agenda. He added, 'Better make the most of it you silly cow.' Sylvie found it hard not to laugh at this pathetic bully, and wondered about his parental background, in the way you would expect her to wonder. Even in the direst circumstances, her sense of equity and fair play never left her; sometimes you wondered if she would offer to defend someone who had tried to murder her. She probably would. Fizzer had often thought about such a possibility, even mentioned as much to Sylvie, but she would only smile and make no comment.

The next problem was that Hacker, having arranged the seizure of Sylvie, had no plan for her future, and given no further instructions as to what was to be done next. His first idea had been that he should have her executed as quickly as possible, but he then realised that such a course of action was unlikely to pay off all that well. Should the shit hit the fan it were better that Sylvie were alive. Ask for ransom? He wasn't sure about that either. Too dodgy, if you asked him, he would have told you.

No, what it was all about, was revenge: he wanted old fashioned revenge and that would do. He wanted to put the frighteners on Fizzer, to teach him a lesson, then call it a day and walk away from it all in the clear, he hoped, having frightened the bejaysus out of Fizzer. Alternatively he might arrange Sylvie's release, so that she would be found staggering around in the roadside not too far from a public telephone. He hoped that Tel might knock her around a bit just to show Fizzer what was what. Teach the bastard and his bloody brief a lesson.

Tel had this in mind as he spoke to Sylvie and grinned to himself at the thought of giving her a few whacks when the right time came along. Hacker had emphasised that he was not to injure her too much, just to make sure that she felt it, be sure of that, he had said. Sylvie sensing that something like this was on the cards, now found herself shivering whenever Bro looked at her. And then she thought of Fizzer's recollections of what had gone through his mind when he'd killed Zeinab the Arab terrorist during the hijack in Damascus ... *all of a sudden he lost patience with the whole crap deal. Too bloody much as it happens. He was tired of it all; tired of being patient, tired of being the hero, it was time for someone* else to do this crock of shit, tired of sweating on his pension, tired of wondering where his life was going and all, and where was Sylvie, and where was his life? He wanted to blow the back of Zeinab's head away with two straight shots into the face, right between cold black open eyes remaining open. *Foot and eye. Die, you bastard die. I'm going to kill you murderous Arab whore. That's for the poor bastards you lot top whenever it suits you. Why should the Israelis have all the fun shooting all the fucking ragheads?...like the tops sliced off soft boiled eggs, revealing shiny pink brain tissue below...* She remembered that and the references to the killing and how he'd said that he'd enjoyed slaughtering Zeinab as if she were a pig, and wondered if this meant that Fizzer was as bad as they were? In a way, yes, or was it no?

And then she remembered that this place had once been a pig farm. Tel had given her that useful piece of information as soon as they arrived. Just the sort of thing he would have told her. You might have predicted that. And she shuddered and prayed that something might happen soon. *Please God let something happen to stop all this, and let someone try to get her out of here.* She felt the terror edging inside her gut. Panic was something that she had never experienced and now she was starting to sense its nearness. She was not feeling as tough as she'd felt even a few minutes ago. It was the pig farm bit that she didn't like, and she knew it. *Please God get me out of this dreadful place someone,* and she near enough cried that out, but didn't.

As it happened if Bro had known how things were going at that moment with Hacker, he might have been forgiven if he had experienced a moderate loosening of the anal sphincter. The team at work in the interrogation suite in the basement at The Box had now gotten well past any fragments of resistance that The Hacker might have been able to offer. The Hacker was unmarked and, guess what? He had coughed in spades: every bloody detail. Imagine that. How do they do it? It was as simple as that. So much for heroic resistance and family loyalties. At this stage Hacker would have gratefully given them Bro's collar size if they'd asked him for it. When he came round from the Ketamine and other assorted chemicals they made damn sure that he overheard everything, including noisy references to his possible disposal in a variety of environments, ranging from the base of a flyover on the M20 extension to a range of slurry pits and coastal sewage outlets. And all this said, as if they were talking about getting an end user certificate for weaponry to be used in a worthy cause: it was all extremely correct and detached.

The Hacker's level of uncertainty was now so high, he now had no way of telling whether any or none of this background noise was to be taken seriously. With this bloody maniac Fizzer in charge, there was no way you could tell any which way things would go, that was how he saw it.

Which was exactly what Fizzer and his crew wanted. 'Let's hang this asshole out to dry as soon as we can,' said Fizzer, and he meant it. How much more simple things become when questions are answered. 'OK lads, let's get down to this bloody pig farm as quickly as we can, right and get it sorted?' said Fizzer.

'Hold it, Guv do you really think that you ought to do that?' said Dave, 'I mean I'm not sure if you should be there when we get things squared away – might be a bit too personal maybe, know what I mean?' But he knew that he was wasting his words.

'Don't be so bloody sensitive,' said Fizzer, 'I mean it isn't as if I meant any of them any harm now is it? For Christ's sake they've only kidnapped my wife.' Dave replied, 'Now you put it that way, I see what you mean, but I'm sure it's against all sorts of regulations.'

And they both laughed at the very notion. Now what? For a start they knew exactly where Sylvie was being held. As soon as Hacker made even an oblique reference to it, they were on to it in one, but it was good to hear it from him in person. It had been passed to them about six months previously by an obliging grass.

'You can't beat a good informer. Everyone knows that,' said Fizzer, 'Where would we be without the maintenance of industrial discontent amongst the toerag fraternity I wonder?' But Fizzer also knew that in police work as in war, things never go entirely according to plan nor expectation. This was something that was one of his best cards. Rigidity wasn't in his bench manual. He said, 'OK I think it's time we moved. These guys aren't going to wait for us.' Dave replied, Sorry to be a pain Guv, but aren't we rushing in a bit. I mean we need more of a planned operation here surely?' Fizzer said 'Planned operation? For fuck's sake Dave, we know where she is, we know who's holding her. We just go and get her. You don't think that I haven't got a few watchers down their way do you?'

'I was only trying to make sure Guv, I have this idea that we might be rushing in a bit, I mean it's not like a normal hostage operation is it?' Fizzer replied, 'OK, so we're not negotiating. Agreed, but this one's not some smart terrorist or a few bad ass IRA Provies with college degrees and tweed jackets: this man is a stupid fucking dummy who by all accounts has trouble wiping his arse.' Dave said, 'I know, but the guy can still work a shooter.'

'I know it.' said Fizzer. 'That's why I want his balls in a sling.' And so they moved on down to the car park. Dave started to walk toward their parked cars, 'Don't be stupid Dave,' said Fizzer, 'No need to send a bloody telegram who we are, don't you agree? Lets just walk around and we can take our pick, or even hot wire the Director's Ferrari if you like, or even a couple of cars, then no one knows what's happening.'

Dave said 'Are you crazy Fizzer? That's bloody brilliant that is, taking someone else's motor. The Commissioner will do his nut. What's got inside your head Guv? What happens when they go missing and they can't find their motors? They'll love that?' And not believing what Fizzer was saying as he comes back with. 'It's lateral thinking Dave. As soon as we pick up the motors, I'll call someone personal in my division who'll put the word around, and the rest is down to us. They wont even go posted as missing, and even if we bend them a little they can be straightened out before morning and there won't even be a paint scratch on the buggers.'

And he added laughing, well he would laugh wouldn't he? 'Plus these are quicker motors than ours. We're doing them a favour? Anyway why should the villains always get the best cars?' Dave's thinking one minute, well you have to laugh and the next, there go our bloody pensions and he says,' Sometimes Fizzer, I wonder if you're a bloody psychopath too.' Fizzer said, 'Not a chance my son. I failed the practical didn't I?'

As they drove down the M 20 Fizzer said, 'It's a routine piece of action Dave. We go in one on one via the front end and snatch her back in one movement. We don't need a fire fight or any big police action here. It's too bloody messy and it's bad for the image. We can't have the *Independent* on our backs, what do you say?'

As things turned out it wasn't quite as smooth as all that, as Tosher and his pal Thicko had been obliged to return because Tosher had suddenly discovered that he'd left his pills at the farm at his last visit or summink. They had no business being there anyway, but Tosher being high on all sorts of shit most of the time, became all obsessive about one special sort of tablet, well to be honest it was more in the nature of a capsule like Doc, as he'd said to the pillhead Doctor in Muswell Hill who wrote scripts for anyone like a man with no bloody arms didn't he?

It was like a more acceptable sort of tablet from the code of best practice from the British Pharmacopoeia, that he wanted him to have, he would tell you, well he would wouldn't he, once the *News of the World* had rumbled him, more in the way of an antidepressant you might say, he said as he sweated praying for the time to come for him to get the next half bottle of vodka down his neck, and stopping the shakes before he puked up, and hoping he wouldn't shit his trousers before he got it – Oh yes he really was trying to help these troubled people, victims of peer group pressure, poor troubled souls, and anyway, paying him would help them to examine themselves. Well really he'd meant to help them to hadn't he, but he needed to get hold of the money, so he just sold them any old crap he could lay his hands on from the grab bag. Which only goes to show if you want a good pusher, if such a thing exists, your best bet, is a bent pisshead doctor and no mistake...

'Hang on,' Tosher had said, 'I must of left me tablits down the bloody farm.' And said, 'We got to go back then innit.' and so back they went. Next thing they're roaring up the lane, Tosher's out the car and yelling blue murder for his pills as he bursts through the door, since no one answered the bell what with Fizzer and Dave being in the bloody place and they've decked Bro, so that up till that moment things are looking pretty good, except that Bro had put a slug in Dave's leg and he's rolling in bloody agony.

Sylvie is safe or so it appears, that is until Tosher storms in and says, ' Where's my fuckin' pills then Bro, you 'ad them did you, you dumb sod, that it?' Tosher immediately realizes things are not how they were when he left and, acting quickly, pulls out his shooter and says, 'Right Mr Edwards why don't you drop the bloody shooter, and if it comes to that I don't mind shooting a copper, know what I mean?' Fizzer says more or less laughing, 'Don't be such a stupid git Tosher.'

And Tosher laughs like the clappers, not knowing what a mad bastard Fizzer can be when he wants to, hence the bloody name squire, as Fizzer goes for him and catches the, not so quick, nor yet so fit Tosher near enough off his guard. Now Tosher is down with Fizzer's foot in his mush, and his shooter is on the deck and he's trying to grab it. Thicko has already done a runner as soon as he hears the noise, 'I'm out of here,' he shouts, and he's down the lane straight into the bloody ditch. Talk about the Keystone cops. And that's how it was, confusion, panic and no one exactly knows what's going on, just like a battle in a way, which it was. Now it gets serious.

'For God's sake Sylvie shoot the bastard,' said Fizzer quietly, 'he's dropped the bloody gun - you cop hold of it and shoot the man before he does it. Dave is out of the picture. Just do it or we're buggered in heaps...'

'I don't know that I...' and then she knew once and for bloody all that Fizzer's and his pals lives were really much awful than she had ever known: worse still, their violence was now her violence; never a happy discovery. And that perhaps the world was a better place with a few villains less.

And so she squeezed the trigger exactly as Fizzer had taught her. The recoil was less than she'd expected but she was far too astonished by what she was doing to be bothered by that, as she saw the back of Bro's head splashing all over the floor behind him. His mouth had sagged with disbelief when her first shot went in through his upper jaw, right in the midline, quite a small hole it was, and she watched all this in slow motion as he coughed and puked up a mouthful of blood and mucus mixed with chewed up pizza, which she could smell as it oozed and half gobbed out of his disintegrating face, as she squeezed the trigger again just to make sure that the poisonous little shit died, exultant now and laughing, as she rid the world of this cruel little half-witted piece of garbage.

And he sort of groaned and gurgled, again and it was like he was trying to say something, like he was sorry that he had bullied her, sorry that he had made her afraid, and he coughed once again as his crappy life ended. Many scattered fragments of his skull, and fragments of brain tissue splattered and squished about. Some bounced off the wall and hit her in the face.

You notice things like that, she realised, since she now had the time to think about that, and she thought Christ what could I say to Fizzer about violence now? You wouldn't think you had the time to think about anything, and yet you did, and she reflected, you knew bloody well what was happening, and you were scared bloody shitless. No question And all over in a few seconds. I'm alive and he's dead.

'Hold on hon,' said Fizzer, 'the fucker's dead or hadn't you noticed. You, I mean we, can't go on like this or you might get to like it and we don't want that, now do we? None of us do, don't you see, like I told you, it frightens you as you do it, I mean like it? Doing this thing: once and for all, none of us do. I hope you got hold of that. It all happens too quickly and we respond. It's the training you see hon, and that's all there is to it.'

Thank you very much, she's thinking, unable to speak, I just killed someone. Some years ago he was a tiny baby and his mother probably thought him the most beautiful child ever and she held him in her arms and fed him and raised him, and I just killed him.

But then when Fizzer picked her up off the deck she was badly shaken up but amazingly unruffled. Fizzer said. 'OK I'm cool, Sylvie, how about you?'

'I'm all right actually,' she replied, all of a sudden quite formal in the face of the appalling scenario that she had engineered, 'I would have hoped that you had not felt it necessary to use violence in dealing with these people. They are entitled to fair treatment before the law whoever they may be. Will you never get hold of that? Or is it something that is outside your reach?'

And him with his brains on the deck, and she'd bloody put them there, thinks Fizzer, and guess what, she's talking like a bloody brief again already.

'Leave it out Sylv. These are a bunch of murdering villains who neither know nor care about the fair treatment of anyone. These are people who kill their wives if the toast is burnt, for Christ's sake, can't you see that? Sod it, lets leave it at that, why don't we just agree to differ and call it a day. We'll never see eye to eye on villains, now isn't that a fact?'

'Now that I've seen what's it's all about I'm not so sure about ...' and she said, 'I'm so pleased to see you...' and than she looked as if she might just burst into tears or something, and that was a hard thing for Sylvie: she didn't reckon the tearful helpless woman act one damn bit, did Sylv. 'Take it easy hon.' said Fizzer. 'You ain't seen nothing yet. Don't forget, you just killed someone.'

She almost laughed at that and said, 'That's what I was afraid you'd say. I suppose next you'll be telling me that I'll get used to it.'

'Hon, you just lost your cherry, like almost.' And then he remembered the occasion on the Damascus hijack when *he had said quietly, 'What kept you Jacko?* when Jacko had near enough taken a bullet for him.' He remembered how he'd felt then, and looking at Sylvie, he knew that was how she was feeling right now, and buttoned his lip for once in his life.

'In any case,' said Fizzer, 'By the way, and I shouldn't be telling you this Sylvie, but if you hadn't killed him, or even if no one had, he would have lost the use of his legs forever and ended up in a place that no one would ever find out about because it doesn't exist. Whichever way you look at it it's a crap world.'

Sylvie said 'What happens now?'

'We wait till back up arrives and then we get you out of here to safety. And then I meet Mr Sarno and the rest and we work out what happens next. Something really bad is about to break. I got a text from FXS. It's bad Sylv, by the sound of it: you could say that's all we bloody need.'

'You mean to say you're going straight off just like that?'

'You know Sylv that it's the job I do. FX doesn't even know I'm here. Not that it would make any difference.'

'I know.'

And so Fizzer and Dave took her back, not home, but to a safe house for twenty four hours, leaving the lads to get things cleared up. And already Sylvie was recovering her self-composure, which is amazing she thought, considering all that had happened. She said in the car, 'I suppose your people will be needing me to make full statements and so on, I don't feel up to it at the moment, but I'm sure I'll be fine in the morning.' And she thought they say that the feeling is a bit like just after you've climaxed, but didn't like to think that.

Fizzer smiles at her and at Dave and said, 'I wouldn't worry too much about that Sylvie, wouldn't you agree Dave?' And Sylvie felt a chill round her guts or somewhere. She was part of all this now, not just the violence, and that had been bad enough. But she remained silent. Their violence was her violence now.

And after a minimal de briefing, despite her protests and demands for inquiries and independent tribunals, she realised once again that what it came down to was that Fizzer and his sort of cops were bad boys, even intolerable, but that when judged by their clear up rate, it was a whole different ball of wax, as FX had once said to her; she remembered that. An uneasy truce you could say, but then that had been her life with Fizzer for as long as either of them could remember, and she had realised that it wasn't as bad as all that.

When talking of her friends such as Xanthia and Rebecca Piker, who cared one way or the other, what they said or thought? She said as much to Fizzer. 'So bloody what,' said Fizzer, adding, ' they can suck my dick if they feel like it, it's all the same to me.'

CHAPTER TWENTY ONE

'They've found Stanni: that's the latest,' said Ted, 'Well to be exact, not found him, but there's been a sighting. Talk about laugh the guy on the phone could hardly speak.'

'Tell the others.' Said FXS, 'and get on to it, I was starting to worry. It's not like Stanni to bugger off like this, how dare he? We want him back here'

'Here's the deal,' said Ted. 'One of our people sighted him, cop this Guv, being driven down the A30 in a W Reg Ferrari.'

'I bet it was red.' Said FX

'Too damn right. Imagine Stanni in a red Ferrari. And the best thing is he was being driven by a wild looking babe.'

'Well that's a relief. I always felt he was living far too dull an existence in that ghastly place with his gang of loony relations. The mother is something else I'm told. May one ask who is the woman who is driving our Stanni in her motor and why?'

'It's registered to a Tracy Suggs.'

'Let's hope he hasn't really taken up with someone called Tracy. I couldn't bear it. Do we know her?'

'So far nothing. I'm getting Fizzer to talk to the people in the restaurant where she pulled him. It's one of his places.'

'I wouldn't worry overmuch. Knowing Stanni, I'd say he'd call in soon and claim his travel expenses.'

'Let's hope so.'

'He's a conscientious chap and won't be carrying anything that might embarrass, you can depend on that. All the same I'll be relieved when we know something more definite. Are we looking at a kidnap? Or is it a pick up?'

'I suspect that it's both. And another thing, I recommend that his family should be kept out of it. The last thing we need is the police on their doorstep saying he's now officially a missing person and next thing it's in *The Sun*.'

And so quite out of the blue, to no one's surprise Stanni, somewhat shaken up, called in as calm as you like, saying he'd been sort of kidnapped, and was picked up at the Fleet Service Station on the M3, and brought in to a safe house to be debriefed by Ted.

'What the hell have you been up to?' says Ted. 'and if it comes to that where did you get that bloody suit?' he added inconsequentially. 'I've never seen you wearing one before this.'

'Well to tell the truth dear boy, I hardly know what to say,' says Stanni. 'The suit was a present from Miss Tracy Suggs if you must know. And anyway what's wrong with it? It looks pretty good I reckon.'

'Don't be bloody ridiculous. You'll need to do better than that.' Ted had a strong feeling that this conversation was likely to lead nowhere. Stanni seemed to be oddly preoccupied and behaving in a manner that could only be described as totally bloody stupid, as he later described it to FXS. But Stanni was not in the least bothered, and he went on, 'I know but I think we can disregard the whole episode as far as security is concerned. The whole thing was what one might call a lucky adventure. I'm far more interested in the Jokemaster thing, about which I have my own explanations, I may add, based on high quality SigInt, in case anyone is interested, and you can tell Mr Sarno that from me with bloody knobs on. I don't waste my time in Deptford with all that fancy equipment you gave me you know.'

'Balls to the Jokemaster. I'm perfectly aware of that Stanni, and the equipment wasn't given to you: it's entirely that you are authorized to use it on official business which you bloody well signed for.' thinking what the hell am I talking about here to this bloody idiot, I'm as bonkers as he is the way I'm going on, 'but you should have been in touch before long before all this happened if you have something really good. It's written into your contract. You know that bloody well:

and in case you'd forgotten, it's gone well past the Jokemaster scenario, we're looking down the barrel of a major bloody disaster involving anything these buggers may want to throw at us.' Somehow Ted could never be as patient with Stanni as FX seemed able to manage. There was no place in Ted's life for the supposedly gifted amateur.

'You mean the Middle Eastern guys who want all the dosh or we get wiped.'

'No need to make it sound like someone is asking for the overdue rent. Do you, have you ever, taken anything that we do here really seriously? Sometimes I have to ask myself that one.'

'Ask Mr Sarno.'

'The next thing is that FXS and I have decided that that your family need not be notified until we know more about all this,'

'I doubt if they noticed my absence.'

'And that goes for your wife.'

'Oh her,' said Stanni, 'I don't think that matters a great deal you know. I think we can leave her out.'

'I'd rather gathered that impression,' said Ted, wondering why, and now realizing why it was that Stanni was forever showing people pictures of his wife. She must have buggered off years ago. You could hardly blame her: Married to him and with that shower of freaks hovering about telling her how wonderful he was day and bloody night. Drive you bloody crazy more like.

And he said, ' All right, what have you got?'

'Merely that the Jokemaster scenario is diversionary, these people in the house, Spudder and pals,are a bunch of eccentrics who used to work in a circus as it happens- I bet you didn't know that, and they were recruited like I said by the Middle Eastern crew and used as a front. Casual hire I suppose you could say'

'We know that, and save us the jokes pal,' said Ted, 'and in any case you should have told us all this as soon as you picked it up.' But he knew that it was pointless to proceed for the moment. 'What I cannot understand is what all this fun and games with the young woman is all about. Tell me.'

'I think she wants us to get married or something,' said Stanni, 'at least that's what she says. I've met her family you know, they seem nice people. And I think I could help her with her career plans if it comes to that.' If this goes on thought Ted, we'll have to get him sectioned under the Mental Health Act and put away till he calms down, or we'll be the laughing stock of the world. He hardly dared ask Stanni what Ms Sugg's career plans might be. If FXS gets on to this I'm finished. He could just imagine the de-briefing with FXS asking his usual carefully chosen impenetrable questions about whatever happened to the tracking system and how did he get that far out of London and without any one of us knowing. It did not bear thinking about.

Ted said, 'What do you mean "or something" for Christ's sake' Next thing I'll be asking him what the devil do you mean Sir? And have you taken leave of your senses?'

'Will we ever know what the Stanni thing was all about?' asked FX. 'Well we can't be much use if the world's greatest intelligence service is unable to explain the fatuous behaviour of one of its more cretinous part-time employees.' said Ted.

'You never really liked old Stanni, did you?' replied FX.

'You might say that. I always felt that he was a well meaning amateur who would, given time, come to a crappy end. Still at least he doesn't qualify for a pension.'

'I suspect that Stanni's "adventures" will turn out to have an innocuous explanation in which banality will triumph over the most prurient of our fantasies.'

'Speak for yourself.'

'My word we are touchy. As far as I can make out the whole Stanni escapade is of no significance from our point of view. This woman has no connections to anything that need bother us. I think he just got picked up by a wacky woman who fancied him. OK so she's an odd young person, but that's not a crime surely? Maybe Stanni needs someone like that in his life. Maybe we all do. He's not going to confide in her ... *by the way darling I work for MI6 isn't that great* ... you can bet on that. People talk to Stanni: all he does is bang on about things that no one gives a toss about, and so they don't have to listen to him, just blather on and tell him all their secrets. That's why we hired him in case you'd forgotten.' And added, 'Truth is stranger than fiction.'

'You don't say,' said Ted.

CHAPTER TWENTY TWO

It was not quite what he had expected, this house of assignation. His Excellency had anticipated a more *Grande Luxe* establishment, something classy of the sort he had seen in certain sinful movies of a decadent Western type. It was clean and well kept but it appeared to be somewhat tacky in its choice of furnishings and fitments. Still, had it not been selected for him by good people in whom he placed an implicit trust? This and similar reflections calmed his mild apprehension as he looked around for the welcome that he was nervously anticipating. Another thing that fuelled his uncertainty was that you entered the place through a rather down at heel entrance through what might, at one time have been a garage, and not only that, you entered through a door in a wall at the end.

Not at all what he had expected. Odd. Never mind, it merely showed you to be on the watch for these deceitful people and their knavish tricks: he relished that fragment of colloquial English; no doubt a relic of Imperialist slang dating from when the hated West exerted its baleful influences. And smiled at the thought.

A charming lady greeted him. She was seated by the bar on a stool displaying her elegant legs, the devil at work again, he thought, Western decadent whore no less. ' Good evening lovey,' she said, 'We were expecting you. You must be His Ex...' He cut her short, 'Please be assured Madame that we must remain discreet in the execution of this matter which is of some delicacy, I assure you. It would not do to compromise oneself in any way.' As he said that, he smiled uneasily, as he was now beginning to feel vaguely apprehensive.

This was definitely not what he had in mind at all; there seemed to be a failure of the correct protocols that one would expect in these matters - it was hard for him to put his finger on it. 'Oh that's all right Dearie,' said the woman, 'Can I get you a little something until the young lady arrives. She is going to entertain you this evening I understand, and it will help to calm your nerves and keep you handy.' And she laughed, rather too coarsely for his liking, for he was a person of delicate sensibility until the moment might be deemed appropriate, when he wished it be known that he could be a veritable tiger of the bedchamber.

'Thank you very much,' he said, 'A glass of your champagne would be most welcome.' The woman laughed and uncrossed her legs and said, 'Well we usually find that our clients like to buy a bottle of fizz, just to break the ice as you might say.'

He replied, 'By all means.' All the while wondering where all this was leading. This was definitely not a high class establishment. The woman smiled at him again, he was beginning to find her behaviour familiar and tiresome. She didn't seem to know her place in the scheme of things. No respect, that was it. That was the way he saw it.

'Excuse me Dearie,' she said. 'Didn't you once come into the Metropole in the old days?' and winked. Gracious heavens, was there no end to the fatuity of this ancient harlot? 'I don't think that I have ever been to that place of which you speak,' he replied politely. 'Funny thing you saying that,' she said ' I could quite fancy you myself. I could have sworn you came in there once in the old days when we use to have the place in Brighton. Quite a lot of your fellow countrymen used to be clients, if you get my drift. In fact I said as much to Reg when you came through the door.'

He was so bemused that he was about to ask who Old Reg was, when a striking looking young woman came through the door. 'Oh hello,' she said, 'Sorry I'm late, but my cab got held up. My name's Maisie, and I'm from Charlton. Pleased to meet you I'm sure.Shall we sit down or do you want to get on with it, know what I mean? Sharon here told me all about you.' She laughed, as did Madame Sharon. 'I hear that you enjoy a bit of rough. Is that right?' His Excellency was about to reply when they were interrupted by the arrival of the champagne which was brought along by another young woman dressed in a shameless Western fashion, and who appeared to have difficulty in restraining her laughter every time that she looked at him.

He was now feeling even more unhappy. He had been led to expect a meeting in a high class apartment, not in what appeared to be a seedy nightclub that had obviously seen better days. Nevertheless, Miss Maisie looked promising, so he decided to await developments. Sharon said, 'You must be famished, poor thing. Would you care for a sandwich or something? Or maybe some fish and chips. Reg does a nice bit of cod.'

He found himself saying that he had had something before he came out, and Mme Sharon said that she supposed that they'd better leave these two lovebirds to get on with it. With this Maisie started peeling off her kit and handed him a selection of condoms, saying. 'I really believe in safe sex don't you dear?' And added, 'Why don't you drop your pants darling, you'll feel better – everyone else does at this stage I find. Now which way do you like it?'

The other young woman deftly undid his fly and his trousers slid gracefully to the floor. His Excellency was horrified, and he became even more so when the door burst open, and a number of uniformed police officers came in noisily, and one of them shouted something about arresting everyone present for keeping a disorderly house, whilst another took a video of the scene.

'Right you lot, Madame Sharon and the young ladies you are all under arrest for keeping a common brothel,' said the leader turning towards His Excellency and saying, 'And what about you chum?' His Excellency replied, 'This is an outrage. Do you realise you could provoke an international incident if you continue in this fashion. I claim Diplomatic immunity and wish to leave. My driver is waiting for me.' The officer who appeared to be their leader said 'Forget it sunshine. Sit down, you are my friend, in extremely deep shit right up to the bloody eyebrows and your best bet is to wind in your neck.'

'How dare you.'

'How dare my ass. All the diplomatic immunity in the world won't protect you from the consequences of your involvement with a dangerous group of people. And it's no good denying it, we know you're in, and you know what I'm talking about, so let's just cut the crap shall we? If you listen to me though, we might possibly be able to cut a deal. You help us and who knows, we might be able to help you?Don't help us and you're as dead as my Auntie Nellie in Bootle.'
H.E. said 'This is outrageous. What deal had you in mind?'

'That's more like it Your Ex. Perhaps we could talk somewhere else.' And added calmly. 'Why don't you sit down and have a drink while I attend to things?' With that Fizzer turned away and said to Sandra, 'Thanks a bunch Sandra. I should move on before Ted gets here. I asked the guys to call him as soon as we'd got things settled.'

'You're a cool bastard, you really are, aren't you?' Sandra replied, still finding it hard not to laugh at the absurdity of the whole situation.

'This is an outrage,' chipped in His Excellency, 'You told me that your name was Maisie, and now you say it's Sandra.'

'Maisie is my professional name, duckie.' said Sandra and she walked out, 'and not only that, she had the bloody nerve to wave her ass at him,' as FX said when he saw the video.

'The point is, and for Christ's sake stop keep saying it's an outrage, it's you being caught bang to bloody rights in breach of your protocol me old son, and you know it,' said Fizzer laughing now, 'The point is that you don't really have any choice here. I hope that I made that perfectly clear. Now what's it to be? The full SP, or do we let the media in on this? It's no sweat as far as I'm concerned either way.'

'Which is?'

'Now you're talking my friend. All we do now is get you to give us the information we need about your pals who are causing all the trouble. They'll not know a thing about it, and we can tidy things up and return you safe and sound to your people, and that will be the end of the story.'

'How do I know I can trust you?'

'I'll tell you, you really got some nerve. You've been in with a bunch of criminals who are planning to blow us all to shit and you ask me that. I don't know where guys like you are coming from. After you give us the full SP, all we need then is a signed statement as well. As it happens we've brought one, all written up for you. All you have to do is read it and sign the bugger, and then we can all go home.'

'You seem to have it all sorted, as you say it.'

'You got it.' And with that Fizzer says to FX, 'I think we're in Mr Sarno. Our man is just about to cough.'

'What's that you're saying?' asked His Ex.

'Just calling the top man, that's all to let him know that everything's taken care of.'

'What do you reckon now Guv? I mean the way I'm seeing it OK, so His Ex is near enough in the bag, but we've still a way to go and not much time.'

'I think that the answers will be found in the Funnies' house.'

'You say that but it's a long shot, worth a look I suppose. Not that I fancy just barging in there on a hunch in case we end up looking a right bunch of idiots.'

'I don't think we have any other option at the moment.'

'We should put a small group into the place: the last thing we need is a gang of muscle- just a few well trained specialists who know their asses from Shinola.'

'Sorry Guv, you got that one wrong; not that it matters. Who do you suggest?'

'Well I understand that Fizzer is looking for the next stroke: once he'd pulled Sylvie back there was no holding the man.'

'It's a revenge thing I suppose. I'm not sure that I'm happy with that.'

'The revenge bit is over. This is strictly business. He said so and he assured me that he was as calm as you like. He sounded fine. He is a funny person. At first he comes on as the definitive total hardnose who doesn't give a shit: next thing he's all soppy and talking about defending the Queen's Peace - says he's paid to keep it. I mean he actually said that to me.'

'Not to be taken seriously. I thought the army were paid to do that; in any case the police are renowned for their loyalty to the Crown. Some of them reckon they'd rather do a Royal Visit than pull a villain,' said Ted, somewhat stuffily. And FX laughed and said, 'Come off it Ted.'

As the evening wore on, in a very short time H.E. was in a state bordering on panic. The ghastly policemen and his crew had dumped him unceremoniously outside his residence and had disappeared, as mysteriously as they had appeared at that dreadful club. How he regretted his folly, for making a statement under duress, and all for the sake of an evening in the company of an infidel whore.

He resolved to change his ways and vowed as much aloud, as it turned out greatly to the amusement of an unexpected witness. 'I thought that we agreed that we would never be seen here together in any way shape or form,' said H.E. who rather took pride in certain variants of colloquial English. 'You will be wise not to argue, Your Excellency,' said Zuheir, one of his paymasters, 'and may I recommend that you place your hands above your head and get into the car. We have to settle certain matters, as I am sure you will understand. It is now the time to visit some of our Western collaborators and as they would say " tidy things up", you follow.'

His Excellency, now suspecting that things might be getting out of hand, said huffily, 'I cannot see that such a matter is any concern of mine,' He didn't like the look of this man, and his unfriendly, even threatening attitude was greatly at variance with the kindly interest these people had thus far displayed. He had wild ideas of trying to call the police on his mobile phone, but realised that this was not an option even worth considering faced with two guys carrying shooters. Zuheir's pal, an even more menacing looking cove, said to him 'Move it *habibi*.' And so His Excellency moved reluctantly towards the long trail home. 'But what about the cause, the liberation of Islam and its empowerment...' he asked. The first man only said, 'Balls to that chum. We need the money, then we talk about the cause.'

CHAPTER TWENTY THREE

'The last thing we need is a, "come out you bunch a crazy assholes we got the place surrounded", performance, make you bloody sick,' said FX.

'You joking Mr Sarno,' said Fizzer, 'That's not the way we do it and you bloody know it.'

FX said, 'Actually I was joking. You realise Mr Edwards that this probably is the big one: if you pull this off, they'll make you head of the Met.'

'Sounds like bloody Roy of the Rovers,' said Ted, but covered his ass by saying, 'Don't forget Guv we had wondered if this bunch might possibly be gifted amateurs.'

'Very nicely put Mr Sarno,' said Fizzer, 'but may I be honest and say that as far as being head of the Met goes, I'd shoot for a guaranteed pension and a sodding big lump sum.' Fizzer still had misgivings about the whole enterprise. First he was doubtful about the intelligence gathering, in that he had never been entirely convinced that he knew what was meant to be going down here. How did the stuff with the Funnies and the terrorists tie in with the Jokemaster scenario for instance? What he'd heard so far had been unconvincing, although he knew from what had come out at the last briefing that there were real and present dangers around, what with the demand for the money with Plague, smallpox and chemistry coming in by air, if no one delivered, let alone nuclear shit. Whose aircraft and how would they get hold of the aerosols and the delivery systems?

It sounded convincing as a threat, but thinned out when you asked where the technology was coming from. Somehow it didn't hang together enough for Fizzer, who considered the possibility of a hoax was well in the frame. Right from day one he'd felt that they had all been rushed into action with an insufficient data base, though his knowledge of FX's reliability and his respect for him was much higher than it had ever been.

The horrors of Sylvie's kidnapping and rescue were fresh inside his head, and he was still flying high on the outcome. OK so she was well tucked away in a safe house, but the the inevitability of her killing the dumb shit Bro had shaken him up more than he had dreamt. He had always said to her that something like this could happen, and now that it had, it had become something that both of them would have to live with. And suddenly he was aroused when FXS said, 'It's too late to worry about trivia. Lets rock and roll.'

So that was the end of the briefing. As he went out the door Fizzer turned and said, 'OK so that's it. Can I say this for the record Mr Sarno and Mr Blunger, cop this, I'm confident that we can pull this one off – you guys worry too much.'

FX says, 'Whatever you may think of Fizzer, one can't fault him for lack of confidence.' But Fizzer was up and away.

Back at the House in the Town, Jack Spudder was irritable and put out. Right out of the blue the entire communication system had gone down. He had called British Telecom who had at first seemed to be blithely uncooperative, and then, to his surprise, after a check by the operative, their mood changed to one of friendly compliance. Jack didn't have enough street sense to be alerted by this sudden change in tone. Oh yes, they would certainly send someone around soonest. Jack was pleased. Now and again these people respond to quiet authority. The sudden failure of the system was a tiresome matter and he was greatly relieved when the BT Ford Transit arrived.

The man from BT, obviously the foreman, well he seemed to be an affable person who engaged Jack in a discussion about the likely causes of the problem and its rectification. It was all related to faulty relays in the system, happens all the time, it's the poor workmanship and poor quality control Guv, that and a memory problem, I've told them a thousand times but did anyone listen I tell you if it wasn't for the wife and kids I'd find another job: all will be taken care of in no time at all. And he said 'Don't worry Sir, we'll soon get it sorted, it's a relatively minor functional breakdown we're looking at. It's a new system, these things do have their teething problems.' Would he ever stop and just get on with it, thinks Spudder. 'Oh yes, says your man.' It's a doddle I reckon and we'll be happy to be of service here now and in the future, as and when needed.'

As he said this Fizzer was eyeballing the place and calling FX and his mates, saying 'Right lads I'm in.' On Jack's return Fizzer said, 'I'll just fetch my mate Dave.' Two in says Fizzer as he reflected instantly on the fact that the model of the house interior had been as misleading as ever. Models don't give you the smell and the grime, and the videos not much better. The place was far more cramped than he had expected. They always were.

Around the corner the rest of the crew waited in a Dry Cleaners Ford Transit. And now, noticing this door marked 'Storeroom' which, as it happened, he'd already noticed, Fizzer said 'Tell you what it is Guv, I think we'll need a look in there, my floor plan says that's where your main fuses are, and we may need to take out your electrics for a few minutes.' Jack Spudder really didn't want him to do that and said, 'I don't think the main fuses are in there actually, my man.'

And then they then got into a pointless argument about the situation of the main fuse box. It never occurred to Jack Spudder to ask how it was that Fizzer had a floor plan of the place... 'Very good. I like that,' said FX as he listened, 'blind the buggers with science and they'll believe anything that's said.' While all this was going on Dave was bringing in the rest of the crew around the back of the house.

Fizzer says ' This guy looks a right fruitcake to me.I think we'll need to string him along as much as we can,try and get something out of him. So far no one else has, apart from the girls and good old Gilli who gave them all a shot of jungle juice.I would mind giving her...Oh forget it. And a fat lot of good all that did except tell us which caterers they used to dope the punters at the reception. Jesus Christ give me strength.'

FX said, 'I call that bloody ungrateful.'

And Fizzer continued, 'Tell you what Dave, you stay here and have a look in that room and I'll chat up the rest of them.'

'That'll be the day,' says Dave.

'Right,' says Fizzer, 'I think we've got it near enough squared away already. I fancy a cup of tea, or would that be totally out of order Squire? Nice place you've got here Guvnor. What is it, like IT then, you're doing here?'

Jack Spudder was disarmed and outraged all at the same time at the request for tea and he feebly requested Nansi Shafter to get some tea for Christ's sake, so they could get rid of this lot and get on with it. And added incautiously, ' Don't forget the chopper will be arriving in about ninety minutes.' Time to turn nasty now.

'And what chopper might that be?' asked Fizzer, all bristling with the adrenaline going, and his Heckler and Koch at the ready, 'Not that Ms Fatarse is interested in choppers.Cherry biting more in her line I'd say.' And he said 'OK folks, fun time is over - let's have you face down on the fuckin' deck double quick, and don't give me any crap about your rights. As far as you lot are concerned, you don't have any, so it's down on your faces if you please.' He laughed, 'In case you don't know, they reckon I've got a short fuse. That's why they call me Fizzer.'

By now Dave and the rest of the crew were positioned all over the place, in and out, back and front, all exits covered and it must have seemed like plain sailing until *the bloody ragheads arrived on the scene* as Dave later said in the

Debrief. 'You can take that out of the record' said FX, 'No need to upset sensitive minorities now is there?'

Fizzer only said 'I don't give a shit one way or the other Mr Sarno. Maybe it's time you and your pals woke up to what these sons of bitches are really all about at the end of it all. You guys really freak me out sometimes. Where do you fuckin' live and earn your money? These sods want our asses and they want us all fuckin' dead if we dont join their religion in case you hadn't noticed. That's the full SP Mr Sarno.'

'I thought that he put that rather well,' said FXS, 'Let's hope he delivers.'

'He'll deliver,' said Ted.

But things did not go exactly to plan, any more than they do in set piece battles; it was merely that, as usua,l Fizzer was ready to take a sensibly calculated risk, plus he was helped by a large piece of luck. He knew that his best plan was to divide the opposition before they could get anything together.

As soon as Fizzer started to move, Jack Spudder froze while Nansi Shafter took off saying 'I'm out of here Jack, stuff the bloody helicopter.' And she's straight into the hands of the back up crew. So far, you might say that things were looking good, or so it appeared until, from nowhere here comes Zuheir and his associates holding His Excellency in front of them with a shooter up his ass.

'I thought we were meeting at the helicopter,' says Jack. 'Fuck the helicopter,' says Zuheir in an accent more reminiscent of Basildon Town than Riyadh, 'Don't believe everything you hear on the phone, or pick up on the internet, and in any case my name's not Zuheir, Your Excellency, it's Kevin.' He looked around, ' OK you bunch of assholes, now hear this one.I and my mate here are no more fuckin' Arabs than Mickey Mouse. All we need is a bit of time to get out of this bloody place and we're sorted.' He glared and added 'Well just because I got Arab parents doesn't make me a fuckin' coon does it. Know what I mean, innit?'

His Excellency now looked as if he was about chuck his lunch, as Zuheir aka Kev continued, 'Anyone moves OK? His Excellency gets it right up the throat right.Got it?' FX said, 'I told you this lot were amateur night. Friend Fizzer could see this lot off with a feather duster.' At this stage Fizzer was totally unmoved, making no response and nearly bursting out laughing until he got serious and loosed off a full magazine from his Heckler and Koch.

'Goodbye assholes' he said, 'No one ever dreamt it would be this easy. Nobody lives.' The firefight with the terrorists was brief and bloody. After Kev had tried to lighten things with a couple in the general direction of the crew at the back, it all began to go seriously downhill for the enemies of the State. 'One down,' says Dave, 'Well let's do the bloody rest,' says Fizzer ' and tidy the place up, that's what they pay us for. Goodbye *habibi* – you didn't know I spoke Arabic did you shithead?' Down they went, every dead one getting one or more through the mouth.

The final body count included Jack, four of the idiots from Basildon, leaving Nansi and the last two who were picked up by the back up crew.

'What's it all about? Who the bloody hell are these people?' asked Ted. 'Don't be defeatist Ted, it's not like you at all. We will know soon enough,' said FXS impatiently. 'This sort of thing is best pushed to the final limit. That is one sure way of discouraging people from engaging in similar stupid enterprises, at least that's how I see it. The news soon gets round amongst the forces of evil.' Ted's wincing.

'Once it gets this far, I feel we need as high a body count as possible. It always seems to work you know.' He smiled, 'Hard cases make bad law you know, isn't that what they say?'

He added, 'Frankly I don't think we will hear too much more of this somehow. We were instructed to clear this lot up as a being a matter of highest risk to National Security presented by the nature of the threats and we have achieved that. It was an unacceptable degree of apparent risk. The fact that I had assured the suits that this lot might well be a bunch of amateurs, and that they are just that, is probably irrelevant.' And he added, 'I think we've done rather well, and that Fizzer as usual has been brilliant.' He had agreed with Ted that the few survivors should be kept indefinitely on deposit against the future. They had already left in an unmarked Transit en route for limbo.

And so it was agreed at the Formal Inquiry that there was no evidence that any force that might have been employed could be construed to exceed in anyway shape or form what might be deemed to be beyond the limits that might be deemed acceptable, given it was unlikely that weaponry had discharged itself accidentally on this or any other occasion, and that, given the exigencies of the needs largely, if not entirely, dictated by the unusual nature of this unfortunate confrontation, that the unnamed and unidentified Security Personnel involved were therefore absolutely exculpated for any alleged deficiencies in the discharge of their onerous duties, and that the leader and his second in command would be recommended for promotion, as would all the other members.

As to the nature of the serious injuries inflicted on an unnamed Foreign Diplomat from a Friendly Nation who had incurred severe gunshot wounds, his claim for Diplomatic Immunity was rejected out of hand, and not only that, after recovery, it had been agreed that he would be handed back to his employers who would, it was understood, arrange for transportation to his point of origin and also for him to obtain rehabilitation in his own Country where such facilities were reputed to be freely available. Also – there was no helicopter.

CHAPTER TWENTY FOUR

Diarrhoea usually strikes around Day Two of a stand off, particularly if it's on a wet hillside, by which time the team leader is bloody glad that he knows how to build a shithouse. Steve knew all about that and had bought large quantities of bog paper and Immodium. Next there was his choice of place. It might be thought a shade odd that Steve should have selected his hideaway in a disused earthworks near an island prison. But he was confident that he could defend himself from his enemies when the big day came. It was at the head of a disused quarry which provided him with an excellent field of fire.

And this place was on the island in which Steve found his refuge, a bleak place off the Dorset coastline where a hundred years ago the locals had been described as ... *'An exclusive community'* ... *recluses of unpleasant habits who keep to themselves, are jealous of strangers, marry their own folk and possessed of curious laws and still more curious morals ...The people ther be politique inough in selling their commodities and sumwhat avaitoise...'* It was a wind-swept landscape – barren and dreary.

The gigantic ugliness of disused stone quarries is hard to conceal even if they have tried to pretty things up with gallows -like derricks at the roadside. It looked as if whole towns have been removed from the stony bowels of the rock. In the middle there were deep pits of stone and huge slopes of rubble tumbling down to the sea in one of the most dangerous stretches of water in the English coastline. Everywhere on this island there are chasms with clean cut sides like docks that have never seen a ship.

The cranes and derricks wave their spiky arms like a bunch of nasty black insects. Rusting out- of- use remnants of steam engines and blocks of stone lie all over the place. And if that were not enough, every now and again the sea mist shakes with distant gunfire, for even though the navy left long ago, they still fire spectral coastal guns.

The island prison population is still on site since the early nineteenth century when it was built by convicts, when its reputation for flogging and death was at its most vile in the days when it was a staging post for the poor sods who awaited transportation. And now you could see it from across the bay; its grim Victorian outline and tall chimneys dominating the misty skyline by day. You could sense its menace at night. The two entrances were starkly depressing. One was approached by a narrow twisting road and then suddenly around the corner there it was. The main entrance was even grimmer. Squat and forbidding it said, 'abandon hope all ye who enter here.' Game set and match.

The second prison was set in the middle of a fortress. You would have thought that no one could ever escape, but they did, and never got beyond the causeway that led to the mainland. You might think that things have progressed since the days when tourists took dainty convict teas. They used to watch the cons returning from a day's grafting down the quarry complete with armed guards and the lads all in yellow suits slashed with broad arrows and Glengarry caps. Nowadays it's more sanitized but it's as useless as ever. We have advanced that much. As fouled and grim as they were, at least *in the good old days* they made no pretence about it. You just got a dreadful time, and if you survived hard labour you were lucky.

What a miserable place it is, and how grim it must have been on a summers day to be there, and to get a whiff of the jolly Weymouth beaches visible from the island top on the heights over the Chesil Beach, and the beautiful bay and radiant coastline to the east. The oddest thing about this sour place is that there is a pretty beach there: the cove of Church Ope. A miniature dell, a picturesque place – another wayside attraction. For years the people quarried the stone by hand and shifted it by hand, no wonder that their descendants seemed solemn and dour. Hardy people in a hardy place thinly populated with people occasionally seen on the unwelcoming streets, faceless stone houses with porches that looked like stone coffins, everything conspired to give the place a sinister air which suited Steve perfectly. Even the main drag, the inaptly named Fortune's Well, is built on a precipice where rooms look down on serial descending backyards, and narrow lanes dropping down to nowhere.

Hardly the place for a wounded spirit, but it suited Steve well enough. The pubs were sullen and gray. At first you might wonder why anyone would want to live in such a place, that is, until you had met Steve. He looked like the ideal resident, a harmless eccentric, a bit on the solitary side, bit of a loner, you could see that, but probably a decent bloke, unhappy love affair sort of thing.

If you'd lamped his armoury you'd have thought again. His three AK 47's, four Browning automatics, and the grenade launchers, not to mention the Glocks and the eight pump- action, large -gauge shotguns. Everything was coming along nicely thank you for Steve who was getting ready to conduct his researches into OOBE's, which in case you didn't know, means Out Of Body Experiences, something that occupied his thoughts with all the intention of a firmly held delusion. For was he not mad? Well not according to his internet psychic mentor who would have told you that Steve was a specially gifted person as he was pocketing the last of Steve's life savings via the internet and a nice little earner it was.

If you had asked Steve about his OOBE's he would have told you all about it, ' *Well you see it's like a special field of energy you see, like it gives you a clearer perception of and a better interaction with the extraphysical helpers who contribute to a unique defence of the group. It's an energetic field produced by the holochakra and the ectoplasm of the epicentre of the energy... 'it sort of acts like a way to focus your attention on the extraphysical reality, giving you a positive mental saturation – influential in assisting the projective process.'* If you told him that he was talking a load of bollocks, he would have looked pityingly at you. At this stage you'd have been well advised to change the subject since there was always the possibility that he might just turn nasty. To be fair though, he had now reached a stage where his anger and paranoia were less directed at any one person and more at the world at large. It was all about the State, the Organization, the Big Business consortia, them out there. Steve had become a fully fledged conspiracy Theorist.

He didn't believe that there was a conspiracy of lizards running the world, but he knew that out there was a big secret, that it all tied in, that meaningless coincidence was full of meaning, that power was no longer in the hands of the individual. That's what he knew, and it would have all passed unnoticed if he had not decided to act on it. Especially since his skills in the use of weaponry were so well developed. He was now well beyond being another dangerous crazy bore. Mad people live in a world that is boring, bleak and awful, and this is how it was for Steve, whose life had now become a nightmare of threatening conspiracies, of shadowy doubt and fear. Suicide might now have become his only escape route. They don't tell you that one too often. But now, Steve with his armoury was a much more potentially deadly person than ever before. But he went down the pub of an evening, would you believe. And played a fair old game of Pool,and the locals got to like him. And it was here that he arrived gradually at the notion that it was time for the big show down.

He started off by rigging elaborate alarms systems and a seven hundred watt public address system in case he needed to tell everyone what was coming down, just to be on the safe side. The other thing he did was to have a good look at the security systems in the two prisons on the island. He was knowledgeable about such matters and tested the prisons carefully by breaking into each of them and getting out without being noticed.

And then once again quite impulsively, he called the whole thing off, collected all his gear into his gigantic camper and was gone in a flash. And all because a harmless drunk stopped for a crap outside his place. That was too much for Steve and he was up and away like shit off a hot shovel. It was the drunk that caused it all, as Steve immediately realised that it was a sign – the devil's excrement.

In no time he's racing South West along the A35 until there right on the edge of Bodmin Moor he saw the very place he was looking for - his new home. You approached it after a mile or two along a narrow road flanked by gorse bushes and pools and there it was by the roadside. Now he had become the classic gun toting loner holed up in a shack in the foothills of the Appalachians, except that he was in a disused café high on the wilds of a stony hilltop, well away from anyone

No one had ever known, or had forgotten how or why the café had been built. It was a relic from the long past, put up by someone who had the crazy idea that this remote place might make an ideal stop for *Teas Light Refreshments and Minerals*. It even had a disused concrete boating pool, long since dried up and reeking. Stuck in the middle of nowhere, it had the unlikely name of the *Kosy Kafe, Sandwiches our Speciality*. It had been a failure from day one The neon sign was still there: surely no one would have imagined that. Imagine will you a neon sign not far from a set of disused cowsheds there's this neon sign that said '*Kosy Kafe All Nite Opening,*' Did anyone notice that this must have seemed too crazy to be real? You approached the place along the long winding road from the main highway .Once again Steve had found an odd place, but it had a friendly deserted atmosphere that suited him.He could keep away from people here and not be noticed.

The real story of the Kosy Kafe All Nite Opening was as innocent and as daft as you like. It had been put up by a guy who had sold a failing menswear business in Darlington after a holiday in the West, in the hope that he might capture the holiday trade. It closed and then remained empty until the Sixties, when it re-opened and became a bikers caff where harmless bikers drank and swore, pissed on their leathers and had gang bangs. For a time they had a certain notoriety, even their own vicar, The Rev Mike 'Leathers ' Hanshaw, until they too faded away. It was all sort of a big story for the local newspapers and then silence and that was it.

So when Steve moved in, no one noticed except the Estate agent who had unloaded it on him. He's a loner, they said, but harmless, it's a free country; not that they particularly liked strangers, but he didn't come across as a threat somehow. At the time when Steve took it over, the windows had been boarded up for God knows how long: there were faded posters advertising rock bands that must have been doomed; bands with names like *electric zebra* and *holy mutton*.

But it was home sweet home for Steve. In no time he'd settled in there. Another lone eccentric. And the sad thing was that probably for the first time in his life, Steve was really happy and content in his safe house, with his armoury, his collection of Captain Scarlet videos and Mystery Comics, all waiting for the Big Day. Steve settled in, and in no time, his alarm systems were ready. Outwardly it was still a disused café, but in the store room Steve had used his electronic skills to construct a secure alarm system and two banks of video monitors. This permitted visitors to come along in the daytime. In this way local trades people and the mail would not be suspicious of the new neighbour. From Steve's point of view everything was now pretty much on the hunky-dory side.

All he had to was to await the inevitable confrontation with the nameless forces of Global Conspiracy. At the same time he preserved his islands of relative sanity, watching videos, going down the nearest pub a few miles along the road and playing pool. He got to know some of the locals who sensing his need for privacy, respected it in a way that he found oddly touching. And now he felt less afraid of things and of life in general – up to a point. Living in the country seemed to suit him this time, in a way that it had never done before. He began to think along these lines as he started to speculate about when the Day would come. It had to be soon.

He'd worked that out from chat rooms on the Internet where it was generally agreed there was little doubt that the Veil of the Temple would be rent in two pretty bloody soon. All that concerned him was the manner in which this end game might be played. It would be even more helpful if he knew the date when it would all come down, so he might just be ready for the dissolution and the big shoot out: meet the new dawn in some degree of peace or something like that. But before that might come about he developed another area of interest.

Steve enjoyed watching the telly of an evening. However his interests were less in the line of Costume Drama, soaps or Big Brother, but more in the area of Current Affairs, as he was ever on the look out for any sign of the rending of The Veil of The Temple and anything that might have to do with The Great Ram, for, despite his improvement in terms of having become calmer, he was still extremely mad.

And then, quite by chance, he happened to read one of HE's more zany writings on the subject of the Arab- Israeli conflict, and out of the blue, he developed the absolute conviction, like a bolt of thunder striking him down on a golf course, that HE was The Great Shaytan and that he, Steve had been called by the Almighty, and by the great Ram to dispatch this ghastly heretic and sinner from the face of the earth. Which is what psychotic people sometimes do. It was as simple and as deadly as that, and he decided that the only course of action would be to arrange an exit visa for him as he had been trained to do.

The real ending was much more mundane.

FX had said, 'For the sake of completeness, I think someone ought to go and see Steve and let him off the hook. It's all ancient history now. Send someone down to tell him that he can get on with his life, and no hard feelings, sort of thing so long as he keeps his head down.'

'I don't think that will work Chief. The poor guy is crazy.'

'Well at least let the records show that we had a go.' Said FX. 'I think we owe him something.'

And so they sent someone down to talk to Steve and explain how things were. The guy was able to find Steve without too much difficulty, since he'd been tracked a few weeks before, and the people had been undecided about what should be done, and so they asked FX to sort things out. Unfortunately Steve completely misconstrued the visit; he spotted the guy approaching. It was most unfortunate as it happened to be on the day that Steve had decided this was definitely the day, no doubt at all, it was definitely the day when the Veil of the Temple would be rent in twain. In a way you could say that the bloody veil was rent in twain if you counted Steve's head as a Temple. Steve took a shot at the visitor who promptly shot him stone cold dead in reply. No drama, no Gotterdammerung ending, just a simple headshot. George Jorgensen had been proved right after all. Poor old Steve, he never really hacked it, the poor dumb shit.

CHAPTER TWENTY FIVE

FX said, 'My only comment Ted, is that our biggest mistake was our failure to make a proper appreciation of the situation the way we have been trained to do. Next we threw common sense out the window, and talked ourselves into assuming that the scenario was far more complicated than it was and read too much into nothing. What was all that about for God's sake tell me? We made a right dogs bollocks of the Jokemaster diversion. A total bloody waste of time which did not please the paymasters, I can assure you. One of them went on about travel expenses till I could have throttled the stupid bastard.'

'Hold on Guv, it's lucky they never heard you when you were over the top and came on with all that crap about the bloody aliens. To be honest I thought you were losing your marbles.'

'Not so fast Ted,' says FX and snappy with it, 'Been reading Karl Jaspers have we? Is that it?'

'Well after some the stuff you talked me up with for Christ's sake, and what about all that old shit about the entire universe on the small side. Talk about carrying physics to absurdity.'

'I think not Ted, and in any case even now we don't know exactly where Maestro Spudder and the brothers come from, now do we?' Ho bloody ho, now he's shifting his ground Ted thought, as FX changed the subject and said, 'Now you see why I think so little of the banality of our de briefing rituals.'

He looked out of the window, 'I gather that Fizzer was in good form,' and trying too hard to sound as breezy as you like thinks Ted, 'I suppose it would be an academic question to enquire about the extent of his personal body count.'

Ted replied, 'By his standards he did well; he accounted for His Excellency severely wounded, most of his left lung gone plus his spleen, half his liver and God knows what else in the bucket, but he's expected to recover and be so fortunate as to spend the rest of his life in an underground prison in his beloved homeland. I mean, as a display of fancy shooting it was great, but we could have done with a few more surviving witnesses. And the bloody rest dead in the firefight except for the odds and sods now in The Greenhouse. The Government officials from The Kingdom were really pissed off about His Excellency until they discovered the full SP, I can assure you. And I could say, leaving unanswered the question of fundage of the whole bloody thing.'

'Oh I say, how jolly rotten,' said FX, 'if it's any consolation the bloody man was never His Excellency anything -not even a junior minister, just a small time nebbish with friends and a taste for getting ahead. He's the only one who refers to himself as His Excellency. What I can't understand is why they never sent him straight home and put him in a hole before we got to him which is what they will do. One would have thought that someone would have rumbled that he wasn't exactly kosher, if that is the appropriate word.' Ted said nothing, stared a bit and said, 'I believe so. You really didn't like that bugger did you.' And thought, "how jolly rotten." I wish to Christ he'd spare us his public school act, it gets right up my wick.

'Your man knew too much about things that were none of his business and in the end it was too much for him. Plus he'd been supplying whores and God knows what to influential people, and all that crap and more. He's not a nice person really.'

'I thought they did that all the time though, I mean it's their equivalent to Disneyland. Are their hypocrites worse than our lot? I doubt it. Anyway no one gives a shit apart from *The Mail on Sunday*.'

'Well there's one major consolation,' continued Ted, 'which is that everyone agrees that the bloody Pink Lady should be shut down once and for all. Never liked the place.

Arranging that is HMG's way of placating the man's bosses who don't like to admit that he was ever in such a place. It's a Loss of Face thing. It must have been a right laugh.'

'Do you have to talk like that Ted. Be fair,' said FX, 'and not so fast about the PL. You could say that in its way the place may have helped to prevent a major conflict, not quite World War Three but bad enough.'

'That's what I mean,' said Ted, 'second rate.'

'Take it from me Ted,' said FX, 'someone will find a use for it.'

'I don't care Guv, all that much,' said Ted, moving on, 'There are still too many unanswered questions about the whole affair. We should have done better.'

'So what,' said FX, 'There are always loose ends or had you forgotten? I don't wish to bang on about it, but at least we were both right when we ID'd this lot as a bunch of amateurs who can be as dangerous as anyone. Kevin and his pals, I ask you, posing as Fundamentalists and taking in His Excellency - a right laugh if ever I saw one, but he was like all of them, entirely in it for the money, like Bill Poynton, like Croke P, like Hacker, you name it. Greed, one of the Seven Deadly, as my teachers called them. They'll have plenty of time to think things out in the Greenhouse will your man Kevin and the Essex Arabs. And while we're on the topic, is that bloody tunnel still open?'

'Of course.'

'And still connected to the railway and so on.'

'Best not to know. They probably closed it.' Why is he asking all this, he knows the bloody answers? As if it mattered a damn. He probably thinks it's all to do with aliens and UFO's. He'll be looking at bloody anorak websites next. What have we come to? He worries me. No question.

FX had always said that The Great De-Brief process could too easily degenerate into a waste of time and an ego trip for the self righteous, but on this occasion, the untidiness and uncertainty of the whole series of events had demanded a real time De-Brief, which caused a few raised eyebrows and anxious moments. FXS was able to deflect certain of the more tiresome critics amongst the suits, except for one member who became unexpectedly excited about the firefight and said it might have contravened certain unspecified regulations of which no one had ever heard, and then excused himself from the conference room in some haste, prompting one unkind critic to liken him to Lord Justice Goddard, of whom it was said that he had to change his underpants every time he sentenced someone to be hanged by the neck until you are dead, and may the Lord have mercy on your soul - Oops.

Most important of all however the meeting enabled FXS to carry off the final showdown between himself and the suits with a typical FX *coup de maitre*, 'It was me against the World on behalf of us all, I thought it was touch and bloody go. One of them nearly passed out when I showed them a video of the *firelight* as he believed it was called; and that bloody did it Ted.' He laughed 'Yes,' he said, 'I assure you Ted, that by the end of the meeting, a mere eight hours, I promise you, I had the whole bloody lot of them eating out of my hand and making all sorts of promises for the future welfare of all of us, come the great day. All we have to do now is wait.'

Ted felt inclined to ask what FX meant by that but decided not to. FX said 'I'm pleased that you didn't ask me what I meant by my last remark. For the moment you and I have had enough of all this: we should have breakfast or something.'

As it was now six in the morning and as Ted had been hanging around waiting, he agreed, 'One thing Chief, do we have to go to that bloody caff of yours.I fancy something a bit more flash.'

'I agree,' said FX, 'we both deserve it. I thought we might try that place in Smithfield where you can get pissed as soon as you arrive and eat yourself into the coronary care unit at

Bart's in five minutes flat. Lets go there and forget all this crap for a while.'

'You worry too much about the unanswered bits Chief - at least they had no access to nuclear capability.' says Ted.

'Now you're talking like the cousins,' said FX, 'I agree. But they did have more than enough anthrax in aerosols and bloody smallpox to have killed thousands, so the people at Porton Down reckon, though I remain sceptical about the efficacy of weapons that can blow back in your face. I would have been scared shitless if it had been Sarin, other chemicals or worse.'

'They did have those two aircraft,' said Ted. 'latest mark Learjets they'd pinched from Duxford, the cheeky buggers.'

'All we can do is wait. I suppose we could sweat them, but what's the point? They'll cough sooner rather than later. OK any links with known major terrorist groups have so far not been defined, and probably may never be. I suspect that when we know the full story, it will be they are a group of smartasses who got ideas above their station, managed to get financial support from we all know who - a government which is now piously wringing its bloody hands. But at the end of it all they weren't, thank God, quite up to it.'

'So Messrs Spurlow and Nansi will also stay on ice in The Greenhouse in the company of the Essex shower until such time as their physical status has returned to normal, and they feel able to cough.'

'You got it. They're as boring as the next villain.'

Lucy and Gilli remained at the Centre where Lucy interested herself in reorganizing things and finding out more about Purdue for whom she had developed an affectionate respect based on his laconic attitude, and his ability not to take things too seriously. This developed into a good humoured relationship in which for the first time in her life, Lucy was being not exploited, a welcome change of direction. She found that the life at The Center was more than acceptable, at times it was amusing and made her laugh out loud, and the place benefited from her administrative skills. Also she was able to tighten things up and get rid of certain dishonest staff members who were contributing nothing to the place and robbing the tills, nicking food and anything they could lay their hands on.

Purdue took it all calmly and said, 'I tell you what kid about this whole thing, well heck, it got that bunch a screwballs off our back now didn't it?' Ordinarily Lucy would have objected to bring called 'kid' but with Purdue it somehow didn't seem to be important.

Next thing, Gilli slips away, more or less unnoticed and with no warning.

'She might have said something.' Ted near enough wailed when he heard about it. 'What did I say? She's a Company person. Stood out a mile I reckon.'

'You always did fancy her didn't you Ted? They never do in my experience, I mean remember to tell you they're going' says FX.

'To be bloody honest, now that you ask, yes I did fancy her,' said Ted. 'But I'm too old you see.'

'I do see,' said FX gently.

And yet no one was surprised when Gilli was next heard of in Los Angeles on her way to an interview at the Department of Marine Biology at The University of Southern California. FX had a final bash at establishing whether or no her links with The Agency were temporary or substantive, but was unsuccessful 'We've not heard the last of her Ted.' He said, 'If that's any consolation. No question, she was an interesting person.'

Ted said nothing.

Lucy missed Gilli far more than she would have believed but was able to keep in touch with her. And the next news was Gilli inviting her to come out to California and try a new life in the USA. Lucy is still considering that possibility. Purdue would like her to stay at the Center.

FXS continues to keep an eye on matters of National Security with Ted. For as FX said, 'It's probably what we do best, wouldn't you agree Ted, and occasionally one has the opportunity to meet quite interesting people, and in any case, it's all we know about. If we were fired, all we could do is work for Securicor or some bloody gangster in Chislehurst, imagine that, or I suppose if the worst came to the worst, we could always drive mini cabs or something, or minibuses.' and added, 'another thing Ted, had you noticed that Tracy Suggs is the dead spit of Melanie Griffith?'

Ted said, 'I think you could do better than that Guv.' He needs a holiday he thought, it's all getting too much for him. I said so as soon as this lot started.

Fizzer carries on as usual, living in hopes of making it to his pension and keeping it going with Sylvie. He bade farewell to his arrogant would be substitute, who was transferred to another Force where his rehabilitation is proceeding satisfactorily.

Ted and Sandra continue to get along quite well and that suits their needs, says FX. Now and again he says, 'It's really time you settled down Ted. It's good for the reputation of the Service.'

Stanni hasn't completely resolved matters with his family who, after holding an all day family encounter group, decided not to write to the *Guardian* about the fact that they had been denied access to the knowledge of their son's mode of employment by a secret agency. 'Is this a police state?' asked Big Daddy, and further, he said that this gross interference with their civil rights was but yet another erosion of their civil liberties and a glaring example of creeping fascism for anyone who had eyes to see, until they received a discreet visit from Fizzer who straightened out the misunderstanding. 'One felt such a sense of the primitive in his presence didn't one?' said

Cynthia, and shuddered. They agreed instead to meet Stanni's prospective in laws. All went well until they had a collective swoon when they met Tracy Suggs and her family who had arranged a luncheon at The Tudor Barn Restaurant near to the Sugg's family home, and there was no claret on the wine list.
'They do a nice Sangria or a Sancerre I believe.' said Mr Suggs.

Big Daddy nearly wept.

Tracy's parents think highly of Stanni. 'He's a bit of a funny old thing, and a bit of a stick in the mud by all accounts, but very clever with it, and really rather a dear, if a little on the eccentric side for the likes of people like ourselves and Father, but I'm told by Tracy that his boss, a Mr Sarno, is a real gentleman, which is nice,' says Tracy's mother, and I'm sure he has a steadying influence on our little girl, which is what matters, and that's what Father says, though I wish sometimes that she had stuck to her job in the Bank.'